ALL THE
TEETH
IN THE
WORLD

JOHN C. FOSTER

JOURNALSTONE
YOUR LINK TO ARTIST TALENT

ISBN: 978-1-68510-142-8 (tpb)
ISBN: 978-1-68510-143-5 (ebook)
Library of Congress Catalog Number: 2024947260

First printing edition: January 24, 2025
Printed by JournalStone Publishing in the United States of America.
Cover Artwork: Nicholas Day with Don Noble
Edited by Sean Leonard
Proofreading, Cover Layout, & Interior Layout by Scarlett R. Algee

JournalStone Publishing
1400 North Wood Rd.
Murphysboro, Illinois 62966

JournalStone books may be ordered through booksellers or by contacting:
or
JournalStone | www.journalstone.com

ALL THE
TEETH
IN THE
WORLD

CHAPTER ONE

1.

He lied.

"I'm hunting."

"Is that legal?"

"No." Muscles in his jaw bunched as he smiled.

He ran into the two women the minute he stepped out of the pines onto the open slope, a treeless expanse spreading out like a baseball field cut into the forest on the side of the mountain. He should have circled the snowy clearing, sticking to the concealment of the trees. But cutting through the open made for easier travel and he was tired.

The women weren't a sign, just bad luck. An accident of timing. And he had his story ready.

He wanted to scream.

He widened his smile instead.

The women wore expensive North Face gear and rented snowshoes, struggling through deep drifts when they spotted him. Breath clouded around their heads and their faces were pink with cold above bright scarves. One was tall. One was short. They looked like Connecticut.

"You don't need snowshoes?" the short one said. Her winter hat sported cat's ears.

"No." He slung the compound bow over a shoulder and pulled out a leather-wrapped flask. Unscrewing the silver cap, he helped himself to a burning slug of whiskey, hissing as it hit his throat.

The rapid tapping of a woodpecker erupted from the trees.

"Well, shit." The short one decided he wasn't sharing and sat heavily in the snow. Pulling a knee up to her chest, she struggled against the straps imprisoning her foot in the snowshoe. "These suck."

"We're supposed to be snowshoeing." The tall one sounded upset, and he pegged them as a couple. "Looking for winter birds."

He pointed down slope and the tall woman turned to look. Far away, it was a bright red drop of blood against the white blanket. It flung itself into the air, brilliant in the sunlight.

"Cardinals are brighter red in winter," he said.

"Heather, look!"

But the short one, Heather, said to him, "Are you going to the lodge?" One snowshoe was dangling by straps from a boot and her cheeks were red from more than cold. Icy grit stung their faces as a gust stirred up snow devils. They all turned away from the wind until it died.

"No." He put away the flask and adjusted the coil of rope around his shoulder. "I'm looking for a hanging tree."

"A what?" Tall said.

"Climb the tree and tie off," he said. "It's easy to slip or fall asleep while you wait."

"For what?" Heather tossed a snowshoe away in triumph and it stuck tail-first into the snow.

"Deer."

"Which isn't legal," Tall said.

"Right."

Tall didn't believe him and that was all right, the ruse didn't have to last long. She was about to press him when Heather interrupted, "Can we follow you?"

"No," he and Tall said in unison.

"Go that way less than a half-mile down slope and you'll hit a road. Easier walking and faster than backtracking to the lodge."

The sky overhead was so blue it was blinding.

"Are you sure—" Tall began, but he smiled.

"Yes."

Heather stood and her boot sank in the snow. Tall caught her when she wobbled, and Heather asked, "Can you help me with the other one?"

Tall nodded and turned to him. "I'm Tia, what's your name?"

She would report him when they reached the lodge.

"Leslie Ward."

2.

Clouds of breath streamed from Leslie's mouth as he trudged through the snow, numbing himself to the cold with pulls from the flask.

The trees were more diverse on this stretch of mountain, and when an old maple spoke to him, he considered its offer. It was black with years and leafless in death, bent over the white ground as if bowing at his arrival. He rested his compound bow against the bole and sat cross-legged among the roots where he set to work on his rope, his dexterity not helped by the whiskey. Shame danced like heat lightning through his thoughts.

A stick cracked beneath a sly step and tiny hairs rose on the back of Leslie's neck.

Had the women followed him after all?

He stood, bracing a hand against the tree as he cast his gaze about, but saw nothing beyond the white humps of bushes and the dark exclamation of the trees.

He stared into dark hollows beneath the surrounding pines as a chill sunk fingers through his coat and into his middle. There were bobcats in these woods, and he had seen bear tracks near the cabin. The yipping of coyotes sometimes carried over the mountains at night.

Snow tumbled from a nearby bush.

He wrenched a stick free from the snow and flung it at the bush, which detonated in a white explosion. But no animal showed itself and he decided he was suffering from nerves, a subconscious survival instinct attempting to distract him from his chosen path.

He leaned his back against the trunk and slid down the smooth bark until he was sitting again, trying to complete the noose before second thoughts derailed him. He was offended that uncertainty chose this moment to step on stage, this moment when he deserved to be alone with the forest and the snow and the yawning cavity inside him. His belly squirted juices and he remembered he had not eaten breakfast, which spawned images of scrambled eggs in a yellow pile beside brown sausage links glistening with grease. The scent filled his nostrils, sage and pepper and pork, and he could hear the rattle of cutlery on plates—

He suckled his flask and burned away the assault with whiskey. Cheap stuff. Deliberately unceremonious.

Tears of self-pity leaked into the stubble on his cheeks.

Enough.

Finishing the noose and whiskey in that order, he tossed aside the flask and stood.

He gripped the tree with cold-stiffened fingers, struggling up the trunk with the rope in his teeth. Snow laden branches shook free their burdens in a series of muffled whumps that sounded like applause.

No thinking, just do it.

He straddled a thick branch a dozen feet up, clinging with his thighs as he tied off the rope.

No thinking.

A nearby tree shivered and dropped its load of white. Powder swirled up in a cloud around its base.

What if the women had reported him and someone rushed right out?

The thought of being caught, of being stopped, filled him with dread. Shame suffused him. Even with his diminished reputation there would be press coverage. Pictures. Humiliation.

The plan was to stand on the branch and leap, ensuring a broken neck. According to his research, it was critical to tighten the noose and place the knot to the left of the neck, beneath the jaw. Even in the depths of despair, the thought of slow strangulation horrified him. He closed his eyes and braced his hands on the branch, breath hitching and now sobbing, yes, sobbing. Maudlin and pathetic and desperate as he stood up on the branch.

A snarl unfurled like a rusty zipper with great metal teeth.

Leslie's eyelids snapped up and he saw movement, furry and dark against the snow. It was sliding over the ground like a shadow, like an oil slick, darting from tree to tree as it approached, and the snarl leaked forth again, now like a motor revving low and ugly. Hungry.

He swallowed and brought the noose over his head, balance uneven as he slid the circle of rough rope down his face, past his eyes, beneath his nose and finally his chin—

A howl split the air and cut through him like a shard of glass—

He slipped.

There was a moment of weightlessness before a wrenching stop and pain exploded through his neck. He swung away from the tree trunk, clutching the rope above his head to lessen the agonizing pressure on his throat, bicycling his feet and gurgling as he swung back—

The impact against the maple's solid trunk was enormous, a blow against his entire body that slammed the breath from him and stole his ability to scream.

A weight struck his legs, yanking at his pants, a barely noticed sensation amidst a million screaming nerve endings until the unmistakable feeling of teeth cut through the noise. An incredible pressure that punched daggers of bone through fabric and flesh and he voided himself as a hissing cry escaped him.

Bristling animals crashed into Leslie as he spun helplessly at the end of the rope, snarls crowding his ears. Dark spots swarmed over his vision until the noose, never tightened, surrendered its jealous grip and Leslie fell in the red mist of his own blood.

CHAPTER TWO

1.

ONE WEEK LATER.

The plastic identification badge crunched beneath a black motorcycle boot as it was left behind, an afterthought, a life over. The sound was overloud in the thin air of winter, as footsteps scraped over salt and ice that stretched across the grey parking lot beneath a gunmetal sky.

Percy Cronk lifted his right hand and studied it as he walked away from his life. Wondering if the hand that plucked the lanyard from his neck was a betrayer or liberator, clearly acting of its own volition because how could a man—

"Percy!"

His strides lengthened, the thickness of his build belying the true length of his legs as he passed between the grey humps of inexpensive cars. No one who worked at the White Heart Recovery Center drove luxury vehicles and—

"Percy, stop!"

He turned quickly and, if a person didn't know him, threateningly. Visible breath jetted from his nostrils in a bullish snort, beard bristling like a boar's stiff hair.

She was small, half-Vietnamese, her brown face tightening against the cold as she ran after him without a coat, the glass doors banging shut behind her with a sound that made him grin with finality. The white teeth bared amidst the curling hair of his beard made her slow, and she raised one hand as she approached. He recognized the conciliatory pressure, as if he were a patient having a psychotic break.

"Percy," she said. "You can't just leave without saying goodbye to the circle."

He stared over her head at the two-story brick building, an old school they had refitted into a drug treatment center with money from Dartmouth College, an extension of the School of Medicine. The best thing he had ever done in his life. He dropped his eyes before he could give names to the empty faces filling the windows, featureless masks waiting for him to draw mouths that could smile and eyes that could see. His patients. His friends.

"Kai..." He stopped, vocal cords wrapped with emotion. The ghosts were staring down at him from the upper stories where the patients lived two to a room. Pale ovals behind grimy glass devoid of individuality.

"She's inside. I can't see her now," Percy said. "You know that."

"What about Mike, Billy—" Kai stopped when his chin dipped and red-rimmed eyes met hers.

"Tell them something good," he said, the words thick and wet. "Tell them something I would say."

"You tell them."

He hadn't seen her pick it up, but she lifted his badge in her hand. It was a rare misplay for the therapist who had talked so many people back from the edge of the yawning, hungry crevasse. Anger suffused him. Shame. Terror at moving from this spot with no concrete sense of his own identity.

"I blew it again," he told her, and she nodded, knowing what was coming. The therapists at White Heart leaned on each other hard and, after several years, were closer than any family.

"This is what we do, Percy," she said. "We fail and get back up and fail and get back up."

"They've reassigned my entire course load." He remembered the shame of the meeting. Squirming in his chair like a truant child.

"I know," she said.

The weights that had held him to Earth were gone. He felt as if his feet would find only air with each coming step, that he would drift and wither.

Her hand was so small, delicate fingers resting on the black leather biceps of his biker jacket. "When you left Notre Dame, you started your true work here. You don't need the trappings of a church to be a teacher, and you don't need to be a teacher to be a healer."

His laugh was vicious and she flinched. "I have to go," he said and pulled away from her, backing up several steps until he turned and ran to his motorcycle. He mounted the old Triumph and flicked up the stand with his heel before lifting his weight from the seat and bringing it down with a savage stomp to the kick-starter. The iron horse roared to life. He gunned the throttle, reveling in the rudeness of it until he saw Kai standing where he had left her, arms wrapped around her thin frame.

Her mouth was moving.

He killed the engine and she spoke again, voice carrying because that was one of her gifts. "You fell in love, Percy. Happens to the best of us."

2.

Percy heeled the bike over, taking the curve too fast as trees whipped by on either side and the cold wind burned his face.

It was the right kind of bar for his mood: low, brown wood with pickup trucks in a lot of gravel and frozen mud. He was there to drink, not fight. But one look at the bumper stickers offered all imagined possibilities for the afternoon and he slid to a hard stop, digging a groove through the gravel with his back tire.

When the engine died, the world paused in between breaths. The steady whisper of a northern wind took its rightful place, greeted by the sharp cry of a winter bird. Other sounds shouldered their way into Percy's world: the murmur of voices and the bass thump of a jukebox. He crunched up the gritty wooden steps and pushed through the door into dry warmth and a beery stink, pausing a moment to let his eyes adjust to the darkened interior where neon beer signs and a TV mounted behind the bar offered the most light.

Men were hunched over the bar in fleece vests and hooded sweatshirts. Nobody gave him a second look as he clomped across the floorboards and picked a stool with clear space on either side. The stool shifted beneath his weight and he imagined himself falling backward in an explosion of splinters, so he rose and took the one beside it and grunted to the old guy sitting to the right, "This one taken?"

"All yours, brother," the man said, lightly slapping the bar as if he had been waiting for Percy. The man had a rangy build, his beard not overlong but wild, his iron-grey hair pulled back in a ponytail tied off with a rawhide thong.

"Hey, Jill?" the man said, and the bartender turned around, big tits threatening to tumble out of an over-tight Red Sox t-shirt cut into a deep v-neck, a strip of belly visible around her waist and bulging over the top of her jeans.

"What?"

"Put a drink for this guy on my tab."

"Whaddaya want, honey?" Jill said to Percy, who glanced at the man beside him.

"Why?"

"You need it, dontcha?"

Percy nodded and braced his elbows on the bar. "Canadian Club, rocks." He felt sweat dampening his armpits and dragged the zipper of his jacket down until he could shrug free of its confines, draping it over the rickety seat to his left.

Jill turned away and ran her fingers over the bottles lined behind the bar until she found the right one and lifted it, eyeing the liquor left in the bottom. "You guys gonna drink more CC?"

"Yes," Percy and his benefactor said in unison, and the old guy let loose a short laugh that sounded like the croak of a dying gull. The man smiled to reveal that he had most of his teeth, though they were of a dark and dubious color. "I'm Mike."

"Percy."

Strong hands shook as the glass touched down on the sticky wood in front of Percy. "I'm gonna get another bottle," Jill said, and Mike nodded at the glass.

"Drink it."

Percy obeyed, lifting the shot of brown liquid and throwing it back so that heat scorched the back of his throat and a line of fire carved a path down into his middle. He shivered, only realizing just then how cold he was from the ride. He closed his eyes as the song on the juke stopped twanging away at the air and the murmur of conversation filled the space, the TV muttering like a tiny string section beneath the main orchestra.

Mike said, "Better?" and Percy nodded, opening his eyes.

"Got fired today."

"That sucks."

"Yeah." He glanced at Mike and decided to skip the name of the place, no way to say Dartmouth without sounding like he was big timing. "I did some teaching and some counseling at an addiction center."

Jill clumped back up with a fresh bottle of Canadian Club, twisting off the cap as if she were wringing the neck of a chicken. She splashed a heavy dose into their glasses.

"You help anybody?" Mike asked, knocking his whiskey back with a hiss. When Percy shrugged, Mike added, "My sister is alive because of the treatment she got down in Boston. Sounds like you did good work."

"I slept with one of them." Percy downed his whiskey and his eyes watered. "How'd you like it if a counselor fucked your sister?"

Mike nodded and planted his big-knuckled hands on the bar, shook his ponytail back, and Percy thought he might get that fight after all.

"Fucked her?"

"Yeah."

"This is my sister we're talking about?"

"Yeah."

Mike fixed him with a look. "That'd mean she was alive. That's all I care about."

3.

Percy had no idea that anything was wrong when he throttled down behind the peeling, clapboard structure of Jenny's Eats and parked beside the proprietor's mud colored Jeep in a spot marked NO PARKING—VIOLATORS WILL BE TOWED. A motion-activated security light snapped on and cast a yellow glare across the scene. He hadn't realized it was so late until the bright light pushed back the evening gloom.

He was still swimming in the boozy glow of camaraderie from the bar and had no clear memory of the ride home. But the liquor and company had done their work and blunted the cruel edge of his sorrow. Enough that the smell of frying bacon from the diner wetted his mouth with saliva. He pushed down the kickstand with his foot and jockeyed the bike a little until the metal stand dug into the ice, making a mental note to throw down some salt to thaw out the small parking lot.

Narrow stairs rose beside a metal vent leaking a steady stream of smoke from the grill. He slipped once on his way across the lot, the Frye boots being shit on ice, but managed to wobble to the steps until he could grab the wooden banister and pull himself up in a heavy-footed climb that shook the entire staircase.

A few people, Leslie among them, had complained that the stink from the diner below must be maddening, but Percy always smiled. Aside from Jennifer throwing him a free feed now and then in return for help around the place (like the salting he really needed to take care of), he found the warmth and smell of a kitchen comforting.

His wrenching belch shattered the evening quiet. Perhaps it was the odiferous burp, or perhaps simply that alcohol had dulled his senses, but Percy didn't detect the terrible odor until after turning the key in the scratched doorknob and tracking a trail of slushy footprints through the kitchen.

Someone else was in his apartment.

Hairs rose on the back of his neck. Something animal clawed at his control and he came within a hair's breadth of fleeing back down the staircase.

"Hello?" The word was hoarse with fear. "Is someone there?" He crept forward as quietly as a big man in heavy boots could.

The bright neon of the JENNY'S EATS sign out front threw rays of light across his murky living room and painted the floating girl in an eerie blue glow. She rotated slowly and her shadow crawled across the wall toward him.

As she made the lazy turn, her dress fluttered in the air from an open window, her head tilted accusingly as her black eyes fixed on his.

He dropped his gaze.

One snow boot had fallen off and stood upright beneath her slowly turning corpse, exposing a foot as pale as a sheet of paper. Liquid dripped from her big toe, a final indignity in a life that had known little else.

Forcing his eyes back up, he saw the bed sheets looped over a rafter. The improvised rope fashioned cleverly into a noose.

The same cleverness that first attracted him.

"Oh, Kristi."

Percy lifted her slight weight, feeling the unnatural stiffness even as he wrestled the noose from around her neck and up over a face blackened with trapped blood. "Oh, Kristi." With his arms around her waist, he squeezed a muffled burp from her mouth. Rank air choked his nostrils.

"Oh shit."

He laid her down on the floor, careful to avoid the puddle where she had voided herself. A sob escaped as he tried to make her stiff body relax on the floor, but it had already assumed its final shape. It would not be shifted to comfort the living.

Several times his mouth opened and closed without producing a sound until he pulled the phone from his pocket to dial 9-1-1. "Hello?

Yes, someone committed suicide in my apartment. Yes, yes, I'm sure." The call went the way of such things and ended. Not a minute later he heard the howl of a siren from the center of town, less than a mile away.

He settled on his knees, resting his backside on his heels and relishing the pain of the floorboards against bone. Percy's cheeks crinkled with salt as his face worked through expressions, protected under the shield of mother night in his lonely apartment lit only by the neon glow.

When his phone rang, he expected the police, but it was life, running over Kristi's death as if it were a speed bump.

The call was from a hospital.

"He doesn't know where he is or what happened to him," the hospital administrator said after introductions. "But he said you would come."

CHAPTER THREE

1.

The steel pin pushed through the fabric of the pillowcase with a quiet pop. Nurse Lavoie stepped back to regard the religious symbol she had affixed to the pillow inches from the patient's gaunt cheek. It was to her credit as a woman of purpose that she didn't once consider locking the pin in place.

"We have a Methodist and Presbyterian on call," she had told him, even offering to summon the Catholic, Benelli. But the patient had drifted away on a cloud of opiates after a disinterested, "No thanks."

She reduced his morphine drip after a quick glance at the empty doorway. If his face were as numb as a cotton ball, the point wouldn't be made.

The patient's room (and, in fact, the entirety of Concord Mountain Hospital) was visibly pure and oppressively white, with polished tile floors and painted walls. The nurse uniforms were of a similarly antiquated style in white polyester, with small white caps held in place by bobby pins. Women were allowed to wear trousers, but Lavoie preferred a nurse's dress. The robin's-egg blue of patient hospital johnnies existed in stark contrast to the institutional sameness of the place.

"Right," she opined, tugging his blanket up below his chin.

Afternoon light streamed through the large window and the room glowed as if with visible healing energy. The man was wealthy enough to afford a single room with a view of riotous fall foliage, though poor when it came to friends. A lonely bouquet of dying flowers drooped from a vase on the table beside the bed, but there were no get-well cards. No balloons. To Nurse Lavoie's knowledge, there had been no visitors.

She adjusted the blinds, severing the bands of sunlight before they could reach his resting form. To help him sleep, of course. Her strong fingers with their square-cut nails tugged at the plastic restraints binding his wrists. It wouldn't do for the patient to paw at his injuries.

"Right," she repeated, crossing heavy forearms over her chest to survey the man.

Bandages covered the gaping ruin of his left eye and the fabric of his gown bulged over numerous dressings. His angular face was windburned and his unshaven cheeks hollowed by starvation, the bony nose and knuckles scabbed as if he'd been brawling. He hadn't been awake long enough to take solid foods and had eaten nothing during his time in the wild.

"Depraved" was a word outside of her vocabulary, but "queer stuff" was solidly in her wheelhouse, and Lavoie had it on good authority that the patient sleeping the sleep of the innocent (hah!) was not above including such in his books, ugly stories about ugly people doing ugly things.

"Right." Lavoie tugged at the privacy curtain on its curved rod above the bed and stepped into the hall, shoes squeaking on the polished tile. Her shift was more than a half-hour past finished and she had meatloaf waiting at home.

It wasn't until she was in the hospital parking lot that her narrow lips curved into a smile. She couldn't wait to feign surprise tomorrow morning.

2.

It was two hours past midnight, and the third-floor hallway of Concord Mountain Hospital was dimmed to help the patients rest. The low lighting lent the alabaster hallway an unsettling quality, a thought Mary Cavanaugh had never shared aloud, and she was in the habit of counting scuff marks and muddy shoe prints as an anchor to reality. A nursing assistant working her way toward an RN, she kept on the move with a coffee cup in hand.

Mary was at the nurse's station pouring creamer into her cup when a man cried out down the hall. Hot coffee splashed over her freckled forearm.

"Shit!"

She sprinted down the pale corridor, flat soles of her tennis shoes slapping against the floor, polyester slacks *shush-shushing* where her thighs rubbed together.

The cries were leaking from room 3G, and she hit the light switch before snatching at the privacy curtain.

The patient was writhing like a fish on a dock, hands opening and closing in the plastic restraints. Red flowers bloomed on his pillowcase and a fat black spider clung to his cheek.

"God!" she swore upon realizing that it was not a spider at all.

Pinned to his bleeding face was a cheap dime-store cross.

3.

Hospitals breed gossip more quickly than disease, and Concord Mountain Hospital had a bad case of Leslie Ward.

It was not true that flowers were wilting more quickly since the arrival of the patient in 3G. Nor was it accurate that infant deaths had risen due to his presence. The two mothers who lost their babies suffered from heroin addiction, and neither premature birth had offered much hope. It also wasn't true that the cross affixed to the patient's cheek had been smoking on contact with his blood. Still, when Dr. Martinho questioned Mary Cavanaugh about the incident, the nursing assistant grew a shade paler beneath her freckles and blurted out, "There's something wrong with him, can't you feel it?"

What was true, and this Dr. Martinho knew because she had been an attending physician on the night of his arrival, was the horrible story of his missing eye.

The missing eye had been caked over with a bulging, hard pack of mud when the EMTs rolled him into the Emergency Room. It was as if a miniature beaver dam had grown on his face, built of dirt, leaves, and crusted blood.

After applying a wet cloth to soften the pack, she had carefully picked apart the mess with tweezers and a scalpel, leaning close enough to feel the heat of his rank breath. When the scalpel released a spill of maggots, several tumbled into her long red hair while more slipped into the open collar of her blouse. She had ignored the shouting intern and the wriggling mass of larvae on the table, working deeper and with greater speed until she realized that the hidden eye socket was empty save for a triangular piece of bone.

4.

There was the very real threat of a lawsuit and Dr. Martinho had to tread carefully. "Nurse Lavoie had no intention—"

Leslie Ward held up a long-fingered hand, the knuckles rough with scabs.

She tried again. "You're in no condition to leave, Mr. Ward."

"I'm checking myself out."

"You can't even stand."

Sitting on the hospital bed in his jeans and plaid shirt, laundered since his arrival but still torn and ragged, he looked like the survivor of a train wreck. His right eye was covered by an ill-fitting blue eyepatch and gauze peeked out from the socket beneath. A circular bandage covered the puncture wound on his cheek, and his lips and gums on that side remained swollen. Closing the wounds caused by the steel pin had required stitching.

Leslie slipped his bare feet to the floor and stood, forehead sheened with sweat. Face to face, Martinho realized they were of a height, five foot eight or so. After his thinning in the woods, they might even be close in weight. Still, his presence was overwhelming, made more frightening by the dark aspect of his remaining eye, flooded from burst capillaries. The white had gone a deep ruby, transforming it into an eerie, glinting orb in the shadow beneath a naturally fierce brow.

"You can't drive."

"I have a ride."

"You need shoes."

"My ride is bringing them."

Struck by the memory of maggots spilling from his face, Martinho looked at the chart to escape his monocular gaze.

"Doctor," Leslie said quietly, "you can't legally keep me here against my will."

"You still can't remember that week in the woods and your chart from New York describes frequent bouts of depression. I can send you to CPEP and they can keep you for three days mandatory psychiatric evaluation."

"My lawyer is also from New York and she's very good."

"I'll bet she is." Dr. Martinho glanced out the window.

The truth was that she had taken three scalding showers after treating Leslie Ward and still awoke to sweaty sheets, scraping imaginary maggots from her hair. She wanted him gone, God how she wanted him gone, but he was in no condition—

"Am I interrupting?"

He was big in a black leather jacket, dirty jeans, and heavy Frye boots with brass rings at the ankles.

"Leslie, you look like crap." Percy smiled through his salt and pepper beard.

Leslie chuckled through his pain and leaned back against the mattress. "You bring my shoes?"

Percy held up a canvas backpack. "I had to break a window to get in, but I grabbed your Nikes."

"Thanks." Leslie turned to the doctor who had crossed her arms, clipboard tucked against her chest like a shield. "Dr. Martinho, meet the improbable Percy Cronk."

Dr. Martinho sighed. "I want you back here in a week, and you're to stop at the pharmacy on the way out."

Leslie grinned, though the effect on his battered face was more macabre than reassuring.

5.

More than one member of the staff surreptitiously followed Leslie's departure as Percy wheeled him across the lobby.

He was a writer, a *student of the human condition* he might say after a few drinks. As such, Leslie was aware of the doctor's distaste. He was aware of the deliberate cruelty of the Christ-happy nurse and her cross. He was aware of a wall of feeling when Percy pushed the wheelchair into the crowded lobby, the skipping of the record, the momentary hitch in motion as the staff, moving as a single organism, recognized something horrible. The rolling wave of animosity unmanned him. He didn't understand it. Felt it unfair the way a child understands unfairness as a palpable and elemental thing. He wanted to flee. Maybe to cry. To ask why.

Instead he kept his crimson eye fixed on the floor, ignoring the buffeting of their collective gaze.

The glass doors whooshed open as the two men approached and cold autumn air struck him with a slap, odors of loam and leaves washing away the fecal, chemical stink of the hospital.

"Ready to go home?" Percy asked.

"Hell yes."

CHAPTER FOUR

1.

The rear window of Percy's Pathfinder was molten with the glory of the setting sun and Leslie squinted against the orange flash from the rearview mirror. He lifted a cup of coffee and sipped, wincing at the heat against his lip, allowing the steam to rise into his widened nostrils.

His memory of the strange and palpable dislike from the hospital staff was already fading. Written off as nerves. Traumatic leakage from his subconscious.

"I haven't had a full night's sleep since they found me. Sometimes no more than an hour." Leslie fiddled with the eyepatch, unable to get the band around his head to sit comfortably. He wondered if he should buzz his hair off or grow it longer to conceal the band. The patch was the robin's-egg blue of the hospital gowns and he loathed it.

"Nightmares?" Percy drove easily with his left wrist draped over the top of the steering wheel and waited for him to talk.

"I wake up so full of adrenaline. Can't get back to sleep."

"Do you remember the dreams?" Percy blew on his coffee and spilled a little on his wrist. Leaning against the pull of the seat belt, he licked the liquid off. His eyes were drawn to the unmapped depths of the forest, an endless procession of tall trees passing outside his window.

He imagined being lost and alone out there.

"I never remember much," Leslie said. "Just a sense of running, always running."

"That's what you did in the woods?"

"I guess."

Leslie focused on the broken yellow line stretching down the road. The eastern sky ahead of them existed in a bluish gray place that refused definition, having lost the sun but not yet found the stars.

"Did you speak to a psychiatrist at the hospital?"

The hollows in Leslie's cheeks deepened and his skin was sickly in the green glow of the dashboard lights. "The shrink said—" His dark eye bulged. "Look out!"

Leslie braced a hand against the dash and his foot stomped for imaginary brakes while Percy cut the wheel, tires screeching. The deer was frozen, staring at them, eyes flaring a brilliant white from the high beams in the split second before the horrible crunch, the sound of breaking glass, and clatter of a tumbling hubcap. They experienced an eternity of spinning, screeching craziness.

"Hoh," Percy said, a meaningless noise in the abrupt quiet after they slid to a stop, even the thrum of the engine muffled as the car sat sideways across the road.

"Fuck, you okay?" Leslie glanced back to see distant headlights approaching. "Gotta move." Percy feathered the gas, turning the wheel to pull onto the grassy shoulder. His left hand felt over the steering column until he found the button for the hazard lights.

Doors opened on silent hinges and they stepped out into the cold morning air as a lone car whipped by, the wind of its passage rocking the Pathfinder. The hazard lights flickered over the scene and the metronomic clicking struck Leslie as a deliberate effort to reinstate order after the long seconds of chaos.

He examined the front of the car and saw the cracked left headlight, the bulb dead and smeared with a liquid that appeared black. He was not sure what he expected to see, but the impact had seemed so much more profound.

A breathy, almost human groaning arrived on the breeze before the familiar scent arrived, hot and metallic.

"Stay here," Leslie said and hurried back down the shoulder with what speed he could muster, imagining how he might transport the animal to a vet, wondering if regular vets treated wild animals...

"Oh no." Percy jogged up behind him. Leslie sank to one knee, reaching out carefully to avoid the spreading rack of antlers and touch the creature on the neck. The fur was rougher than expected, the flesh beneath taut like a spring. He felt the racing of its pulse and the warm cloud of its breath.

"The spine looks broken, what should we do?" Percy asked. "We have to get it in the truck."

Leslie licked his lip. "Percy." He looked at the big man's red-rimmed eyes and knew his friend didn't understand.

"Wait here." Leslie pushed up to his feet with a grunt and dragged his gaze along the tree line beside the road. "Wait."

He struggled down the shoulder toward a gap in the forest edge where a field of dead cattails raised fluffy tips over the open expanse of a snow-dappled marsh, stalks bending in the wind. He spotted a suitable rock and pulled it free from the earth while beads of greasy sweat oozed from his forehead. His shoes crackled over the frost-tipped grass as he trudged back up the slope.

"I don't understand." Percy put a hand on Leslie's shoulder, but Leslie shrugged it off, never taking his eyes from the deer.

"Say something if you want," he said, but he didn't give Percy a chance, sensing his friend's confusion. He lifted the rock over his head and swung it down with a grunt, dropping to his knees to add force.

The sound was like a melon striking pavement and the buck jerked, pedaling its front hooves as Leslie lifted the rock and smashed it down again, teeth bared.

Percy grabbed Leslie beneath the armpits and wrestled him up to his feet.

"Why did you do that?" The setting sun cast sparkles across the spreading pool of blood.

"It was dying. It was hurting."

Leslie was struck by a memory. He spoke to the sanctity of the carcass at their feet.

"The last thing I remember was shooting something," Leslie said in a monotone. "A bad shot, my arrow was stuck in his ribs and he howled. I remember him rising up on his hind legs. A rack of antlers so wide, wider than any I've seen..." Leslie shook off his reverie.

"What else do you remember?"

"Running. Snarling. I remember how much the teeth hurt."

"Is there more?"

"Snatches that I don't trust. It's like whatever is in the blank spot is metastasizing into something surreal, my imagination filling in the gaps."

"Do you want to remember?"

Leslie scuffed a line in the dirt. "I think I have to."

"I'll help if I can."

Leslie shook his head, a childish twist of guilt on his lips before he looked away.

24

"I broke his antler," he said and bent, picking up the deadly thing. The thorny mass of horns was already cold to his touch and he was surprised, remembering the warmth of the deer's neck. "Come on."

Leslie walked back to the idling Pathfinder and opened the rear hatch with a pneumatic hiss. He placed the antler inside.

2.

The sky was closer in the White Mountains, and the night above was awash with a spray of stars. The black waters of the lake lapped gently, the moon's reflection dancing with the movement of a breeze that caressed the tall pines and set the white birch trees creaking.

The cabin was small and isolated, herded against the water by the encroaching wall of the forest. It contained two rooms with electricity provided by a generator, though more often than not Leslie was content with the orange glow of his fireplace and glass-shrouded oil lanterns. The cabin was called Stone's Throw and the lake was called Moon Lake for obvious reasons. Percy called it *Nibi Tibik-Kizis*, which he said meant "Moon Water" in the old Algonquin tongue. Leslie always meant to look it up but had decided at some point to leave it be. He liked the idea that the lake had an older name and that people before him had enjoyed its solitude.

"I thought you gave Jordan the condo," Percy said, and mist rose along with his voice. He sat in his usual rocking chair on the porch facing the lake, a bottle of Redbreast Irish whiskey clutched by the neck in one big-knuckled hand. The chair groaned in distress as he rocked steadily back and forth, but Percy had long since decided it was simply a complainer and would not give up the ghost while he was sitting and drinking.

The familiar sound comforted Leslie.

"She got the condo, I got the cabin," Leslie replied, holding a wooden match to the end of his cigarette and dragging deep. He shook with a racking cough that was painful to hear and shivered in the crisp air. The doctor was right; he had no business leaving the hospital. "I have another property in Brooklyn. Been waiting for a developer to buy it and put up a new building. I'll go there."

"Good place?"

Leslie shrugged and jarred loose another cough. It was reflective of their natures that he kept his blood-filled eye fixed on the dark water while Percy glanced up at the stars every time his chair rocked back on its runners.

"I thought you liked it here."

Percy handed over the bottle and Leslie swallowed a healthy draught. "I was running, man. Had to get out of New York."

"You gonna tell her you're coming back to the city?"

The glowing tip of Leslie's cigarette moved from side to side. "This one time after we'd split, we had to meet up to go over some papers—this place in Greenwich Village—and I asked what she was doing that night. She told me I didn't get to ask that anymore."

"Fuck." Percy leaned over and his chair cried out in protest. Leslie relinquished the bottle and listened to the pleasing gurgle of whiskey as Percy tilted it back.

"So I guess that works both ways," Leslie said.

"Fuck."

The orange tip of Leslie's cigarette nodded up and down. Something splashed out in the lake and ribbons of smoke drifted from his nostrils. He shivered again. "It's gone bad for me here." He looked around at the looming trees surrounding the cabin, pale birches scattered among them like a giant's finger bones.

"You sure that's not the trauma talking?"

"Nope."

The silence was full of their presence. An aura composed of tiny sounds and movements, breathing, the inaudible wrinkle of skin as faces tried on and discarded expressions. They were more pack than friends. Inseparable during their years at Dartmouth, the literature major and philosophy major walking in lockstep, leaning on each other to survive the crushing workload and the fledgling, inevitably doomed relationships with women. Leslie had made the observation during a class reunion and Percy laughed, which was Percy's default setting. That was alright. Leslie hadn't minded because when he named Percy as *pack*, the big man's spine had unconsciously straightened, his jaw and lips tightening. For the briefest of moments, Percy's eyes flickered with a sentiment long since lost by men. Percy understood. Leslie was safer in Percy's presence than with anyone in the world, and that included Jordan, who had been his wife.

"I wish you weren't so fucking dumb." Whiskey sloshed as Percy slugged. "You still can't remember anything more than you told me?"

Leslie's smile was a will-o'-the-wisp. "I remember crawling out of the woods chewed up like a fucking dog toy." He flicked the cigarette away and it arced over the railing like a shooting star. "Used to be I thought I'd find another book out here in the quiet. Something found me instead." He sat up straight. "The woods scare the shit out of me now."

They passed the bottle back and forth in silence for a while, the only sound the creaking of Percy's rocking chair, until the big man said, "Brooklyn, huh?"

"Brooklyn."

A splash out on the water.

"Fuck this," Leslie said. "Tell me what's going on with you."

Percy sank down in his chair with a crackle of wicker and his bearded face was hidden in shadow. "Same shit, different day."

"Oh, fuck you."

Percy shook the nearly empty bottle. "I'm cold," he said. "Let's head inside and make ham sandwiches."

CHAPTER FIVE

1.

Awake. Thank god. Away from the teeth of his dreams.

The weak flame of relief was doused by a repeat of the sound overhead, and Leslie sat up, blankets pooling around his waist.

A footstep.

Impossible—

Boards creaked as a man walked across the roof.

Leslie's single eye scrabbled at the murk as his head whipped back and forth, panic clawing at his fledgling consciousness. Moonlight drifting through the window was a weak ally, and Leslie's lone pupil engorged until the eye was black, the eye of a night thing—

Bare legs slid off the edge of the mattress and sleep-numb feet found the rough planking of the floor. He followed in a boneless slide until he was crouched by the side of the bed, just another creature in the dark fearing the step of a man—

A predator—

It's found me. It got a taste of me in the woods and followed me. Found me.

Fear sank barbs into his lungs, allowing only hurried sips of air. The wounds on his body throbbed with memory. He remembered pain so great he lost his humanity. Remembered howling like an animal.

Remembered the horror of being eaten.

Breath whistled past his teeth. His body thrummed with blood spiked by nature's amphetamine, adrenaline that constricted the vision and strangled the lungs as it pumped fuel into the big muscles of arm and leg.

Oh fuck, that was definitely a step on the roof.

He crept on the tips of his fingers and toes, chin lifted to maintain his watch on the ceiling lest it sprout some *thing* that dangled from the rafters. Red-eyed and silver-drooled.

Fuckmefuckmefuckme.

The clamor of his pulse was loud enough to register on the Richter scale. Painful tension was all that prevented a gleaming trail of urine as he made it to the door, mind locked on one thought.

The gun over the mantel. Double barreled. Twelve gauge.

The gun.

The door latch clanged like an iron bell and he froze, biting back a whimper, his mind a tiny craft swamped by waves of adrenaline so that fight or flight became flightflightflight.

The gun.

Fingers and toes tickling the ground like a spider's legs, he slunk along the floorboard down the narrow hall. A splinter stabbing the meat of his thumb was ignored. He let it drink.

An open doorway to his left. The bathroom was a black maw where—

A face floated in the dark! He jerked away from the pale smear of flesh and found his shoulder blades pressed against the wall as it disappeared.

Jesus, he swore silently. That was my face in the bathroom mirror. A scuff from the roof overhead injected new urgency into his veins with a flood of adrenaline.

The gun. Only the gun mattered.

He pushed his head into the sprawling savannah of the living room, heavy with the smell of the fireplace. He made out the faint glint of windowpanes on the front door and swiveled his head, preparing to stand and snatch the g—

A man was sitting at the table.

Leslie froze in a half-crouch, thighs trembling with effort.

Silver drips of moonlight trickling inside teased him with details. A square, dark back. The slack drape of an arm.

A drunk slumped over his table?

He had no neighbors.

Percy? No, that was last night. Percy had gone home.

His craven mouth opened to call out, a foolish betrayal of the whole. The hand, quicker, clamped itself over his lips.

The man did not move, but Leslie did. He lunged, grunting with effort as he snatched the weapon from the hooks. He backed away blindly from the man in the chair, hand feeling behind him for the counter—

His fingers pressed into yielding flesh.

The air was shocked from him in a whistling gasp as he twisted at the waist, swinging the length of metal and wood in a wild arc until it hit the fat, glistening orb of flesh with a meaty smack. The ham on the counter detonated, chunks of fat flying free like a rain of shiny grubs.

"Oh god."

He staggered, stepped on a slick piece of meat, and felt his knee wrench when he went down. He jerked the weapon up, jabbing the business end toward the intruder at his table as his thumb raked back over the twin hammers—catching only one—to prime the shotgun.

He crushed the trigger...

The weapon produced an oily click.

"Oh, fuck me."

And yet, a moment later, the intruder remained in his seat and Leslie's vision adjusted to the gloom. "Shit." He limped over to the bulk of the Carhartt jacket draped over the back of the chair. He jabbed it with the barrel of the gun (his need to double check would not be denied) and grinned—a little manically, perhaps—but grinned, jabbing it again, the garment he'd bought so he wouldn't look like such a city slicker.

He wondered if he would ever tell anyone about what happened. About the comic absurdity of his terror. Face still flushed with embarrassment, he imagined penning a piece for *Vanity Fair*...

Creak.

The spit dried in his mouth.

The sound from the front porch was so familiar that Leslie realized he'd been hearing it for over a minute. The steady sound audible before he attempted to murder the ham and the jacket.

The sly squeak of a board. The rhythm of the rocking chair on the front porch.

The lid over his good eye blinked, cleaning the orb, the torn remainder of the other twitching in poor imitation.

His knees popped when he sank low to creep forward, breath rattling in his lungs as if he were sprinting uphill. He worked his dry mouth, sandpapery tongue smacking.

Below the left window. To the side of the door.

The fear reared over him. Looming. Unmanning. Fat and swollen like a tick. He fought against the terrifying weight and raised his head, a rabbit cowering beneath the shadow of a hawk.

Movement on the porch. A seated figure was rocking gently, a silhouette against the moonlit snow.

Leslie ducked below the window. His throat was a desert canyon, unable to produce sound. He lifted his head to look again.

The empty chair was slowing to a stop.

Leslie moaned, sliding down below the window. He crawled to the door and reached up on his knees to run his fingers over the deadbolt.

"There was no one in the chair." A mantra.

He leaned his back against the solid wood of the door, good eye closed, shotgun clutched in a white-knuckled grip.

2.

The trill of birdsong came to him through the window, and the morning sunlight cast a handful of diamonds across the sparkling snow.

Stiff and sore, Leslie shuffled to the bathroom, fingers and toes numb with cold. He pulled the string beside the mirror over the sink and leaned close to the glass, the harsh light carving canyons in his haggard face. He was brushing his teeth when a thought struck him and a mouthful of foaming toothpaste spilled into the basin. He turned his head on a creaking neck toward the far wall where he had seen the face peering at him last night from the dark. The face he had thought was his own, reflected in the mirror.

There was no mirror on that wall.

But there was a window.

3.

When the teapot whistled, he poured water into a large, clean mug and while it cooled, dropped several cotton balls into the water as he breathed in the steam.

He wasn't sure he could do this.

In the bathroom he removed the blue eyepatch the hospital had provided and drew in a breath, releasing it slowly before looking at the slightly gummy conformer in his empty socket, the skin around it going green and yellow as the bruises changed color. The stitches on either side of his socket had yet to dissolve and gave the appearance of insect legs sprouting from his contused flesh.

He scooped out the plastic conformer and braced himself for the sight of the pink meat beneath, but it still came as a shock. His inner workings were hideous. But he had practiced at the hospital and filled another container with hot soapy water, placing the conformer inside where it bobbed innocently.

Using a single cotton ball for each wipe, he began inside the eye and swiped outward. First cleaning the mucus from his eyelids, then the socket itself.

He almost broke at that moment, convinced of his horrific Frankenstein ugliness, but he proceeded, cleaning the conformer and replacing it, then putting the stupid blue patch back in place.

He had pulled on yesterday's clothes and found his phone, summoning Percy's number from his contact list.

Percy would take him back to the hospital.

When it vibrated in his hand, he twitched in shock but answered without looking at the caller, sure that some psychic connection had sent his friend to the rescue already.

"Percy?"

"It's Angie," the voice crackled back at him, cutting in and out because of weak reception.

"Angie?"

"Yeah, your agent, remember?"

He could feel the unexpected stretch of a grin, followed by the pain of dry lips splitting.

"It's good to hear your voice."

"Hah! There's a first. Say, when are you coming back to the city?" She was closer to sixty than fifty and talked like a tough dame in a Chandler novel.

"End of the week." He felt steel bolts lock in place as he cornered himself with his own words.

"Good, call me before you get on your way." He heard the unladylike slurp of coffee. After three that slurp might be gin. "Listen, kid, I want to be able to tell people what you're working on. There's a little buzz with you going wildman in the forest and all."

"I, ah..."

"You are writing?"

"Yes."

"Gimme something."

"It's a, uh...it's a Buddy Paretsky book." He heard a hollow wind blowing through the connection. "Hello?"

"I'm here," she responded. "I thought you were done with the Paretsky stuff. Random House doesn't want Paretsky."

"I know, I just…" He fought against the cold weight forming in his belly. "It's the voice speaking to me now."

Her sigh was epic, longer than he thought possible. "After what you been through? Of course that's what's speaking to you. We'll talk about it back in the city."

Leslie brushed at the sweat dampening the hair at his temple and studied the moisture on his fingertips, trying to prolong the conversation. "You hear back from the movie people?"

"I will by the time you get to the city."

"Okay."

"I want to see you as soon as you get home. Let's do that cheese place."

"Artisanal?"

"I'll have my girl get us a table." They bullshitted for another minute before she said, "Hey, kid, you alright?"

He noticed a trickle of blood on a knuckle. The scabs kept cracking in the dry air. "Yeah, Angie. I'm good."

CHAPTER SIX

1.

Leslie's last week at Stone's Throw was an exercise in the practical management of fear.

He saw hate in the black eyes of a bird.

He heard cruelty in the laughter of the loon.

He went out during the day—only the day—to practice driving, his head swiveling to watch the trees until he was safely inside his car. Parking was trickier and he bumped his fender several times, but he discovered that while his depth perception up close was off, after twenty feet or so it was just fine.

Good, he could drive. Which meant he could flee if that thing came back to the house. He knew it was probably a raccoon, maybe smelling the ham left out on the counter. He knew it. Still...

He was inside before dark.

He retreated from his traditional evening habit of a smoke and a cocktail on the porch and stayed behind closed doors with all the curtains drawn. The porch ceded without a fight to his nocturnal visitor. He spent evenings listening to music and writing notes for his new project at the small dining table with the genny running to make the place bright.

Angie wasn't happy, but the truth of the matter was that the new book was speaking to him, shouting at him like no book in years. Yes, it was a Paretsky book, but it was such a relief to have some kind of story pulsing through his veins that he chased it down and set to work. He'd come up with the idea during his long days and nights in the hospital, swimming through opiates and pain.

Was the wellspring of words tapping into his trauma? Of course it was. He'd paid with a goddamned eye for this story and it demanded to be written.

No way to know, however, if anyone remembered Paretsky and would want to read it.

2.

The shotgun, loaded, was always within reach.

The cabinet that contained his recurve bow, lighter than the one he lost in the woods, was open at all times, the upthrust ranks of aluminum-shafted arrows shivering in the firelight as if eager to fly. He had removed the target heads from ten of the arrows and replaced them with four-bladed hunting tips. The recurve bow, faster than the compound weapon, was strung and remained so though it was bad for the wood. It was modeled on a tool from an older time, four feet long with an eighty-pound pull. It had been hand-crafted for him by a bowyer in Vermont and the guard was made of polished bone. If he found himself unable to reach his shotgun, he would go for the bow.

This was how he managed his fear.

On the third night, he remembered the antler brought home after the accident with the deer and set aside his notes. He discovered where Percy had hidden it in the closet and placed it on the table.

The genny chose that unfortunate moment to hiccup and the lights dimmed. A pine knot popped in the fireplace and Leslie found himself standing rigid with the shotgun at port arms until the lights steadied.

There was wine aplenty and he selected a bottle of Syrah from the wooden rack, putting the double barrel down only for the two-handed operation of using the corkscrew. With the deed done, he retrieved the weapon before pouring a glass with his free hand.

He swallowed in a great, throat-churning rush.

More wine gurgled into the glass.

He returned to the table and was struck by an instant revulsion for the antler. The brutality of the animal's death was etched in his memory and echoes of the horror were reflected in these remains, the velvet that once fed the antler now desiccated, shrink-wrapped skin on the way to mummifying. He muffled his urge to throw the antler outside and sipped his wine. Ran a finger along the thing. He would face this fear, safe inside with electric lights and a firearm beside him.

The wine curdled in his stomach and he asked himself, "What happened in the woods?"

He remembered antlers on the biggest buck he had ever seen. Antlers so wide they belonged on a moose. The Hart of the forest.

3.

As the sun fell on the fifth day, the eerie laugh of a loon's tremolo skipped across the water and the flesh over his spine crawled. The hyena-like cackle was followed by the long, wailing howl of the bird, so much like the call of a wolf. A second wailing cry snaked between the trees and he dropped his load of firewood, stumbling through the fall of logs as he pounded across the pine needles until his boots thudded up the steps and he was inside, slamming the door and pressing his shoulder blades against it as his hand groped for the deadbolt.

4.

That night, he took a call from the Leech.

"Oh my god, how are you?"

The man reminded him of someone from the movies, but he couldn't quite remember who. The voice so unctuous and fawning that Leslie had no equipment for dealing with the fathoms of bullshit it contained, so he took it at face value and offered a few edited answers.

"Jesus fucking Christ, it's like something in one of your books," the Leech continued, stepping on the description of Leslie's prognosis. "I mean, if they'd been people out in those woods instead of animals."

And there it was, the reason for the Leech—Norris Chapin's—fawning attention. The books Leslie wrote. No, not even that. Chapin didn't give a hoot for anything written by Leslie Ward. He wanted Buddy Paretsky, the fiction who wrote fiction. Depravity.

"Tell me the truth," the Leech said, as if he could recognize a truth. "This is going to come out, right? I mean, not in some real-life *48 Hours* TV episode, but on the page?"

Leslie knew it was a mistake. As much of a mistake as answering the call. But he was lonely and frightened and if he called Percy, he'd break down and beg for a rescue.

The Leech was someone he affectionately despised, so he answered the call and the questions, and when the big one came, the one the Leech had been working up to, Leslie said...

"Yes."

He didn't remember the rest of the call, eager to crack open a bottle and expel the taste of the conversation. A whore rinsing his mouth after a blow job.

When it ended, he did just that, popping the cork on a cheap Temperanillo—he'd no sooner drink a good wine after talking to Chapin than he would drink it with bubblegum in his mouth—and dug out his laptop.

His fingers knew the URL and soon the grey page of the ParetskyBytes message board came up. He had to create a new profile so no one would know he was lurking. Two minutes later he was logged in as TasteofSkin (it was that kind of message board) and scrolling down the first thread that caught his eye.

BIG NEWS! A new thread stated, started by EyeofGod, aka Norris Chapin. Questions popped up like kernels in a hot pan, Chapin's own particular brand of fan gathering like a cloud of flies.

A NEW BOOK!

The thread exploded with incredulity and excitement and ultimately the question Chapin was waiting for.

WILL THERE BE A NEW MOVIE?

Video clips of Chapin's work—Chapin and Leslie's work—began appearing in the thread and Leslie clicked on a few, the sedate atmosphere of the cabin churned by tinny screams from the laptop's small speaker.

5.

On the seventh day, Percy took him to the train station in Boston.

CHAPTER SEVEN

1.

Her name was Lavinia and she was holding a sign with his name upside down, waiting near the Dunkin Donuts in Penn Station. It was exactly the type of thing Lavinia would do, he was to learn, to be in the right place at the right time and somehow still not get it quite right.

She was bent forward in the manner of tall girls uncomfortable with their height, hair pulled back without thought, narrow glasses perched on an improbably small nose, wearing a vaguely brown dress beneath a brown leather bomber jacket complete with a somewhat chewed fleece collar. She looked for all the world like a person constructed by two different factories with competing design theories, one opting for the neat porcelain teeth and pert features of a child, the other going long, focused on length of spine, of arm, of finger.

"You Angie's girl?" Leslie said by way of introduction. She glanced down at her sign as if for confirmation, noticed her mistake, and righted the sign before reading it to double check and then squint down at him.

"You hurt your eye."

"Yes."

"I'm Lavinia."

He held out his free hand. "I'm Leslie."

"I know that." Her bony hand unfolded and wrapped around his.

They stood there for a moment as commuters hurried by, the noise of Penn Station wrapping them in a cocoon of privacy.

"Do you have a car?" he asked.

She tilted her head as if he'd asked an unusual question. "Of course. Angie said take care of you."

2.

Turbulent storm clouds shrouded New York City where cruel, sparkling towers gouged the belly of the sky. The tallest buildings had already vanished into the thunder-tossed maelstrom, losing ground in the endless struggle between earth and air.

The sprawling immensity expanded along 7th Avenue and threatened to consume them as if they rode a leaf on a river of quicksand. Once the layered skyline had suggested infinite possibilities to Leslie. Now the jagged structures resembled a mouthful of uneven teeth and the tallest spires rose like outstretched claws.

Still, the muffled cursing of the town car's driver and the bleating horns when they pushed into Manhattan's traffic brought a smile to Leslie's lips. Hordes of shouting sports fans were vomiting forth from the many mouths of Madison Square Garden and he wondered who was playing.

He rolled down his window to drink in the cacophony and inhale the odors of exhaust and stone and millions of New Yorkers living in one place. The crowded sidewalks became a single omnipresent organism with a thousand faces.

Coming to New York was a good idea. Exactly what he needed. He wanted a hotdog and to see a Broadway show. He would tell himself this until he believed it.

The drive to Brooklyn was something of a blur as they pushed east across midtown to the speedway of the FDR, taxis and other vehicles racing past like streaks of light. The driver exited without needing to be told a few miles south and they ground their way slowly through a strip of projects into the warren of the Lower East Side, routed through narrow plywood canyons protecting construction sites until they burst forth onto the wide lanes of Delancey Street and joined with the flow of traffic arcing over the East River on the Williamsburg Bridge.

3.

Leslie would tell himself later that it was simple relief at not being treated like a leper, but he found himself warming to Lavinia. The tall, awkward wreck of her. Like the errant hairs escaping her ponytail, tiny details of word and deed escaped her control as if intent on ruining her mimicry of a human being. She conducted herself as if she were accustomed to an atmosphere of differing density and averted her gaze from him as if her eyes were used to light on different frequencies.

And so as they rode in the upholstered comfort of the hired town car, Leslie found himself considering the tall girl contorted into a corner between seat and door.

"Emily Dickinson had a sister named Lavinia," Leslie said. "She—"

"She found her sister's poems in the bedroom after Emily died," Lavinia said with all the joy of a student reciting an encyclopedia entry. "Eventually she gave them to Mabel Loomis Todd and Emily's mentor, Thomas Higgins, who published the first editions of Emily Dickinson's poetry."

Leslie tried to wipe the surprise from his face before she could notice, but she had her eyes trained on a distant horizon.

"My parents named me for Lavinia Dickinson."

"They did?"

"Or the character from *Titus Andronicus* who has her tongue cut out. I'm not sure what message they were trying to send."

"That's odd," he said without thinking.

"Yep."

Leslie touched his eyepatch as if for reassurance and surprised himself by asking, "You're a poet?"

"Yep."

He winced inwardly; *Here's where she asks if I'll read her work.*

Instead she said, "Mostly I work with strays. The last census counted almost 2,000 loose in Brooklyn alone."

"Writers?"

She smiled as a teacher would to a slow student. "Dogs."

CHAPTER EIGHT

1.

The neighborhood had changed while Leslie was away.

Industrial storage bays, liquor stores, and storefront churches were giving way to the bright lights of farm-to-table restaurants and absinthe bars, appearing in the poor neighborhood like an eruption of acne. Manhattan hordes were sweeping in to buy up brownstones and push out families with their Manhattan money and Manhattan expectations.

That longtime residents of Bedford Stuyvesant would see him as just another well-heeled interloper was something Leslie still struggled to accept.

The car slowed and eased into an open spot beside the curb.

"We're here," Leslie said and stepped out into the cold night air.

The building greeted him like a hyena hiding amidst a group of children. He froze, vision narrowing, hackles raising on the back of his neck and bristling on his forearms. The suitcase in his right hand gained weight and he fought the urge to duck back into the idling town car.

The neighboring structure housed brand-new condominiums. It boasted six stories of wide picture windows transforming living rooms into storefront displays of life for the young and trendy. Behind the windows, elaborate light fixtures were visible, shelves of glossy books, big screen televisions, and well-appointed kitchens with hanging copper pans. The eye danced from window to window with a natural voyeuristic pleasure, viewing without guilt, perhaps aspiring.

Lavinia heaved more suitcases and a taped cardboard box from the trunk and stacked them on the sidewalk in front of the building beside Leslie's home. "What a great building."

"Just went up this year." Leslie smiled and kept his eye on her face when he pointed to their destination. "I'm in here."

269 Macon Street was a chilling shock to the system, cold water dousing bright enthusiasm. Old and uncared for, the building hunched

a full story shorter than either neighbor and was fronted by chipped red brick that naturally accumulated grime and resisted washing. If this were a street of children, 269 would be the building they told stories about, daring each other to pass on the sidewalk, perhaps to run up the seven steps of the stoop and bang a fist on the peeling black paint of the door.

In the rosy glow from the car's tail lights, she smiled. "I love the old architecture."

Leslie shot her a look to see if she was gaslighting him, but her eyes were on the building. He wondered what she saw.

A building is inert and incapable of personality, but Leslie felt the malignant regard as he drew closer, his own footsteps muffled while the whistle of wind in the building's eaves gained in strength. The front door was the gaping mouth of an idiot, the steps its lolling tongue. Meager light shone from windows on the lower two floors, but the upper stories were shrouded in gloom, glinting window glass like the baleful stare of eyes, too many eyes, a spider's count of eyes.

Malignant, yes. Malignant and somehow stupid.

Something changed in Lavinia's breathing and Leslie was struck by the premonition that she would warn him not to enter.

"The work around this door is beautiful," she said. "You should get a high-pressure cleaner."

Surely she was kidding. He pushed through the metal gate fronting the tiny, bricked yard. Green eyes flashed and the shadows on the steps took form, flashing across his vision.

"Holy shit!"

Lavinia clapped a hand on his shoulder, though whether it was to steady him or restrain him, he wasn't certain.

"Just a cat," she said. "There are so many feral cats, it's terrible for them in weather like this."

Leslie remained still for another moment, tilting his head back to rake his eye up the five stories of red brick, his weakened gaze probing for more surprises. The building was a dilapidated structure on a dilapidated street but seemed eager to suggest something to anyone wise enough to listen. Suggestions in the detailed molding, now chipped and weathered. Hints in the lettering carved into the stone over the door, battered by wind and time until Leslie could no longer read it. He was reminded of the Sphinx, who must warn travelers of their danger before it devoured them. He was reminded of the rattle on a snake.

With his vision cut in half, it was as if he saw the building for the first time.

"Let's go in," he said, and the two of them collected his things. Leslie let the gate swing shut behind them with a crash, releasing flakes of rust.

He placed a foot on the first step but a vertiginous drop stopped him and he paused again, feeling as if he were spinning. He blinked furiously to steady himself and saw the building lean impossibly. Precariously. He blinked again and raked his gaze along the neighboring structure, noting the straight vertical rise alongside the red bricks, meaning that 269 was as straight as they were. He had a feeling that if he looked away and then back, the building would fall into a heap of bricks. Were he to do it again, the construction would return.

"Are you okay?" Lavinia asked.

In an earlier century, even a writer might be so lacking in cynicism as to give greater weight to his impressions and avert the events to come. The house did not want him. But he was a modern man, a champion of the material, and resisted the intelligence of nerve endings.

Leslie shook himself free of reverie and struggled up the seven steps and into the building, ushering Lavinia through with a comedic display of clumsiness before closing the door behind him with a hollow bang.

"Put the box down, I can come back for it."

"I can do it."

"Leave it, it'll be safe."

Lavinia turned toward sitcom laughter leaking from behind the only apartment door on the first floor.

"Sounds like the super is home." Leslie shrugged. "He drinks."

Leslie ascended the listing staircase, but Lavinia wrinkled her nose at the smell of old smoke. "Someone burned their dinner?"

Leslie trudged up risers covered in a filthy carpet of no discernable color. He saved his wind until they reached the third-floor landing and pointed up the next flight of stairs.

"I have the third and fourth floors," Leslie said, pausing to catch his breath as Lavinia turned sideways to move by in the narrow hallway, her body radiating unexpected warmth. As if reading his mind, the tall girl blushed, her high color visible even in the light of the single overhead bulb.

"There's a fifth floor," Leslie continued. "Untenanted. There was a fire up there last year." He pointed at the dark staircase at the end of the landing, leading up.

"And the super hasn't made repairs?"

"The super... Well, you'll meet Gordon." Leslie grinned. "He doesn't want anyone to live there."

"Why not?"

Leslie turned his key in the lock and heard the greasy thud of the deadbolt. He pushed open the door with a scream of unoiled hinges and stepped into the pitch darkness, reaching for a wall switch. He flipped the switch and was confronted by an unexpected swarm of shapes before a blue flash and sharp snap doused the light.

"Shit."

Lavinia's hand emitted a glow as she held a bright phone aloft. He stepped inside as far as the weak light allowed and extended a tentative hand toward a wooden dresser. "Huh. Looks like Gordon has been storing furniture in here." His voice disappeared into the vast space and he was reminded of a great cave, high ceilinged, the ground a maze of boulders and stalagmites.

"You were telling me about the fifth floor," she said. "Why can't anyone live there?"

"The fire was caused by a suicide." Leslie was deliberately blunt, hoping to dampen her curiosity so that she might share his unease. "Gordon says the top floor is haunted."

Lavinia looked around.

"Cool."

2.

They discovered a dining table amidst the clutter and cleared several throw pillows from it by the simple expediency of tossing them across the room.

Lavinia discovered a black iron candelabra with five melted candles and produced matches from the pocket of her bomber jacket. Leslie was amused that she tried to hide the pack of cigarettes in the same pocket.

The candles provided a shifting orange light that left the high ceiling and the outer edges of the room in darkness, as if they stood on a disembodied floor surrounded by a sea of night. Leslie said this thing and Lavinia ducked her head as if to blush.

While she searched through the bag of groceries for a promised wine bottle, Leslie tore open the cardboard box that had arrived with his luggage and lifted an old black Remington typewriter from inside, setting it on the table with a metallic bonk.

"This house likes candlelight," Lavinia said, and Leslie wondered what things the house might *not* like.

Shadows eddied in a dark tide around the flicker of their candlelight as Lavinia poured a Bordeaux into red plastic cups. She splashed a few red drops on a stack of typewritten papers Leslie placed beside the Remington. He shrugged, shoving the stack closer to the typewriter. "Don't sweat it, it's shit."

"The book isn't going well?"

"They haven't gone well for years." Leslie tilted his cup back and swallowed the expensive wine with gleeful vulgarity.

"What's it called?"

"*All the Teeth in the World.*" Leslie grinned toothily.

They both turned at a musical chime to see a cuckoo clock mounted on the wall. It was in the shape of a red barn and they were delightfully startled when the mechanism whirred and a farmer appeared from the miniature barn doors, pursued by a farm wife carrying a kitchen knife. Leslie laughed at Lavinia's startled expression, eyes twinkling.

"Is this—" Lavinia laughed in delight when a steady *BONG-BONG-BONG* drifted down from upstairs.

"There must be a grandfather clock upstairs," Leslie said.

They waited for the noise to abate and Lavinia glanced at the cuckoo clock in time to see the farmer and his wife retreat back inside the barn doors.

She ran the tip of a long finger around the rim of her cup and opened her mouth to speak but said nothing. As if receiving a secret signal on her personal wavelength, she stood, her shoulders hunched.

"I should go."

Leslie stood more slowly, knees protesting. "I... Thank you for all your help."

"I should go."

At the door she paused. "I have to feed the dogs." She pulled the door open just wide enough to slip through and then she was gone.

CHAPTER NINE

A blanket of white lay across the mountains, draping a hush over the world. The snowfall was gentle and, if a person were to hold completely still, might speak to the listener in the whispering hiss of flurries.

Percy stayed in second gear and rarely exceeded twenty miles per hour as the snowflakes darted through the beam of his headlight and melted into blooms of fire on his reddened cheeks. The Triumph's guttural coughing was an offense against the winter peace and the great pines lowered their branches in disapproval, boughs weighted with snow that blew off in sparkling clouds in the wake of his passage. A frozen river paced him for a mile, snaking alongside the road, black patches of water visible where the ice had broken away. It was down slope to his right and littered with round stones. He fought the temptation to gun his motorcycle over the edge. The river would not carry him away.

Miles from the nearest town, Percy saw not a single vehicle on the remote road. He was grateful that a lane had been plowed not long ago as he ground through a fluffy inch of the stuff. He had his helmet on his head and sunglasses to keep the snow out of his eyes. The Triumph's saddlebags were filled with things taken almost at random from his apartment, which was still cordoned off with yellow police tape.

Rumors of his departure from the clinic were already moving through the community and cast Kristi's suicide in the worst possible light (as if it were possible to make it worse). During his last conversation with Jenny, he saw accusation in her eyes.

The wooden sign for STONE'S THROW thrust itself up beside the road and he rumbled to a halt, dragging trails through the snow with his boots until he was fully stopped. The half-mile of winding drive to the cabin was a private road and Leslie had made no provisions to have it plowed, so Percy confronted eight inches of snow on the weaving path as it climbed around a sweeping curve until it vanished into the towering pines.

He pushed back the left sleeve of his leather jacket with a gloved hand and used his thumb to wipe snow from the watch face. Not quite four o'clock. Just enough time to turn around and reach town before dark...

Or to walk the Triumph up the drive to the cabin.

He swung his right leg up and over, careful not to slip, feeling the pull of wet denim against his thighs. This was not overly smart, pushing his motorcycle deep into the wilds during a mountain storm, but God protected fools and drunkards, right? He was already a fool and if he made it to the cabin would avail himself of whatever spirits Leslie had on hand.

He turned the wheel left and pushed, grunting a cloud of breath as he fought inertia. When a foot slipped, the effect was instant. He fell chin-first against the Triumph, face slapping off the seat as it crashed down in an explosion of snow and he fell beside it.

Groaning, he touched his stinging tongue and came away with red on the fingertip of his glove. The snow fell from above in endless waves, a freezing starscape that invited him to close his eyes.

He sat up and spit a wad of red phlegm onto the smooth white ground, looking back at the track of the Triumph's tires leading down to the road.

"Dammit." He stood, shaking off snow like a hibernating bear. Spit some more blood and heaved his bike upright with an angry burst of muscle.

Upward. Quiet. His breath loud, glasses fogging until he took them off and stuck them in a pocket. The edges of the road were invisible so he kept equidistant between the trees on either side. Snow tumbled from an overloaded branch. Sweat gathered beneath his helmet and his breath froze in his beard. He was already tired, lungs laboring. But he would not allow himself to rest.

His mind wandered as he walked, and he remembered a film by Martin Scorsese. *The Mission.* No one liked it but him, but he liked it enough for everyone. In it a soldier, a terrible person who committed himself to God, suffered his own form of penance when he scaled a cliff while hauling the brutal weight of his armor. Soldier and mercenary become mystic. Percy was traveling in the opposite direction, mystic becoming fool. But the penance was the same, and so he struggled and he slipped and his beard froze on his face and tears that began as a reaction to the cold leaked hot and free when sobs overtook him.

In the healing solitude he gave himself over to the pain, the selfish anger at his loss, and because he was human and writhing in his own torment, only last did he think of the lost soul who hung herself in his apartment.

He sank to his knees, the weight of the motorcycle heavy against his shoulder, feeling the damp through his jeans, cold before his legs grew strangely warm and then numb. He had no will to move and considered letting the Triumph topple. Of sitting and hugging his knees to his chest as the flurries buried him beneath their downy shield. He thought of his friend then, lost and injured yet never stopping. He wondered at the essential difference between Leslie and himself as tingling comfort replaced the shivering chill in his middle. What kept Leslie moving when he, Percy, was ready to—

Blinking snow from his lashes, he cocked his head at a furtive sound.

The rippling laugh of a loon sent a shock through his body, and Percy released his grip on the Triumph. The battered motorcycle fell in a snowy explosion.

The laugh rang out, high and shrill. Percy's head jerked to the right as if pulled on chains and he shrieked at the sight of her, hanging deep in shadowy spaces between trees, her body swaying and white. He scuttled away and landed on his backside, feeling the concrete reality of his bulging wallet digging into a buttock even as Kristi Sugar dropped to the ground, dress flaring. Exploding into a cascade of white snow.

The white mantle flew off him as he surged upright, stiff-legged from cold and fearing the wrenching pull in his back as he heaved the Triumph up and began a lumbering run up the road while the breath rasped through sandpaper lungs and the tears froze into icy rivers in the seams of his face.

He alone broke the quiet, but Percy could not escape the feeling that he was being watched. He would flick his chin to the left or right suddenly, as if to surprise something in the open, his gaze raking the trees high above ground in search of that terrible floating form, every snow-covered knot of wood her face, every powdery cyclone her fluttering dress.

The gloaming deepened into night, always an early guest in the winter mountains. He snapped on the headlight and found comfort in the special blindness it offered, rendering unseeable everything outside that yellow cone of brilliance in which the snowflakes danced. If Kristi

Sugar was out there, he could not see her, and in the way of children, he hoped she could not see him.

Because her angry spirit would *demand* regard, just as her living self had sought attention.

After an eternity of pushing through a state beyond exhaustion, Stone's Throw humped up out of the shadows.

He pushed down the kickstand, staggering up onto the porch with a hand on the railing, lungs heaving like a bellows.

Numb hands worked the magic of keys and he stumbled inside to slam the door shut behind him with the weight of his body, his movements an exact replica of Leslie's such a short time ago.

As the black spots faded from the edge of his vision, Percy understood what had kept Leslie moving through pain and cold and hunger when the body was spent and hope was lost.

Terror.

CHAPTER TEN

"Here you go." Leslie pushed a twenty through the slot in the scarred plastic window separating the back seat from the cab driver. He stepped out into a blast of Park Avenue traffic sounds and slammed the car door behind him before hopping onto the sidewalk.

The Artisanal's sidewalk tables were empty and Leslie pushed through the glass door into the cavernous, high-ceilinged clatter of the restaurant, struck with the smell of baking bread and bubbling cheese. A cold rush of wind caught his attention and he turned to see a narrow man in a black leather jacket shouldering the door open to leave.

A familiar face, a TV face, but the name slipped his mind even as they made eye contact and each felt the jolt of recognition. "Hey," Leslie smiled.

The younger man nodded and slipped out the door. Leslie caught the eye of a tall woman in a clinging dress posing by the host stand.

"Angie Silver?" he said.

She glanced down at a seating chart spread. "This way," she said, her accent chilled by Russian permafrost.

They weaved a serpentine path among white-clothed tables and wicker chairs toward the arched opening to the restaurant's famed Cheese Cave. Leslie waved when he spotted his agent seated in a red vinyl booth.

"Leslie," Angie called out, throwing a fist in the air as if in celebration, though she made no effort to rise. She was the picture of rebellious, if aging, Upper East Side money. Her hair was colored and styled but long for her age and she wore expensive rings on fingers just beginning to show liver spots. Her makeup had been laid on a bit thick and she'd smeared lipstick on her teeth. Despite the expensive cut of her suit, however, she managed to rumple the jacket and the brooch pinned to her breast was crooked. Years ago over drinks, she'd told him that in a past life she was a bare knuckle boxer.

He believed her.

Leslie thanked the hostess when she lay a menu on the waiting plate and he slid into the booth, pushing his shopping bag ahead of him.

"Domestic chores?" Angie said.

"Trying to make the place livable."

"Lavinia said it was rustic."

"It's downright feral."

"What'd you think of her?"

"Lavinia?"

"No, Marie Antoinette."

"I think there's a lot going on beneath the surface."

Angie laughed, holding a fist before her red lips when the mirth slipped into a cough.

Leslie's fingers slipped on the cool condensation beading the clear glass when he picked up the water bottle on the table.

"I want you to stay this time." Angie smeared butter onto a piece of bread and tore off a piece, popping it into her open mouth. "Settle in. Forget women. Jordan still got that restraining thing against you?"

"I think so. I'm not sure how long it lasts."

"Doesn't matter. Forget about it. Get to work."

Leslie shifted, the healing wound in his side itchy. "I am working."

Angie grimaced and took in Leslie's appearance. "You've lost weight."

"I was getting fat."

"You look like you got a tapeworm. Order a burger."

"I'm alright."

"Eat."

The agent dragged the back of her wrist across her lips, smearing more lipstick. She cleared her throat and took a sip of white wine before nodding as if Leslie had spoken.

"Listen, I won't keep you in suspense. That's your thing, right?"

"Right." Leslie felt the smile stiffen as if it were drawn in quick drying cement. He studied black crescents of dirt beneath his fingernails.

"Warner Brothers went with someone else. They wanted a hot young voice, you know the drill."

"Oh bullshit."

"No bullshit," Angie said, swirling another sip of wine around in her mouth. Her prize fighter eyes glittered above rouged cheeks. "They want someone the kids know."

"I'm a best-selling—"

Rings flashed when she lifted a hand. "The last one was five years ago. You know how these movie jerks are. Philistines."

"I thought you said it was looking good."

Angie shrugged. "It was, but they went a different way."

"Who?"

Angie raised both palms. All she needed was a couple of plates and she'd be a waiter. "That's not what you need to worry about. Order a glass of wine."

"Who was it?"

Angie's fingers tapped nervously on the white tablecloth as if she might need to snatch them away. "McDowell."

"McDowell?" Leslie couldn't fake a smile anymore and didn't want to try. "He was just here."

Leather creaked when she shifted in her seat.

"The guy's a dilettante," Leslie said. "He's a fucking actor, for Christ's sake."

"He's hot since that vampire show and his new book is a best seller."

Leslie's mouth opened and closed before he could curse again. He felt stiff and uncomfortable in his seat. Too hot. Every movement studied.

"Look, you and I know McDowell is just a kid," Angie said.

"A kid you represent."

"Yeah, a kid I represent."

Leslie picked up a roll and tore off a piece, but his stomach rebelled at the thought of eating.

Angie showed lipstick-reddened teeth in a smile. "I already put you on deck for this thing. Said if they needed to punch up the adrenaline, you were the guy."

"On deck."

"Hey, Leslie?"

"Yeah?"

"You want fucking movie money, we need a new book. A thriller. A Leslie Ward book, not a fucking Paretsky book. Write me that fucking book and you get the fucking Hollywood money."

Leslie ran a rough tongue over chapped lips as Angie turned to the bag beside her on the banquette and proceeded to rustle until she pulled out a photocopied story from *Rolling Stone Magazine* and opened it on the table. He opened his mouth to speak and she lifted a finger, silencing him before she began reading.

"'It started out as an experiment,' Paretsky said. 'I wanted to hear a mundane conversation over dinner between the two worst people imaginable. It was *My Dinner with Andre* with a serial killer and a rapist.'"

"I was 26 years old—"

Angie's raised finger. "'It wasn't enough material to be a book on its own, but you remember the 90s and how popular that TV show *Friends* was? I thought about an apartment building, something like a cross between the nice Upper West Side place they lived and the Lower East Side dump I was in at the time, and I recreated the dynamic, except these friends were the most horrible people in existence. Real scum. They had the same concerns and triumphs of regular people but were, you know, a cannibal and a serial batterer and a dealer who sold to kids...like that.'"

Leslie picked up a roll and tore off a piece, placing it on his tongue where it absorbed the spit in his mouth. He chewed, trying not to cough while Angie ran her fake fingernail down the page and turned to the next, the crackle of the glossy paper loud in their tiny corner of the restaurant.

"Paretsky wrote two novels about the apartment building and the books generated intense debate, with the pros regaling them as the most subversive satire since *American Psycho* and the cons calling it everything from exploitative trash to sordid filth. Cult director Norris Chapin, one of the few people to have spoken with Buddy Paretsky in person, adapted the author's original dinner conversation into the midnight movie *Everybody's Fine.* The controversial film followed in the footsteps of *The Rocky Horror Picture Show* as it developed a loyal audience and complex rituals that accompanied viewings. But it was the director's retelling of one conversation with the author that created the most outrage. Paretsky is said to have suggested that the film was best experienced while riding the verge of orgasm, leading to a trend of in-theater fellatio that caused the film to be banned in most emporiums. When this journalist spoke with a long-time fan of *Everybody's Fine*, a man who had seen it twelve times in twelve different cities, I asked him what he'd like to say to Buddy Paretsky. His response? 'I wouldn't say anything, I'd be too busy sucking his dick!'"

Angie dropped the article onto the seat beside her. "This *meshugas* is what you want to return to? Random House doesn't want this. I don't know who wants this."

"What I'm working on isn't about the apartment building...but it's a Paretsky book. It's the story that's speaking to me."

"What if people find out you're Paretsky? What if Walmart decides they don't want to carry Leslie Ward's novels because of Paretsky?"

Leslie leaned back and heard the groan of the banquette beneath him. He rubbed his shoulders against the seat back as if to relieve an itch.

Angie thumped her swollen knuckles on the tablecloth. "You've been in a slump, so write your way out of it, alright? Give me another novel about Tom Flanagan. Get you back on the bestseller lists. Get you back on the movie people's radar."

Leslie experienced a bolt of pain in his empty eye socket and his face tightened.

Angie pursed her lips and shook her head. "What's this one called?"

"*All the Teeth in the World.*"

The agent slapped the table and Leslie flinched as if he'd been struck. "Well, *boychik*, that does sound like Paretsky. What's it about?"

"It's about eating."

"Eating what?"

"People, Angie. People."

CHAPTER ELEVEN

1.

The world conceals its greatest beauty in hard-to-reach places, and Percy was struck by the glorious calm of morning as he stepped out onto the snow-covered porch without a stitch of clothing.

His mind was consumed with the morning. It was a trick he had learned long ago, a method of survival when dealing with the very worst cases of addiction. The sexual abuse. The despair.

His feet began to burn with the cold, his toes numbing quickly as his scrotum tightened and his penis shrank. He chuckled, the humor made visible by clouds of vapor as he strode down the steps into snow that met his shins in a soft embrace and there stopped again to meet this morning, teeth white and bright in the tangle of his beard.

He was right to come to *Nibi Tibik-Kizis*, called Moon Water in the old Algonquin tongue and named Stone's Throw by his friend. The healing energy of the place curled around him and he threw wide his arms, sucking in several frozen breaths that drove away the hangover as steam rose from his naked body.

The sky overhead was clear and blue, and the sun blazed on his red cheeks. He saw the pale moon hanging in the sky as if waiting for him to rise and he greeted it, thanking it for watching over him during his slumber.

New fallen snow covered the frozen lake and he heard the sweep of the wind as it blew designs in the powder, wondering what they'd look like from above.

Another draught of clean air filled his lungs and was released at *Nibi Tibik-Kizis*.

He strode down the slope toward the lake and released a bright yellow arc of urine to mark his territory. That ritual completed, he measured the sensation in his feet and decided that he should retreat, build up the fire, and hope that his clothes had dried sufficiently to wear. Then he would rustle up food from the cupboard.

2.

Percy's Frye boots crunched in a vaguely flatulent manner as he walked across the snowy ground beneath the trees, keeping the lake visible to his left. The boots were tight over three layers of socks, and his torso was warm enough with three layers of t-shirts beneath his motorcycle jacket. He had borrowed a black Boston Bruins hat from the cabin and stuffed his hands into wool mittens he discovered on a shelf in a closet.

His left foot came down on something slick and his heel shot forward before he caught himself on a narrow birch, dislodging a spray of snow that chilled the back of his neck. Birds raised a ruckus in the high branches and he laughed, struck by how much better he felt only twenty four hours away from the implosion of his life. That there would be bad days ahead he knew, and he planned to seek out therapy. But for the moment he turned himself over to the beauty of the place and let its peace infuse him.

He unzipped a red nylon fanny pack and pulled out a Hershey bar, consumed it quickly, and washed the chocolate down with a handful of snow that melted on his tongue. Also in the pack was a small digital camera and, in some vague nod toward wilderness survival, a folding knife and a road flare for signaling or starting a fire.

A cluster of red berries caught his eye and he knelt, awed that nature would produce such vibrant color. While squatting he made out the fading tracks of a rabbit and headed up slope, winding around trees as he followed the path in the hope of photographing the animal.

"The woods are lovely, dark and deep," he muttered, citing the only line he could remember from Frost's famous poem.

Breath huffed from his mouth and his boots shush-shushed through the powder as he paused to study the way melting ice on a tree branch caught a ray of sunlight and threw it back at the world. He produced the camera and took several pictures, though he expected such transitory beauty was not meant to be captured.

A thought of Thoreau's deliberate living curved his lips with a smile and he decided to absorb the moment with his own unaltered senses, without the enhancement or constriction of any device. Wind tousled the treetops and gentle snowfalls scattered flakes that glittered like diamonds. Tree branches rubbed together like the forelegs of enormous flies...

He slowed and stopped, wondering at the odd thought even as he cocked his head to one side and strained to locate the direction of the discomfiting sound.

He would wonder, later, how events would have turned out if he had retreated at that moment.

But like most men touched by magic, he chose to pursue its caress and he pressed onward, the ground dipping and rising until he descended through a hollow lined by crooked black maples that he didn't remember ever seeing before, though he had hiked around the lake more times than he could count and even climbed more than one of the great pines, returning to the earth sticky with sap and smiling from the childish exertion.

He pushed through the skeletal growths of leafless bushes, their brittle twigs crackling. He heard the insectile rustling of branches again and felt another urge to return to the cabin, his joy in the morning gone.

Darkness drew his eye and he sensed as much as saw the way the black maple trees bowed toward each other to create an arched roof with a shadowy bower beneath. Beyond it and shielded by trees was something larger, a hill, perhaps a small cliff of exposed granite—

The noose hung from a branch several feet overhead, gray and frozen into an icy snake. His bowels filled with ice water as he was consumed by his nightmare made real. He turned to leave and saw the dog.

It was badly mangled, the wounds frozen from long exposure as if ready for some macabre dissection in nature's classroom. The snow around it was disturbed but free of blood, adding credence to the idea that the creature was long dead. It struck him as an intentional display, the body of the deceased laid out for viewing, the branches overhead forming a natural chapel.

It was a strange enough sight that Percy pulled out the camera. It was then, when he zoomed in, that he saw the aluminum shaft of the arrow standing up from the beast's rib cage.

Leslie's arrow. There were two dozen just like it back in the cabin.

Percy shivered with the knowledge that the pack had come for Leslie here, within running distance of home.

Switching the camera to record video, he approached with his gaze aimed through the device, weirdly eager to show Leslie that blood other than his own had been spilled.

Gloom beneath the bower shifted and Percy realized that something lurked in that hidden chapel. *Several somethings*, he amended when the shadows oozed apart with the viscous separation of a lava lamp.

They were black and numbered seven. Tall wild turkeys, their scabby heads rising as high as his own breastbone, the skin dark as if diseased, the feathers tattered and darkened with mange.

Low, gulping sounds leaked from their throats as they made their way toward the dog, closing in from all sides before they paused.

Seven heads swiveled toward Percy.

"Screw this," he said and jerked open the zipper on the fanny pack to pull out the road flare. He twisted the end and jerked it hard, holding the thing away from him as it flared into red incandescence and sparks hissed against the snow. He counted to three as if it were a grenade and threw the flare with an underhand toss. It bounced into the weird chapel in an explosion of sparks.

Ruddy light danced in avian eyes.

Percy lifted the camera and snapped a hasty shot, the flash startling him and causing the turkeys to release a chorus of their ugly, gulping calls as they trundled forth from the bower, heads bobbing. He backpedaled into a tree and the resulting cascade of snow snapped him from his mesmerized state. Within a moment he was bolting back along the path of his own footsteps until he was back among the pines. Half-shielded behind the rough bark of a trunk, he cast his gaze back along the churned snow of his trail in search of the damnable birds.

There was no sign of pursuit.

Putting the camera back in his pack, he searched about until he found a dead branch sticking from a tree and took hold of it, dropping his body weight against the wood until the thick branch snapped in his grip.

The makeshift club gave him a small measure of comfort on his trek back to Stone's Throw, skirting wide around snow-laden branches that reached down across his path, as if to snatch him off his feet. Wind gusts blew stinging crystals against his exposed cheeks and he gritted his teeth against the discomfort until he emerged into the clearing around the cabin.

CHAPTER TWELVE

1.

Her hair was white, her dog was black, her coat was grey, and she still turned heads at seventy. She wore oversized sunglasses like Bridgett Bardot and traveled the sidewalks of the Upper East Side as if they were her own.

"Madame," George said when she arrived at BXL and followed the sound of his footsteps, listening for the screech of the stool across the waxed floor to orient herself before perching at the bar like a latter-day Bacall awaiting her Bogart. She let one low-heeled shoe dangle off her foot and listened to the conversations around her, joyful in an atmosphere redolent of hoppy Trappist beer and the clatter of plates.

"Bonjour, Catherine," the bartender said.

"Bonjour, Henri," she said with a voice made for a Virginia Slims ad.

"Un martini?"

"Oui."

"Water for Hammet?" George asked, and she nodded, resting her elbows on the bar and chin in her hand as George fetched a water bowl for her guide dog and an ice shaker sang its song.

"Madame," she heard as the martini was placed on the bar. Her fingers felt the cold before they made contact with the stem of the glass.

She knew he waited as she sipped. It was not really possible to hear a smile, but she detected it in his voice as he teased her. "I have olives stuffed with blue cheese today, if you like..."

"Blasphemy." She sipped again and listened to his chuckle travel away as he attended to another patron. She remembered the first time she had asked him about his martinis and he said, "Gin, never vodka, chilled, the bottle of vermouth is lifted and I nod in the direction of France before replacing the bottle on the shelf."

She had asked for three olives and received only two, a fact she noted after her first sip. When she mentioned this failing they became fast friends, and she was in the habit of enjoying one of his martinis every weekday at lunch.

Another martini would have diminished her French and introduced a Virginia lilt to her voice, though that place was long ago and far away in the story of her life. The witchiness had stayed with her, however, undimmed by her mother's religion or her own hedonistic path to the present day.

She heard the scrape of Hammet's water bowl along the floor and the splashing lap of his tongue and smiled. He was a good dog.

Catherine Van Horn didn't think of herself as a witch, though she had been labeled such in her youth. But she did have a knack for knowing and occasionally a knack for influencing. It was the knowing that had drawn her out into the afternoon in search of pain. She was hoping to follow the knowing to a place where she might employ her influence toward the unburdening of the wounded soul that cried silently across the ether.

"Est le bien de martini?"

"It's good, Henri, I'm just woolgathering." She sipped again to prove the quality of the drink and he retreated. They took care of her at BXL and she appreciated it, much as her live-in assistant took care of her at home. But people think too many loud thoughts and following the will-o'-the-wisp of her knowing required solitude with only her good-natured Labrador to guide her.

It wasn't magic, her knack, and it wasn't fortune telling either. She thought of it as pouring her thoughts like water over the world so that they seeped into the secret cracks of things, showing her a side of reality most people didn't realize existed.

A third sip then to assuage Henri's concern and she let her thoughts spill forth, imagined them widening in a pool atop the surface of the bar and sending little rivulets toward the door. "Who are you?" she whispered.

She reached for the money clip in the pocket of her coat and peeled off a twenty, knowing the denomination because that clip only ever held twenties. On the bar it went, and she placed the glass atop it against the chance of a sticky-fingered breeze.

"Hammet," she said, and he whuffed in response, his harness jangling as her hand took hold of the handle.

"Subway," she said, and they walked out the door side by side.

2.

She waited with Hammet on a humid platform reeking of garbage as two trains thundered to a stop and disgorged a sea of passengers before rattling away into the tunnel. Twice she turned aside offers of assistance, the second from a policeman with a surprisingly gentle voice.

The third train was a downtown 6 and she clucked to Hammet, who guided her to a seat on what sounded like a mostly empty car.

It took her three stops before she was able to separate the strands of sound into individual stories. Young girls were gathered at the far end of the car. A tumbling soda can rattled with the motion of the train.

But it was a man she sought, and Hammet, attuned to her knowing, had seated Catherine directly across from her quarry.

She had been blind since birth and her concept of sight was a metaphor, a combination of senses, but she could feel a fever in him and hear his pained respiration, the tiny hairs on her arms quivering in response to the coiled tension of his body. She savored copper on her tongue, a taste of split lips and paper cuts. The whole created a picture for her of a man huddling in a cloud of black insects, millions of black dots that blinded his eyes and clogged his nose.

"Hush, boy," she said and rested a hand on Hammet's shoulders, surprised to feel his ruff bristling.

The lights in the car flickered, and though Catherine couldn't see it, she heard the girls' worried talk. She curved her lips in a smile, letting her breath out slow, Hatha yoga, hoping to slide her pulse in alongside his.

"Hey, fella," she said through a smile, not afraid to use a little sex to get his attention, even at her age.

The pain was immense, the enormity of it registering before she had time to recognize that Hammet had twisted back to close his big jaws on her finger. Existing in a place of deep awareness, she felt the teeth punching through skin, pushing aside flesh as from above and below the deadly fangs sought a meeting in the middle. The proximal phalanx of her pinky provided only token resistance and Hammet bit through the digit, jerking his head back and swallowing her finger in one growling motion.

Blood jetted from her insulted knuckle. Incredibly, she could hear the spatter in the moment before she screamed.

Hammet's muzzle pushed against her belly and his claws dug into her thighs. She released a wail of pure desperation and pushed against his strength. His bite caught fabric and flesh and she hurled herself away, banging hard into a metal pole and tripping when the train rocked on the tracks.

Her rescuer announced his identity with a predatory growl. She heard her beloved dog as his body cracked hard against window glass. The fight was brief and brutal, man and dog sounds blending in carnivorous fury as they banged and cracked off the hard surfaces of the subway car.

Hammet fell beside her and his hot blood washed over her as she clutched her torn belly.

The train slowed and the door whooshed open. Catherine heard voices raised in fear as her rescuer fled, his footsteps fading quickly into the cacophony of the station.

CHAPTER THIRTEEN

1.

Leslie walked north through the splash of red and green neon from a busy pizza joint, weaving around slower pedestrians, momentarily bogged down behind a group of women studying an outdoor flower display, until he stepped off the sidewalk and slid between cars to walk up the street against traffic, squinting against headlights and ignoring the shouted imprecations from passing drivers.

The temperature drop chilled his skin, invigorating him as he trailed clouds of breath, the air blowing from his lungs like a locomotive.

Ten blocks. Twenty. The neighborhoods changed. The fishy stink of Canal Street in Chinatown faded as he found Broadway and angled north and west across Manhattan toward the East Village. He couldn't go home yet. He'd go mad in the confines of the apartment, pacing until he wore a groove in the floor.

His mind was stretched taut, a humming wire white with heat. A strange clarity, a frightening clarity just beyond his reach. He hopped over a puddle topped by a rainbow swirl of engine oil and darted behind a delivery van onto the sidewalk, spying a bar with a green neon sign that announced MULDOON'S SALOON.

He nodded to the broad-shouldered doorman and stepped into an aromatic cloud of beer and grease stink. His shoes thudded on the hardwood floor as he paced the length of the bar, and when a man pivoted away with two brimming beer mugs, Leslie slid onto the stool.

"What can I getcha?" She had on a Harley Davidson t-shirt with the sleeves cut off and the neckline lowered, tattooed stars adorning her cheekbones. He had the urge to fuck her right there in the bar and was shocked at the surge of libido

"Jameson neat." He set a twenty down to distract from the thickness in his voice.

She winked and moved down the bar, taking more orders as she passed. It was an ability Leslie marveled at, remembering so many things in a chaotic environment. His own stint at waiting tables after school had been brief and humiliating.

"Eight bucks." She set a short glass a quarter-filled with brown liquid in front of him, spilling a bit but not enough to mind.

He sipped the whiskey, rolling the first taste on his tongue before allowing it to trickle down his throat. He noticed a split in the shoulder of his jacket. So the crazed events on the train had happened after all.

"Wild." He waited until the bartender looked his way and raised his empty glass. She brought him a fresh whiskey.

The televisions behind the bar were showing a variety of New York teams winning or losing, depending on the sport. It was the kind of programming that didn't require sound and he appreciated having something to focus on.

When he was ready, he ordered a third drink, drifting pleasantly from the booze on an empty stomach.

"Hey, look." The bartender pointed at a television at the far end of the bar. "You're on TV."

He pushed back off the stool, catching it before it could clatter to the floor, and hurried down the bar to stare up at the news anchor on screen. He was standing a little too close to the guy seated in front of him, who turned with a scowl.

"Holy shit," the seated man said, anger vanishing.

The bartender had a remote and she hit rewind, the program blurring back for several seconds before the picture resumed.

Like every other American, he instantly recognized the shaky, handheld footage filmed on a subway car during some kind of tense situation, the chyron WCBS NEWS streamed along the bottom of the screen. The image zoomed past two frightened teenagers to some kind of struggle occurring at the far end of the subway car.

Leslie saw himself onscreen, the resolution terrible but his identity undeniable. Onscreen Leslie was thin and of average height, but he seemed to move casually toward the struggle, gliding as much as walking across the subway car. He hurled the large black dog into a window before seizing it again and body-slamming it across the seats.

"Duuude, you hulked that dog!"

Leslie shook his head. He knew it had happened but couldn't reconcile the man on screen with himself, Leslie Ward, standing in Muldoon's Saloon riding a pleasant high.

"They said it went rabid, man. You saved that chick's life."

Leslie backed away from the shifting images and stepped outside into the bracing air, forgetting the cash he'd left on the bar.

2.

The air cooled his molten skin and he paused to slip a pack of American Spirits from an inside pocket, shaking the pack until he could lip one free. The same pocket held several matchbooks—he was in the habit of collecting them—and his hands were steady as he lit the coffin nail on his first try.

Walking. Headlights on passing cars stretching into yellow streaks of light. The warbling of a siren was the song of the air. He passed 50th Street and realized he was not tired. Not hungry. He could smell the trees only eight blocks away. Rich loam and growing things. The scents should have conflicted with the choking exhaust and the greasy crackle of a kebab cart, but they did not. Nature combined them into the scent that marked the city.

At 58th Street he spied the relative darkness of Central Park and strolled east, delaying his gratification, the feeling almost sexual.

He jogged easily between cars, not waiting for the light, ignoring shouts and blaring horns. Several carriages were lined up along the curb, the head of each horse shrouded in the mist of its breathing. Leslie inhaled the sharp tang of their dung and they noticed him, jostling in their harnesses. Carriage drivers in top hats hurried to soothe them.

The black iron fence stretched out of sight on either side, the dark entrance yawning before him. Dried leaves swirled past his feet, scritching along the sidewalk like the claws of small animals. They smelled of must and decomposition and comfort.

He filled his lungs with the rich odor of growing green things, so much like the woods of his memory.

He slipped the jacket off his shoulders and moved into Central Park.

CHAPTER FOURTEEN

1.

The dancing piano of Chick Corea rolled from the speakers to fill the living room with jazz. He was playing a two month, eighty set engagement at the Blue Note and Jordan wanted to reacquaint herself with his sounds before catching him live. The track lighting was dimmed to supper club levels and she sank into the beige cushions of the couch, her feet drawn up beneath her.

"Christ, when will rosé become passé again?" Chess said.

"I like rosé," Jordan said.

"It's from a box."

Jordan liked the box. The box pleased her to no end though it irritated Chess, who, admittedly, knew more about wine than she. He roamed across the thick living room rug and she chose to follow his reflection in the big living room window rather than Chess himself. Seen in reverse he was just as tall and aquiline, his hair as thick and swept back, but the twinkle in his eye seemed more honest as his ghost produced an imaginary bottle from a phantasmic shoulder bag.

"Let me open the Valpolicella."

"I want to finish the rosé."

"I'll open it to breathe then."

"To breathe."

He wandered into the kitchen and she heard the clink of the bottle against the black marble countertop. The pop of the cork was gentle. The music grew simple, Corea lost in himself, uncaring. She envied him.

"What the hell is that?" Chess called out.

Jordan twitched from her reverie and heard the plaintive howling outside the window. She rose, ignoring the gurgle of pouring wine from the kitchen, and confronted her own image in the window glass before focusing past it to stare into the dark swarm of Central Park.

"I thought we were letting it breathe?" she said.

"I'm weak with thirst."

The canine baying resumed, changing in tone as she swept her gaze down to the sidewalk some five stories below.

It was hard to make him out through the blur of passing traffic and dance of headlights, but she saw a man standing directly opposite her window, leaning against the park wall. She willed him to be gone before Chess arrived, but as if her thought had conjured him, Chess's reflection appeared beside hers bearing two bell glasses of red wine.

"Who is it?"

"I don't know."

"Wait... Is that your ex?"

"I can't tell."

"It's him, isn't it?"

"He's too far away."

"Don't you have a restraining order against him?"

Consumed with his own irritation, Chess missed her silence.

"I'm going down there," he said.

She turned around to see Chess swallow his wine and set both glasses on the obsidian coffee table. "No."

"This is creepy. He can't do this."

"Do what?"

"Stalk you."

"Stop it."

He grinned. "I'm just going down to talk." He was tall and had maintained the build of a university rower even after a decade away from the sport. His cream-colored sweater made his shoulders even broader and she knew from memory that he was a head taller than Leslie.

"Chess, sit down and let's drink the Valpolicella."

He kicked his feet into his shoes and tossed a grin over his shoulder. "The flavors will be open by the time I get back upstairs."

That was the moment she realized there was no future with Chess, not when the door closed behind him, but the moment she saw his confident grin. She knew men well and, after a good deal of trial and error, knew herself. She felt the opening of something in her chest, a gap separating herself from Chess. She wouldn't throw him out tonight, life was rarely so dramatic. She might sleep with him again and enjoy it. Might have dinner with him and attend openings at his gallery, but the apex had been reached and she let out a sigh without realizing it.

She picked up her glass and sipped as she crossed the rug, bare toes scrunching against the fake fur, and ejected the jazz CD from the player. Her fingernail ticked against the jewel cases as she ran her finger down the vertical stack of CDs, looking for something more suited to her mood.

2.

Jangly guitars and Billy Bragg's off-tune lyrics greeted Chess when he used his key to enter Jordan's apartment.

"He was gone." Chess kicked off his shoes and flopped heavily onto the couch beside her, bouncing her enough to spill a drop of red on her collarbone. "Oops," he said, using his index finger to sweep up the drop and touch it to his tongue.

"Mmmmmm," she said.

"Hey." He picked up the half-empty bottle of Valpolicella. "What are you doing?"

Wine-rouged lips curved in a grin. "You're right, it *is* good." She plucked the bottle from his hand and released another cascade into her glass.

"I think I should stay over tonight."

Jordan sighed and her breath tasted like wine. "We need to talk."

3.

Chess left after an angry-fuck and Jordan opened a Merlot, something he wouldn't deign to drink.

She wandered her apartment, naked and smelling of sex, enjoying the prickling of cold air on her skin, the tightening of nipples, hating the stink of him but refusing to shower. Flagellating herself with memories of dissatisfaction.

And of Leslie.

Her office was dark and musty, the atmosphere itself carrying the weight of age. It was the one room she hadn't changed after the divorce. Friends had asked her about it and she deflected from habit, talking about how much influence *she* had in designing it when she and Leslie first moved in together. The truth was simpler and therefore avoidable with determined effort.

The office *was* Leslie, maybe the best part of him. The purest part of the man she had married, the man she had loved and who had loved her before the sky went grey and the water thickened with pollution.

It had been real. It was important for her to remember that it had been real.

She sat in his leather chair, skin sticking to the surface as she shifted her seat. She filled her mouth with wine and let it roll across her tongue, listening, wrapping herself in shadows.

The sound of breathing competed with the mechanical ticking of an unseen clock. The ticking was stifled more than muffled, the unique muting caused by the walls of books but somehow more so, as if the room was not simply surrounded by shelved volumes but by literature of great consequence.

On a writing desk stood a banker's lamp with a green glass shade. On the lamp was a switch that, when thrown, released a cone of soft light across two newspaper articles.

The fingers of one hand deftly unfolded them, trembling as they spread the grey pieces of paper atop the grained maple surface.

From the MANCHESTER UNION LEADER:

Franconia – State Police are searching for Leslie. C. Ward of New York City, missing since Sunday...

She pushed it away to examine the second article.

From the CONCORD MONITOR:

Franconia – New York novelist Leslie C. Ward was discovered on the grounds of Canon Mountain Ski Resort...

After reading the two articles several times and smoothing non-existent wrinkles from the paper, disembodied hands reached through the cone of light for a telephone.

It was an old rotary phone and it took some time to dial the number. Eventually she heard a series of distant clicks and the sound of another phone ringing. A voicemail.

"Leslie?"

She laughed, a humorless, desperate sound, and dragged the glass of Merlot into the light, leaving a wet trail across the wood. "Sorry." Her free hand lashed out at the disconnect.

A dial tone filled her ear.

"I'm sorry it's taken me so long to call." Jordan spoke to the gloom and the clock began to chime. She made a sound that she wasn't quite aware of, an animal sound that would have shocked her had she been sober.

"Please call me back." Spoken to shadows that refused to answer.

The telephone receiver was placed back on the cradle and the dial tone silenced. The stem of the wine glass was lifted in both hands, disappearing from the light. The glass was returned to the surface. Empty.

She stood quickly and the wheeled chair rolled back to smack against the wall as she lurched, drunker than she thought.

Her rapidly diminishing faculties took Jordan as far as the living room, where she fell asleep naked and shivering on the couch in the cruel glare of the television.

4.

"Leslie Ward."

The news anchor's words prodded Jordan from slumber. She opened her eyes, working a sandpaper tongue around her dry mouth, staring blankly at the NY1 news broadcast. She saw the footage of the violent dog attack on a subway train and the equally violent rescue.

Leslie's author photo filled the screen as a disembodied voice described his career.

Pain forgotten, she pushed herself up to a sitting position and fumbled for the remote until she could rewind the segment and watch it again.

"Leslie?"

CHAPTER FIFTEEN

1.

Percy paced the length of the cabin, unable to shake the unsettled feeling that had followed him from the forest. Three times he opened Leslie's liquor cabinet (he had no palate for wine and didn't want to waste Leslie's good stuff) and three times he closed it, citing the grey afternoon light streaming in through the windows as reason not to climb into a bottle.

He stripped down to his boxers and socks and upended the round table before laying down on his back. Lifting the edge, he worked his way underneath the piece of furniture cum exercise equipment. Inhaling sharply through his nose, he blew it out through his mouth and began pressing the table up over his chest, completing ninety-two repetitions as the muscles of his chest swelled and grew fatigued. He lay panting beneath the table for an awkward minute before pressing it eight more times and letting it fall aside with a clatter.

When his pulse stopped hammering, he peeled the socks off his feet, striding outside into the winter to steam until his pores narrowed and the sweat chilled across his bare skin. He collected wood from the shed and stomped barefoot back inside the cabin where he built up the fire and quietly studied the place, noting the evenness of the corners, the smooth joining of the wood. The window frames were perfectly rectangular and the light refracting through the glass, while grey, was typical for New Hampshire in winter.

And still he felt uneasy, as struck by the oddness of his experience as if he had returned to the cabin to find the front door was mounted sideways, or if he had seen a whale breach through the ice of the lake. He remembered Leslie's words. "It's gone bad for me here."

Had Stone's Throw gone bad?

Sinking cross-legged before a fire, what they called sitting Indian style in his youth, he pressed the camera's power button to activate the device and scrolled through his mostly inept photography until he came to the video he was looking for.

The recording was shocking, lit in wild magenta by the brilliant road flare. The black birds loomed large and distinct, even more tattered than he recalled as he zoomed in, the skin of their heads more scabrous, their dangling wattles more oozing. The ruddy glint in their eyes conveyed a frightening intelligence, and though he told himself that was an effect of the flare, something in his core curled in on itself in repudiation of simple logic.

A log tumbled in the fireplace and the flames sprang up, sparks danced in the air, and the cabin was lit with a shocking orange effulgence. Startled, Percy made sure no burning wood had tumbled free and it was only when he glanced back at the images on the camera, the spell of the eyes broken, that he saw past the cluster of wildlife to what the flare's bright glare revealed at the back of the strange chapel.

Stones. Towering stones. Great vertical megaliths of granite supporting what looked like a table stone across the top.

It was a dolmen. A stone construction from the age before recorded history.

Percy's mouth opened and closed as if he wanted to ask questions. He was well-versed in the indigenous peoples of the region, explored as part of his studies at Dartmouth. The Abenaki, Penacook, and Micmacs were known for wooden lodge houses but never for stone construction. In fact, it was this lack of stone construction that enabled European colonists to so easily declare the natives uncivilized.

This dolmen was not unlike its European counterparts. While discovery of Viking landings had been made farther north in Nova Scotia, it was not unimaginable that Norsemen had made their way south into present-day New Hampshire. A place rich with resources and game and sparsely populated by people.

It was a stunning discovery and Percy flirted with the notion of dressing and returning to the woods, this time equipped with electric lights and a shotgun. One glance at the dark beyond the windows dowsed the bright flare of enthusiasm.

It wouldn't do to go into the woods at night.

Not where *they* waited.

Tight muscles in his neck relaxed as he realized that any expedition would have to be put off until the morrow. So deciding, Percy set aside the camera and took up a bottle of rye from the liquor cabinet and sat in his shorts to drink from the bottle, listening to the growing wind and thinking of old religions.

2.

In the shifting glare of the road flare, the seven crept forth from the unnatural bower to encircle the ravaged body of the dog. Their sack cloth wrappings dragged across the snow, moth-eaten fabric trailing drifts of coal dust as they struggled between definitions of themselves, now squat, now man-shaped, now towering and horned with great spreading antlers that scraped twigs from the interlocking maple branches overhead.

The stiff body of the canine folded in half with a sharp crack of ice and its broken jaws released a howl of terror.

"Oh my God."

Percy propped himself up on his elbows beneath the covers, casting frantically about in the unfamiliar space until he made out the open doorway into the main room of the cabin and saw the shifting orange glow from the fireplace, umber hints of detail reassuring him.

A gust of wind howled through the eves and Percy kicked off the blanket. He didn't remember crawling into bed and felt as if he had invaded Leslie's private space in some unseemly way.

The wind whistled into the bedroom and something moved in the main room. Fear seized Percy's breath until he could discern the fluttering pages of a paperback novel on the floor.

He lowered his bare feet and his toes curled against the cold wood as he lumbered out into the firelit space of the living room, a glance showing him blackened logs laced with tangerine as sparks danced up in a whirlwind. His heart leapt in his chest when he saw the front door swinging open before it banged against the wall and rebounded. The spit dried in his mouth and he froze, muscles taut with fear.

The dim light revealed a trail of splotches leading across the floor to the open door. "What?" He snatched an electric Coleman lantern from a shelf and snapped it alight, scouring the shadows from the room with its white glare.

The lantern light revealed pale spatters of bird shit befouling the floor.

A shriek swelled inside his mind at the thought of the large, wizened birds inside the cabin. In three long strides he was at the door and leaned out with his lantern held aloft. Swirling snow devils danced in the yard as the night wind sang. For one brief moment, Percy saw the distinctive tracks of large birds leading up the steps to the door before a sharp gust swept the wood clean.

3.

The pane of glass warmed against his forehead as morning bruised the night sky, painting the snowscape molten. Percy blinked and huddled deeper in his blanket, surprised that he had dozed off during his vigil, dark hours spent staring out the windows in search of the birds.

He coughed and shivered. Took in the open bottle of whiskey on the table, the loaded shotgun resting beside it.

Stage setting for a suicide.

CHAPTER SIXTEEN

1.

Leslie ignored the wall switch inside the door to his apartment, making his way to the narrow staircase by feel and climbing with a heavy tread. He tripped once, exhausted, cheeks crinkled with salt as his face worked through expressions.

His mind leapt to the black dog, crippled after his tremendous throw. He was still trying to understand the moment. The strength. The certainty.

"Lavinia?" He wasn't sure why he called her name. Why he was thinking of the odd girl after standing outside Jordan's apartment. His former apartment.

He was so very tired.

He shambled toward his bedroom, stripping as he walked, discarding the idea of a drink to steady his nerves. He needed sleep to make sense of the evening.

Light splashed in through the window—he had yet to install curtains—but his air mattress was against the wall in shadows and he dropped to one knee and then rolled into bed.

"Ach!"

A *BANG* announced the popping of the air mattress and he arched his back like a man electrocuted. Without conscious thought, he rolled to his hands and knees, scrabbling behind him to feel the wash of hot blood spilling down his skin.

"Shit!"

He scooped up a flashlight and swept the beam over his deflating air mattress.

The deer antler waited innocently atop it.

A chill struck him with the force of an ocean wave, drenching him in icy fear. He felt goosebumps rising along his bare skin and his nipples tightened into painful knobs.

It tasted me.

He bent and picked it up, wincing at the pain of his wounds. The horn felt warm in his hand, rough and ugly, and the wet gleam of blood drew his eye to sharp points. He carried it into the bathroom and placed the ungainly weapon into the tub before turning on the shower to wash it clean.

After several minutes of scalding spray had filled the room with steam, Leslie placed the antler safely atop a stack of boxes and stepped into the shower himself, careful not to slip. He let the hot water mix with flowing blood to clean his wounds, and when he was done, he examined them in the mirror, three separate punctures below his shoulder blade seeping pink. Not deep, but painful.

Bunching a towel against his injury, he cleared boxes off a couch and stretched out on the cushions.

2.

For one panicked moment, Leslie had no idea where he was.

He sat up on the couch, grimacing at the ache from his back, the towel stuck to his scabbing wounds. A floorboard creaked in the hall outside and he froze. "Who is it?" His voice was thin with fear.

There was no response.

He held his breath, imagining a faceless intruder in the hall

(great antlers spreading wide)

on the other side of the door, waiting for him to make a sound. He clicked on his flashlight and the bright circle settled on the doorknob.

It turned.

Leslie lunged, grabbing the knob, trying to remember if he had thrown the bolt, when a blow shuddered the door in its frame and he stumbled back with a cry.

A weapon found his hand. The antler.

His skin shrank from the contact even as his knuckles whitened, grip tightening. He pawed the air with the antler and it was an absurd gesture, an old woman forking the sign of the Evil Eye.

Breath held behind clenched teeth, he turned the knob and threw open the door. His flashlight revealed nothing but the bare wall opposite and he stepped into the passage, blinking against the fluttering cobwebs to shine the flashlight down the hall. The yellow splash of illumination flitted around the blackness where cobwebs fluttered over rotting carpet.

He caught the fleeting image of a pale foot vanishing around the newel post and experienced the hideous sensation of his skin crawling over the surface of his body.

He damned the architect whose whim dictated that rather than a revealing banister, the final staircase should ascend a narrow corridor all its own. Before his flagging courage could desert him completely, Leslie sprang down the hall and crouched at the bottom of the last flight of stairs, his light playing smoothly up each riser until it gleamed off the alabaster flesh of a naked man.

Leslie shrieked and stumbled back, his flight arrested by the crushing contact of his shoulder blades with the wall. His aim dropped during his panic and illuminated only the bare feet as they turned on that top step to face toward him, toenails long and curved. He averted his face even as the light climbed with an addict's trembling eagerness toward the bare legs and flaccid penis of the man, higher over hanging gut and flabby chest to the silent horror of a face.

What Leslie saw was a terrified manikin, jaw unhinged, mouth open wide in a voiceless scream, its eyes blind caverns incapable of sight.

"Gordon?"

A frigid chill rolled down the staircase and the barometric pressure dropped. Leslie had never imagined such an experience, never conceived it possible to be paralyzed by sheer imagination. He was drowning, the hinges of his own jaw loosening, his pupils swallowing his eyes when an incident of biology saved him. A brief, shameful squirt of urine wetted his underwear and trickled in a hot path down his thigh.

"Gordon!" Leslie gathered the shreds of his bravery and crept up the stairs, one eye on the waiting door behind the old man. He prayed then, not to the Christian God but to the faceless deity of children. Prayed that the door should remain closed until he had gathered Gordon to him, afraid that if it should open he would go blind with terror, abandoning the old man to whatever emerged.

"Take my hand." He flinched when the next step screamed under his weight. Tucking the flashlight below his right arm, unwilling or unable to release the antler. He stretched his left hand forth, fingers extended as if to exert a pull, a command.

Gordon's hand inched forward and allowed itself to be gathered in a powerful grip.

"Come!"

Leslie crept backward, tugging the super down the stairs, prepared at any moment to drag him off his feet if the door atop the stairs swung open.

They followed the bobbing beam of the flashlight until he pulled Gordon through the doorway into his apartment. He threw his shoulder against the door, slamming it shut with a hollow boom. Breathing then and not shivering, shivering was too mild a term for what overcame him, a lie. He shook with his weight against the wood of the door so that it rattled in its frame.

He led Gordon downstairs where he set lights to burning. He could smell alcohol on Gordon's breath and recognized symptoms of shock.

"Can you hear me?"

Gordon's eyes rolled toward him so slowly that Leslie imagined the grating of stone against stone. Purplish lips flapped and Leslie realized that the old man had not put in his dentures. He felt a wave of embarrassment for Gordon and draped a blanket over his shoulders before leading him out into the safely lit hall of the third floor. Gordon followed his directions as would an idiot child until they reached the open door to the first-floor unit and entered a living room lit in the flickering blue of a vast, boxy TV of ancient make.

"Holy shit," Leslie muttered as they entered a hoarder's lair. The reek was tremendous, rotting food, the sharp tang of urine, and a smothering stink of mildew.

He couldn't remember the last time he had been inside Gordon's apartment, but the old man had deteriorated since the last visit. Great stacks of newspapers and magazines formed a replica of midtown Manhattan on the floor, his hoarding metastasizing into something huge and awful. A visible manifestation of the madness eating his mind.

Leslie navigated the passage to a ragged lazy boy chair sporting great patches of electrical tape. Gordon's sad captain's chair.

"Right here, man, siddown."

The old man allowed himself to be turned and backed up until the chair touched the back of his legs, at which point he sat with a wheeze. The blanket rucked up against the chair back and piled behind Gordon's head until it draped down over his face. The old man was perfectly still but the sight struck Leslie with the force of a premonition. A desperate tug yanked the covering from his face, but the closed eyes furthered the image of a corpse.

He didn't believe in prescience, but the sight of Gordon's covered face clung to him like a rain-soaked shirt and he shivered in spite of himself.

Leslie decided that sleep was the old man's best ally and was turning toward the television when a heap of shadow near the box uncurled and rose.

White fangs gleamed from the darkness.

Leslie's breath caught in his throat and every muscle in his frame locked. He heard the loud thud of his heart and a plaintive whine, and it took several seconds to realize that the whine was coming from the shadow.

The pitbull shuffled forward with an ungainly step as the thudding resolved itself into the wag of his tail, striking the television with metronomic regularity.

Leslie worked spit into his mouth. "Easy, boy."

The dog whined and shuffled closer, ears lowered as it snuffled cautiously forward, tail wagging with greater speed. In the cruel light from the TV screen, the dog was a terrible sight, scarred and thin, its ribs visible beneath mangy fur. It took another strange step on its single front leg and lifted its snout with another whine.

Leslie felt the jolt as he saw the wet shine of its one eye, the other lost in a snarl of scar tissue.

Surprising himself, Leslie sank to one knee. "What happened to you, boy?" He held out his hand and the dog crept closer, shivering, cold nose brushing his fingers.

A million thoughts crashed through his mind in a tangle, the most surprising was a surge of warmth. A counselor at the hospital said there might be phobic reactions to dogs, but he felt nothing of the sort. Instead, he read the dog's message in the tilt of its blocky skull and the shift of its tail.

"Are you hungry?"

The pit chuffed and pressed its head against his knee, nearly unbalancing him. Skinny as it was, the dog was strong.

"Why don't you come with me?" Leslie felt around the filthy collar for tags and found none as a long tongue lapped his wrist. "Come up with me until Gordon feels better."

He slipped quietly through the maze of moldering periodicals with the dog at his heels and out into the hall, pulling the door closed behind him.

"Do you have a name?"

The pitbull sat and stared up at him, head tilted to the side. Leslie's single eye met that of the dog.

"How about Wotan?"

The pitbull chuffed and Leslie led Wotan upstairs.

CHAPTER SEVENTEEN

1.

The relentless tapping invaded Leslie's sleep. He imagined a gathered army of clocks speeding up, enraged and insane until they burst apart in an explosion of spinning gears.

"Ugnh."

He sat up as morning light streamed in through the window, climbing stiffly from the couch as the tapping resumed in machine gun bursts. Typing. Good, he was writing.

A burst of pain behind his missing eye derailed the obvious question.

Leslie bent with a hand on the small of his back to pluck his pants off the floor, stifling another yawn as he stepped into them and shuffled toward the stairs. He held the rail for balance and walked quietly, determined not to interrupt the writing on his way to the kitchen and the blessed nirvana of coffee.

In the downstairs living room, he hesitated as he saw himself seated at the table, spying his own bare back hunched over the typewriter, his own spiderlike fingers dancing madly over the keys. The scalloped outline of his spine was visible beneath the blue-white skin and the cleft of his buttocks was revealed between the slats of the chair back. He found the sight of himself grotesque and was ashamed at his nakedness.

He made as if to back away, but the damnable floorboards screeched and his typing self whipped about, a clumsy red smear around his mouth, white teeth bared in a grin.

2.

Leslie was shivering in the cold blast of air through the open window. He had kicked off his blankets during the night and beads of sweat were freezing like scattered crystals of ice on his skin. He sat up expecting to hear the crackle of frost.

Raspy breathing drew his attention to Wotan, curled on the floor against the couch. After eating all of Leslie's lunchmeat, he had followed Leslie upstairs and almost immediately fell into a deep sleep.

Leslie had no idea that dogs snored.

Imagining the warm aroma of Guatemalan Blend, he forced last night's dream aside, staggering to the bathroom to release a long, hissing stream of piss into the bubbling cauldron of the toilet. The smell was rank and sharp, the urine of a diseased thing. He flushed it away and went downstairs, bare feet sticking to the wooden steps as he descended.

The Remington squatted on the table, unmanned, the stack of pages unmolested beside it. He picked up his phone, absently noting the low charge before thumbing the button to listen to a waiting message. Angie's words tumbled forth like a waterfall.

"Turn on the TV, you're all over the news. Are you crazy? That animal could have killed you. *Killed you.* NBC called. New York One. *The Post.* I think you should talk to them, but you've gotta call me first. You can use this. Use that time in the woods. You can use this to let everyone know that *you* wrote those Buddy Paretsky books. But instead of looking like a creep, you're the heroic guy who studies his own darkness while rescuing old society broads on the 6 train. This new Paretsky book? The *Teeth* thing? You're gonna write it under your own name. Call me."

3.

Leslie rotated his shoulders as he descended the steps and glanced at Gordon's apartment door, pausing to listen, hearing nothing. His sweatpants were too short, so he rolled them up over his calves, feeling the cold bite of the morning air on his skin, and tugged the hood of his sweatshirt up over his head.

Tapping his pocket to make sure he had his keys and his wallet, Leslie pushed through the door into the vestibule and then through the heavier wooden door into the chill morning.

The sight on the steps slapped him awake.

He shifted his feet as if to retreat, feeling the stickiness against the soles of his sneakers, already leaving footprints in the coagulating gore splashed across the steps.

Wind ruffled his hair as he struggled to make sense of the matted clumps of fur scattered over the risers. He made out a rounded lump the diameter of a fifty-cent piece with claws distended. He stared into the milky yellow eyes of a cat and began to understand.

It was an abattoir. A slaughterhouse. Pieces everywhere. How many were there? He crouched as if to pick up the small, clotted mess of a severed foreleg. Stopped himself before making contact and pressed a hand to his mouth.

Three cats. One ripped raggedly in two. One bereft of limbs. One decapitated, the head nowhere to be seen. He struggled to reconcile the massacre with his knowledge that feral felines fought frequently. Led violent lives.

But they didn't use hand grenades.

"Fuck."

4.

A froth of pink tumbled in a series of small waterfalls down the steps as Leslie moved the spray of a garden hose back and forth.

"Leslie Ward?"

He stopped spraying to look at an approaching man in a flapping overcoat. The man was short and brown, composed entirely of round parts. A round head atop curved shoulders and a round midsection, rimless round spectacles in the style of John Lennon, and Cupid's bow lips that stretched into a curving smile.

"That's me." Leslie picked up a Hefty bag.

"What happened?"

"Like a cat gang fight. What's left of them is in there." He gestured to the row of three plastic trashcans.

The newcomer popped a bright yellow gumball in his mouth and glanced up at the building. "Is this your place?" His words were muffled around the gum.

"Yeah."

"Not Central Park West?"

Tension knotted Leslie's shoulders. "Who are you?"

The round man got his gum chewing under control and offered another smile. "Lieutenant Argyle." His eyes lost their warmth while the smile stayed in place. "I was in the neighborhood and wanted to remind you that while the restraining order has lapsed, it's easy to reinstate."

Leslie's cheeks burst into flame even as cold sweat broke out on his body, a mix of shame and fury tangling his tongue. "Did Jordan send you?"

"Jordan?" Argyle's confusion seemed genuine until recognition dawned. "Oh, no. I'm just here as a concerned friend."

"Of whom?"

"You, Mr. Ward."

5.

Leslie's sneakers slapped the sidewalk as he pounded west on Empire Boulevard, dodged around a line of school children holding hands at Mary Plinkett Avenue and through the iron gate into Prospect Park.

Passersby looked away from his fierce grin and flinched at the sweat flung from his body. He moved in an ecstasy of pain, his hips and shoulders rolling with newfound ease. The body discovering ancient mechanics. The mind giving itself over.

He felt like he could run for days.

This park was wilder than its Manhattan cousin, Central Park, and the path was lined with trees and bushes denuding themselves in anticipation of winter. His sneakers scuffed over damp leaves as he loped past squirrels gathering nuts before the frost. He cruised past happy couples outside the Botanical Garden and slowed as he approached the Prospect Park Zoo.

He fumbled a damp ten-dollar bill from his pocket, handing it to a young lady in a head scarf at the ticket booth. Reluctant to touch the wet money, she nonetheless slid a red paper ticket beneath the window, only to find that he had moved on.

A rank odor lingered in his wake.

Past the splashing sea lions in their watery pool, Leslie followed invisible signals alongside the Animal Lifestyles enclosure. His upper lip curled away from his teeth as the baboon troop began to holler and screech. Something red swam behind his eyes and submerged.

Past classrooms, he found the exit to the Discovery Trail and stepped through over the objections of a staff member.

Gravel crunched beneath his feet as deer flinched away. A porcupine bristled on the other side of a fence and a great, flightless bird trotted to the far end of its pasture.

He arrived at his destination to find the six of them waiting. Reddish brown and small, their black eyes met his as pink tongues lolled from open mouths.

Leslie hunched, chest hitching, riveted on the wild dogs. Dingoes from Australia. Never domesticated.

Time lost its meaning as wordless communication passed between the hunters, two-legged and four.

Smells grew vivid. Hunger clawed at his belly.

An idea struck Leslie. A beautiful, perfect idea whispered to him in a voice as clean and clear as Buddy Paretsky's. He braced his hands on the fence separating him from the pack and fought the urge to grin.

CHAPTER EIGHTEEN

When Lavinia let herself into Leslie's apartment, Wotan let out a delighted howl and darted from the mess with his tail wagging.

Lavinia put a hand to her chest in surprise before crouching down, knees popping. "Well, who are you, beautiful?" The dog snuffled forward. "I bet you're Wotan."

Lavinia scratched the scarred dog behind the ears and under his chin, the pit rumbling contentedly until she stood. "Hey, buddy, I'm gonna take you for a walk but I have to pee first."

She made her way to the bathroom with the dog at her heels and closed the door to keep him out. She ran the water and released one startled laugh before quieting herself. She didn't want the landlord to hear her and storm his way upstairs. Leslie said he seemed less stable than he once was, relaying the story of finding the old man sleep-walking upstairs and discovering the starving dog in his apartment.

She tugged a bath towel from the hook where it hung alongside the mildewed shower curtain and recognized all the symptoms of bachelorhood en extremis. The ragged towel smelled a bit musky, so she hung it back on the hook and scraped water off her face with her palms.

Shadows grew long in the large downstairs room despite the bright afternoon. It was an apartment that relished stale air and gloom. Lavinia felt uneasy, as if she had stumbled into a fox den on a nature hike. She turned on several lights, looking past stacks of books and papers around Leslie's couch until her eyes came to rest on the table and the strange, ritualistic artifact resting beside Leslie's typewriter.

It was a dear antler jutting up from a long wooden trough filled with congealed wax, the stubs of many colored candles rising like broken teeth.

One index finger pressed the hard, rough horn and she pushed gently, rocking the antler in its wooden trough. It made a noise that raised her hackles, scraping and unpleasant. She suspected there was no sound exactly like it.

Lavinia had never experienced the sensation of crawling flesh, but she felt it in that moment, the meat of her finger straining to retreat back up the bone. It was a hideous, frightening feeling and she was struck by her solitude, calling out reflexively, "Wotan?"

She heard the muffled whuff from upstairs and a scuffling sound and headed for the staircase, climbing the steep steps quickly with the aid of her hands.

In the dirty light streaming through the windows, she found the small pitbull curled and snoring on the couch that had so recently served as Leslie's bed. She sat beside the dog and ran her fingertips over his ribs, calming herself as Wotan breathed.

CHAPTER NINETEEN

It didn't matter how rich a person was, how beautiful, how many flowers filled the room...the chemical stink of illness, shit, and death was never completely banished from a hospital.

Argyle looked down at Catherine Van Horn where she rested beneath a thin maroon blanket and thought blasphemous thoughts. She looked old without makeup. Her skin like stretched parchment, the crow's feet around her eyes deeper. It worried him to see her so frail, the cruel IV needle bruising her skin and the entirety of her violated hand wrapped, club-like, in white gauze.

He listened to the rasp of her breathing and the gentle beep of a monitor as he checked the water levels in various vases, refilling one from the sink in the attached bathroom, and then picked up her chart from the foot of her bed to scan the gibberish scrawled upon it.

He was sniffing a blue flower in a bedside vase when he heard, "Did you see him?"

Argyle lifted his fingers away from the blossom and smiled so she would hear it in his voice.

"I found him in Bedford Stuyvesant about to go for a jog."

"Health nut?"

Argyle frowned. "I don't think so. He looked like a refugee. Too skinny. Eyes too wide. Eye. He wears a patch over his right eye and the scars around it are still pink."

"Really?"

"I looked into him—"

"Of course you did."

"—he went missing not too long ago. Some kind of hunting accident."

"Missing?"

"Out in the woods for a week. Crawled onto the grounds of a ski resort and was found by the maintenance crew."

"Where in the woods?"

"New Hampshire. White Mountains."

"Old mountains."

"I don't—"

"Old forest."

Argyle just waited for her mind to spin through its calculations. He'd known Catherine since he was in high school, when his essay won him a full ride to John Jay College, courtesy of Catherine Van Horn. She was a strange one and prone to fugues but saw more and with greater clarity than most people, despite her blindness.

"What is it?" Her left eyebrow raised and she smirked. She could hear his thinking in his silence as well as in his voice. It would be eerie if he didn't love her.

"Something off about him, Catherine," he said, stroking his fleshy chin. "Raised my hackles. I pushed him a little bit."

"Why?"

"That's it, I don't know. It was a reflex. I went out there to thank him. Tell him about you, see if he wanted to visit... Now I don't want him anywhere near you."

"One eye, you say?"

"His ex-wife had a restraining order against him."

Catherine sighed and her hand found his where it rested on the bed rail. "Divorce is an ugly, disruptive event. You know this, Eustace."

She patted his hand before sliding her fingers free to touch the bulge of her gown over the bandages. "I asked them to wait but they said his injuries were too severe. He was in pain."

"Oh, Catherine." His wide hand stroked her silky hair.

"I told them to do it," she said. "Hammet is gone now."

Her eyes filled with tears.

CHAPTER TWENTY

1.

PAGING BARRY WHITE.

Chess stood amidst twisted masses of metal worked into human form, the scuff of his shoes loud against the raw floor and unpainted brick interior of the darkened gallery. He inhaled, flaring his nostrils. It was a practiced movement, developed for this exhibit. He liked to tell people, women, that the metal smelled like blood. That they weren't in a gallery, but a slaughterhouse.

It was important to cultivate an edge.

WHICH ALBUM? he texted back, typing quickly with his big thumbs.

THIRD.

An instant reply earned a smile, his client jonesing hard. He could use the three hundred bucks too.

He did a calculation and texted back a time to meet before jogging through the gallery to his cramped office. He ditched the John Varvatos jacket for his ghetto threads, a leather motorcycle jacket he'd actually bought two blocks away in Soho, a little too thin and too light to be the real thing, but the distressing and artfully applied stains gave it an aura of authenticity.

Chess sauntered back through the exhibit and pushed out through the glass door as a low-slung BMW buzzed past, Mariah Carey leaking from the windows. A quick hop enabled him to snatch the dangling chain and drag down the steel security mesh that protected the gallery. He slammed it into place, stomping the latch once with his heel, then crouched and locked it.

2.

Chess headed south with ground-eating strides, pausing only to check out the legs on a trio of party girls he passed. The redhead was something, nearly his own height in her stilettos. He caught her eye and thought she smiled. Imagined how it would excite her to hear about what he was doing. The kind of guy he was.

That was the kind of girl he needed. Looking for excitement.

Fuck Jordan anyway.

Mist was beading on his leather sleeves and the storefront signs were sprouting Chinese writing well before he turned left onto Canal Street, his pace slowing to a crawl in the bustle of locals and the crowds of tourists come to gawk at them. He could have picked up the train a little closer to the gallery but was less likely to run into someone he knew if he boarded in Chinatown.

It was cool to be cool, but staying out of prison was cool too.

He stepped into a line of people shuffling down muddy steps and slipped around the knot of slow movers as soon as he could, metro pass already in hand. A quick swipe and a turn of his hip and he was through the turnstile, galloping down another set of stairs to the E train platform.

It was only a minute before a blast of damp wind from the tunnel heralded the appearance of his train. He stepped behind the yellow line as it rattled to a stop, the doors wheezing open to let him board. He took the middle in a cluster of three open seats, knees open wide to discourage anyone sitting near him.

Several stops later he disembarked at the World Trade Center, hustling up the stairs into the quieter streets of the Financial District. The weather was getting worse, a cold chill that sliced through his jacket and settled into his bones, and he cursed the lack of an umbrella. But he wanted to hurry and get the job done, and he kept up a good pace until he reached the subway station at Park Place and once again dropped beneath the surface of the earth.

Settling in for the long ride out to Brooklyn's darkest corner, he never noticed the person following him.

3.

Emerging at the Rockaway Avenue station was like stepping into a different reality from the chic fashionistas and bistros of Soho.

"Crap." It was raining in earnest. A dog howled in the night and Chess shivered.

He narrowly missed stepping in a steaming pile of crap and kicked a beer bottle against the far curb where it cracked but didn't shatter.

A crumpled black watch cap came out of his jacket pocket and he tugged it over his hair. There was no hiding that he was white, but he didn't need to advertise in the glow of every streetlight that he was so blond.

After four minutes of quick-stepping past storefronts with boarded-over windows, he had reached Brownsville, one of the most depressed sections of Brooklyn. The kind of place where kids didn't stay home for snow days, they stayed home when it rained bullets. As far from the Brooklyn gentrification fad as you could get and still be in the city.

Chess approached a TV with the screen kicked in piled against a broken toilet and a three-wheeled shopping cart. It would make for a great photo, the kind of shot he'd show to the right kind of lady to let her know he rode the edge. But his peripheral vision had already picked out a cluster of young men on a stoop and he decided that flashing an iPhone wasn't in his best interests.

Fists jammed into his pockets, he didn't notice the figure trailing him a block or so back, anonymous in a hooded sweatshirt. If he knew that the follower had tailed him all the way from Manhattan, he would have broken off immediately, but Chess was working so hard to be alert that he was aware of nothing...

And the follower was talented.

Chess stepped into the doorway of a five-story apartment building at 323 Osborn Street and pulled out his phone, tapping out a quick text.

ALRIGHT flashed across the iPhone screen and Chess ducked through the metal door with the wire mesh security window. Neither the buzzer nor lock worked, but he didn't worry too much once he got inside and pushed through the fire door to the stairwell. People in the neighborhood knew who lived on the third floor at 323 Osborn and only someone serious would cause trouble at that address.

4.

Tugging down the front of his sweatpants, the follower roped out his dick and pissed on the apartment door, adding one more layer of rottenness to the place. It was a powerful, hissing stream that darkened the wood, and when he felt his bladder nearing empty, he elevated his aim to spackle the doorknob, teeth flashing white in the shadows of his hooded sweatshirt.

323 Osborn was a real shithole.

McDonald's wrappers crinkled beneath his feet as the man adjusted his stance beneath a single fluorescent lamp while the dance of light and shadow stretched flickering fingers down the hall. It was a corridor to be mugged in, stinking of old grease and septic tanks.

The follower pressed his ear against the door and felt the thump of the speakers, wrinkling his nose at the cannabis stink that seeped through the wood. The faux-brass number 3E on the door hung upside down from a single nail.

"Hey, what you doing?"

The follower turned toward a heavyset woman peering from a doorway down the hall. He casually put himself back into his pants and tied the drawstring.

"Fuck off," he growled, teeth bright inside the hood. She would later tell her son that *it was a grin full of beetles.*

The woman unleashed a barrage of Spanish, but ducked inside and slammed the door when he stepped her way.

Sticking the end of a cigarette between his lips, the follower spun the flint of a steel lighter until the tip of the butt flared orange. Smoke trickled up from inside his hood.

5.

Chess slammed to the ground as glass shards rained down around him.

Snarls and screams chased him from the broken window three stories above and his bladder voided, the hot liquid drenching his crotch as his teeth ground each other into mulch and his eyes bulged from their sockets.

Fear coursed through him like a hydrostatic charge.

He scuttled away from the flat bang of a gunshot, flinching as something dark filled the window through which he had escaped. He wasn't sure if it was beast or man and didn't wait to see, scrambling on all fours until he could stagger into a limping run, tears of agony streaming from his eyes.

His ankle gave out and he fell again, weeping with the knowledge that he could run no farther. Dragging himself into a dank alleyway, he concealed himself behind a reeking dumpster.

His hands didn't know what part of his body to clutch, the pain blooming from all points, masking the click of claws on asphalt.

But not the growl, a low rumble that sounded like a broken machine.

Chess closed his eyes in horror, but opened them when he felt the weight of a monstrous gaze.

"No!"

It had so many teeth.

6.

Leslie limped down Broadway's trash-strewn sidewalk beneath the elevated train tracks of the J/Z line, hooded sweatshirt plastered to his body by the driving rain. Vague memories of awakening on a train tormented him and he remembered a woman who wore a puff coat over her dashiki watching him with a wariness born of experience.

What the hell happened?

He stopped in front of a waterfall splashing down from the tracks above and sought meaning in the explosion of liquid against pavement. The dark window of a meat store offered no more insight, nor did the Kennedy's Fried Chicken beside it. Across the street was an electronics store and Fat Albert's, a discount clothing store he'd always meant to check out but never had.

What happened?

A passing cab splashed him, but he was too exhausted to curse.

It felt like coming down off a three-day bender, his bones made of lead. Heavier. Uranium. But no memory of drinking or taking anything else. He had no idea what time it was beyond *night* and wondered if he was drugged. He considered resting in a doorway but found the energy to move on.

"Almost there." His hand rasped over an unshaven chin. The few people sharing the rainy sidewalk give him a wide berth. Cats in an empty lot yowled at his passage.

He pushed west onto neighborhood streets, dark and unusually quiet in the rain, no one hanging out on the stoops. Macon Street, home sweet home, was quiet and looked like paradise compared to Brownsville.

The seven stone steps of the stoop were endless, and he paused twice to let the throbbing in his head subside. His thoughts tumbled and splashed like sea otters and he carried a vague sense of shame.

Twice the keys wriggled from his grasp and tinkled on the step before he achieved entry, shouldering through the security door and closing it by leaning his weight against it, the crash when it closed igniting pain throughout his body.

More stairs and then he was home.

A remote filled the living room with Handel's organ concertos and he halted to take in the altar mounted on the table. Had he made that? It was hideous, seven wicks sticking up from the meaty wax of melted candles.

Seven wicks. The number struck him as significant, but his mind was a machine with rusty gears and couldn't build up enough steam to make the connection.

What did I do?

In the shower he hung onto the nozzle with one hand and let his head droop as the hot pins and needles of water washed away the pain.

7.

Leslie reclined on the couch downstairs with the lights off and candles lit, still wet from the shower and shivering as the water evaporated from his pale skin. He was just too damned tired to go upstairs.

He had pushed a stack of books on the floor to make space and they lay scattered around him, proof of his descent into... What? A drunken brawler?

What had he done?

The inebriated feeling had departed and a deep sorrow filled the empty space, a red thing lined with rotting green veins. Each pulse of the sickly organ injected his mind with fragments of memory and he stared at the jagged shadow of the antler climbing up the wall and across the ceiling.

CHAPTER TWENTY ONE

1.

Leslie awoke to the sight of teeth and was not afraid. He inhaled the rank animal smell and was comforted by the dog's hot breath.

"Wotan," he said with a voice hoarse enough to be called a growl. "Hey, buddy." The three-legged dog rumbled deep in its chest and licked his nose before moving backward in its strange, hopping gait.

"Leslie?"

Lavinia leaned over him on the couch, her long hair dangling across his chest as she touched his face. "You're hurt."

Thunder rumbled and rain drummed against the windows.

"Lavinia." He dragged fingers through the hair at her temples and felt the impulse to kiss her, so he did. "Lavinia."

"Leslie."

Lightning flashed through the room. An obliterating white light. A god's light that rendered the world barren.

He blinked away flashing colors as thunder shook the building and he felt the storm's power directly overhead. She said, "You're bleeding," and it was true. The savage wounds given to him in the woods flowed scarlet like pagan stigmata.

"Are you sure?" she asked, and he laughed from deep in his chest, loving her and leading her through the clutter of furniture as if through a forest, the standing lamps and coat racks become trees.

The firelight from the candles was higher now and the antler seemed to shift with their rhythm.

Leslie was awake and not awake. He was at the altar in the woods where a great Hunt had ended, the altar existing in place of his long table. She was beautiful in the firelight with hair like Artemis, the height of towering Skaoi, and the grace of lithe Flidais, and he understood that he had not escaped the Hunt and would never escape and had indeed been taken by the Hunt beneath the towering trees.

Taken as he would take her beneath towering flames.

But because he was still Leslie he said, "Are you sure?" and she answered with a kiss, her tongue rough against his teeth as he gathered her dress at the hips and lifted it, turning her, pushing her down over the altar. He was Leslie in the now, groaning with pleasure as his hardness slid inside her. He was Leslie in the forest, savaged on the altar to the music of his own terrified screams. He was that taker, towering over both Leslies. The white blindness of lightning was his lightning. The growling crash of thunder was his thunder.

She added agonized music to his desperate cries and he continued rutting even when her wild tresses caught fire.

He collapsed atop her and Lavinia fell onto the bony spurs of the antler.

She bucked, caught by the horrible antler like an animal in a trap. A terrible pain scraped the inside of Leslie's skull and exploded out through his ruined eye. He stumbled, twisting. Saw his shadow whirling about the walls as if seeking escape. Fell to his knees as his shade mirrored him.

Leslie screamed.

On the wall, tendrils sprouted from the shadow of his skull, from his wounded eye, branching and twisting high above as if his head were the earth giving birth to the World Tree.

2.

Leslie awoke on the couch and saw the ribbons of smoke rising from the molten sea of wax on the table.

Wotan rose awkwardly from the floor beside him, claws scrabbling on the hard wood.

Leslie was naked and in pain from the crazed night before, his limp penis smelling of sex, his back sticky with dried blood.

He knew something had happened.

"Lavinia?" Wotan perked up his ears but Leslie received no other response.

He lifted the antler from the congealing wax and stood it up.

"Lavinia?"

He wondered if she had left, embarrassed at the suddenness of their sex, returned to her posture of shyness. Padding to the door, he opened it and leaned into the hall.

"Lavinia?"

He would never see her again.

CHAPTER TWENTY TWO

1.

Fat snowflakes slapped against the outside of the windows, but it was warm inside the bar with a fire crackling lustily away in a brick fireplace.

Percy and Mike sat on stools beside each other. The older man had recognized Percy as soon as he pushed inside the dark bar and waved him over. They had several rounds under their belts and Percy wondered if he would be able to ride his motorcycle back to the cabin.

He shuddered at the thought of another night alone with god knew what lurking outside and chased away the chill with another shot of Canadian Club. He hissed, rolling his shoulders and lifting his gaze to the flickering television behind the bar. Recognition struck him like a blow.

"I know that guy," Percy said.

"On TV?" Mike asked.

"Yeah, that's Leslie Ward."

"Leslie?"

"Don't start."

Mike let loose with the seagull squawk that passed for a laugh and reached over the bar to grab the remote.

"Whaddaya doing, Mikey?" Jill put down her book and stirred from her perch behind the bar.

"Looting your register." Mike aimed the remote and thumbed up the volume as tiny colored bars spread across the bottom of the screen. "Percy knows this guy."

"Somebody famous?"

"He's a writer," Percy said.

"Oh," Jill said as if she'd never heard of such a thing. She moved down the bar and rustled inside the largest purse in the state of New Hampshire.

Mike straightened his spine on the stool and crossed his arms over his chest. When his sleeve slid back, Percy caught sight of faded ink work and realized that what he had assumed was a birthmark beside Mike's left eye was in fact a teardrop tattoo. "What kind of stuff does he write?"

"Thrillers. You know, lawyer gets a mysterious letter that says he has to fly down to Mexico and represent a defendant or his family will be killed. Or a guy finds out his wife has another family in another state, and when he digs into that discovers she's got a third and a fourth family and things get weird."

"That would fuck me up." Mike gunned down his whiskey.

On screen Leslie was leaning back in his chair on a studio set made up to look like no one's idea of a living room, relaxed in a tan jacket over an open-collar shirt. His face had filled in some but was still lean and angular, made enjoyably sinister by the black eyepatch.

"...exploded back onto the front pages," the interviewer was saying. His trim blond hair and pug nose suggested an innate gift for entertainment reporting. "After so many years of hiding out, what's it like to get so much attention?"

"I was hardly hiding out." Leslie's smile was devilish, teeth white against weathered skin. "I was rebooting myself up at a cabin in New Hampshire." The timbre of his voice was warm with health.

"New Hampshire." The interviewer's tailored suit stretched when he leaned forward as if to climb over the coffee table. "Where you survived an ordeal straight out of a Jack London novel. The wilderness. Freezing temperatures. Starvation...and wild dogs."

Leslie ducked his head and scratched his temple as if to resist a laugh.

"That really happen?" Mike said, and Jill said, "Shhh," with a look to Percy seeking approval. He nodded and winked.

Onscreen, Leslie continued. "It was something—"

"Will you ever write about it?" the interviewer interrupted.

Leslie shrugged as if easy about the experience. "I might already be writing about it."

A sly grin and the interviewer tossed his head as if to throw back long hair that he didn't possess. "But first you came back to New York and danger followed you."

It was quick, but Percy caught it. A flicker of disquiet rippled over Leslie's face.

A black and white photo filled the screen, the woman striking and glamorous in her large sunglasses. "Catherine Van Horn, a society beauty in her day and a well-known patron of the arts was riding the subway when she was attacked by her own seeing eye dog. Fortunately for her, she was riding on the same train as Leslie Ward."

"Ahh," Leslie said as a still shot from the cell phone video appeared. A blurred Leslie was lifting the wild, black shape of a dog. Mercifully the scene cut back to the interview where Leslie stroked his chin and the interviewer leered.

Jill pulled a tube of lipstick away from her mouth. "Holy shit, I saw this on the news."

"There has been an outcry from animal rights groups," the interviewer pressed. "People saying you hate dogs because—"

Anger crossed his face like a wave scouring a beach. Leslie straightened. "I don't hate dogs—"

The interviewer's hands were raised, placating. "I know that, and that's why we're talking. In fact, you've adopted a dog, haven't you?"

"Yeah, a pitbull named Wotan. I adopted him from a neighbor." Another shrug. "He lost a front leg and he's only got one eye." He tapped his temple beside the eyepatch. "Like me."

"And after all this you decided it was time to come out of your shell on *Meet the Entertainers* with a big announcement."

"It wasn't a carefully thought-out plan."

"But you're here and you have something to tell us, don't you?"

"Yes."

"A new book."

"Yes."

"A very special new book." He grinned as if they shared a secret.

Leslie nodded. "Yes...a Buddy Paretsky novel."

The interviewer looked at the camera as if in shock and the screen was suddenly filled with the tilted image of police raiding a crowded movie theater.

"Buddy Paretsky, the cult novelist who launched the subversive entertainment genre known as *Teatro Orrendo*, The Hideous Theater, in which—"

"Actually it was film director Norris Chapin who—"

"Violent and salacious acts take place not only onscreen, but in the theater itself."

"Ahh..."

"And you're telling us here on *Meet the Entertainers* that you are, in fact, Buddy Paretsky?"

"He's me."

"Buddy Paretsky and Leslie Ward are one and the same?"

"I am Buddy Paretsky."

"Wow." A deep breath, hand placed against chest as if to quell the vapors. "And what's this new novel called?"

The camera zoomed in on Leslie's face in a tight shot so that his toothy grin filled the screen. "*All the Teeth in the World.*"

2.

Percy took the ride into town very carefully. He found a working payphone outside the Roundabout Diner and made a phone call, ignoring the dill pickle stink of the receiver. The frozen phone was painful against his ear as he threw a lifeline into the void.

"Come right now," Leslie said across the miles. "I'll have a Delta Shuttle ticket waiting for you."

Percy's vision blurred. "Thank you." He found it hard to speak past a blockage in his throat.

"Don't fuck around. Don't go back to the cabin," the tinny voice ordered. "Go straight to the airport and get to New York. I've got you, man. You're home free."

CHAPTER TWENTY THREE

1.

"It's cold," Percy said and shifted on the wooden bench, watching a boat trundle and splash across the pond with a load of brightly jacketed tourists. He felt a mild irritation that Leslie, a natural outdoorsman, was unaffected.

"It's in the forties," Leslie offered and Percy grimaced. He studied skeletal bushes that once carried flowers and scuffed a boot through brown and orange leaves below the bench.

"You've put on some weight," he said, eyeing Leslie's cheekbones, still sharp enough to pierce the skin.

"Yes."

"It looks good on you."

Leslie said, "When we— When I lived closer, I used to walk through Central Park when I was stuck on a story point. When I needed to think."

"I'm tired of thinking." Percy shivered in his leather jacket.

A trio of joggers was visible and several graying Chinese women stood in a group, rotating their arms and bending at the waist. Squirrels gathering late season nuts were visible. The buildings of nearby 5th Avenue were visible.

The barrier between the two men was invisible but no less real.

"We need to get drunk." Leslie stood and pulled Percy to his feet. The big man noticed that even during this gesture, Leslie angled his head slightly away to hide his injury.

"Lassen sie uns betrinken," Percy said.

"What?"

"Drunk, ja."

2.

It was a hobbit hole of a place, an Irish pub on 38th Street, dim enough to give lie to the afternoon outside. Dark wood and a tin ceiling, the small fire behind a grate crackling merrily as if specifically designed to provide refuge during a storm. It welcomed them immediately and the short waitress with the red curls walked them around the bar, seating them in a cramped booth. Her hair rested in glorious contrast against the shoulders of her green polo shirt and Percy thought it quite striking.

"Did you love her?" Leslie's words rolled across the scarred wooden table and struck Percy in the chest.

Percy slumped. He knew he needed to speak about it, to unburden, but had expected hours of reminiscing before stumbling naturally around to talking about what had happened.

"I thought so," he said after a moment. "Maybe I was excited by the lure of forbidden fruit. Or just fucking lonely." He closed his eyes at the lie, not a misstatement of fact but of scope. He was unaware of his lip curling in contempt at his own cowardice. He had been more than lonely. Had, in fact, been circling the drain when Kristi Sugar showed up at Whiteheart for treatment, bright-eyed and beautiful and looking at him as if he could change the world.

He changed it for her. Permanently.

Percy sipped a short glass of whiskey to buy himself time, inhaling while the liquid rolled around on his tongue. "I used to drink whiskey with ginger ale."

"You order that here and they'll chuck us out." Leslie gave him time, but another question lingered between them with a physical weight. "Did she love you?"

Percy flinched and attempted a smile but failed, achieving only a grimace. "Maybe I was just forbidden fruit."

"Really?"

"No. She loved me. She trusted me. She everythinged me." The expression came over his face like an assault, his jocular features crumpling, eyes squeezed into slits. He made no sound, but his sorrow, hot and panting, was alive in the air.

Leslie placed his hand over his friend's and clenched it, at a loss for words. But it was the right thing to do and Leslie, aware that it had been so long since he knew the right thing from the wrong, was glad he'd done it. "When I got divorced, it'd been coming for a long time. I knew it was the right thing, knew it...and it still broke me in two. I fought against it at the end, like I'd been breathing poison so long I was afraid of being pushed out into the clean air."

"We're quite a pair."

"I'm glad you came."

"Me too." Percy slid his hand free and cracked his knuckles, earning a wince from Leslie. "I saw you on TV. Paretsky, huh?"

Leslie laughed. A forced sound, but necessary. "We've got a lot of ground to cover." His eyes traced designs in the ceiling. "Paretsky, your love life... Oh, I kind of have a dog."

"Have you talked to Jordan?"

Leslie's eyes focused like gunsights. "No."

Percy waved to the waitress with the glorious red hair. "Two more whiskeys."

3.

The small suite at the Waldorf Astoria overlooking Central Park was luxurious, and if he were sober, Percy would have complained, but he had cast himself adrift on the currents of the world like a leaf on the tide and allowed Leslie to pay for it.

Leslie: "Take the bed, you're longer."

Percy: "That's what she said."

They laughed at the well-worn joke.

Leslie collapsed onto the couch in the living room while Percy poured a rich burgundy into two water glasses he discovered beside the ice bucket.

"Slainte," Percy said and raised his glass as Leslie charted a weaving path to the counter and picked up his own. "Cheers."

They clinked glasses and drank. Leslie spilled wine on his white shirt.

"Well, shit," Leslie muttered and unbuttoned the garment on his way to the bathroom. He stuffed it into the sink built into the marble counter and turned a brass knob to drown the stain in cold water.

"Holy shit." Percy blurted from the doorway as he saw the angry curve of puncture scars on Leslie's back.

"Huh?" Leslie said.

"Just looking at your narrow ass and thinking those coyotes must've been desperate motherfuckers."

Their laughter rang off the tiled walls as Leslie turned off the water and draped his soaking shirt over the shower curtain rod.

"I should have called sooner." Percy lowered his chin.

"You were up to no good," Leslie offered. The weight of deliberate exposure traveled back and forth between them like a tennis ball.

"I should have called to check on you," Percy said.

"You should have called because you were in trouble."

"Well, yeah."

"Yeah, you jerk," Leslie said. "You're not on your own. I got you."

Percy made his way back to the long window in the living room, noting frost gathered on the outside of the glass. The park was a dark sea in the night with the glittering lights of the city beyond. Leslie's ghost appeared in the glass beside him. The city blurred as their breath fogged the glass.

"She's seeing someone else," Leslie said, rolling a sip of wine around in his mouth before swallowing. "Someone who doesn't yell."

Leslie dropped his head. "I gave her our condo because she deserved it, but the thought of some other guy there..." The words caught in his throat.

Leslie needed an out and he thumped his chest. "I'm drunk."

"Me too."

Leslie cracked open a bottle of water provided by the hotel and handed it to Percy, who swished the cleansing liquid in his mouth.

"Can I ask you something?" Percy said, handing the bottle back. When Leslie nodded, Percy tried to hold his friend's single-eyed gaze. "Did you bring a rope into the woods?"

Leslie turned away as if it were necessary to sip the water, but lowered the bottle from his lips. "I brought a rope."

The quiet statement hung in the air as he retreated into the bathroom and closed the door.

Percy made his way into the bedroom, kicking off his shoes in a clumsy shuffle. He stripped down to his boxer shorts beside the bed, listening to the television begin an urgent murmur in the other room.

4.

Percy awoke to whispering. Words. Not words. The pop and crackle of a lusty fire.

Blue light flickered through the open doorway from the main room. Percy remembered that he was in a suite at the Waldorf Astoria and sat up with a groan, stick-dry vocal cords clicking instead of thrumming. He leaned forward and released a muffled fart into the mattress, his hairy belly bulging onto his knees.

A brief explosion of effort stood him up, swaying, a collapsing tree filmed in reverse. He pressed a hand to his thumping temple and stared about the unfamiliar room, the furnishings bathed in the glow from the streetlights far below. The stale processed air of the hotel room was dry on his skin and he wished guests could still open hotel windows.

He lurched with a giant's heavy tread into the main room where Leslie sat cross-legged on the blue carpet before the TV, light and shadow etching his ribs and wounds in black detail. Heavy curtains danced against the windows and Percy felt the breeze chilling his torso as the air conditioning worked itself up to a storm.

Whispering. Not from Leslie, from the TV. The screen showed familiar dark trees rising from the snow and Percy shivered in recognition.

Leslie lifted the remote and the volume bar glowed to life at the bottom of the screen, climbing. The snapping crackle of static grew louder as the speakers strained to pull meaning from sounds that chose to remain hidden.

"You got it hooked up." A pointless statement because the answer was on screen, his badly shot video showing a colorless world of black and white as the camera danced over the eerie bower in the woods.

"You said there were birds," Leslie muttered.

"Turkeys."

Percy rubbed bloodshot eyes and strained to make out details of the gloomy shapes moving within the bower, black things against the double depth of blackness backed by stone. Not stone. Obsidian.

Ruddy eyes glinted and Percy felt his respiration pick up. "There." The shapes were oozing forth from the bower like molasses, refusing definition. "What the fuck?" They circled the pale, hairless corpse of a man, and Percy knew Leslie hadn't pierced a canine with his arrow.

"That's not a dog," Leslie gasped in horror.

"This isn't what happened." Percy felt the prickle of goosebumps across his bare skin.

"It's what you filmed."

"It's not what happ—"

"Look." Leslie pointed a quivering finger at the screen. "Back by the rock formation. The dolmen."

Drops of perspiration sprang from Leslie's lank hair as he shook his head, and Percy saw that his pale skin was slick with sweat despite the air conditioning. Gusts of wind set the heavy curtains flapping.

But the windows were closed...

"What's—"

"Look!" Leslie insisted, and Percy obeyed, focusing on the shifting screen as whispers clawed at his eardrums and an upright shape shifted deep beneath the interlocking branches, emerging from its den. Like the dark shapes of the turkeys

(not turkeys)

this new apparition refused definition. Percy caught a brief glimpse of a hairless torso as twigs fell from overhead, a vast spread of antlers tangling in the interlocking branches.

"Hooves!" Leslie exclaimed, and the door shuddered in its frame. Percy jumped, heart leaping into his throat as the assault resolved into a hammering fist from the outside.

He and Leslie exchanged wide-eyed glances. Leslie paused the video and Percy made for the door, feet tingling against the carpet.

"Ach." An azure spark leapt from his fingers to the metal doorknob. He winced before pulling the door open to the extent the security chain allowed.

It was rare that Percy had to lift his chin to meet someone's eyes. She was well over six feet in her neat Waldorf uniform suit, shoulders straining the fabric of the jacket. Her white-blonde hair was cut into a brutally short brush and her over-plucked eyebrows gave her a look of permanent shock, though her lips were pressed into a thin line.

"We've had a noise complaint," she said, her voice textured with an odd accent.

"Really? I mean, we were watching a video but it wasn't that—"

Her eyes flashed and he stopped. "I could hear it from the elevator, shouting in Swedish it was, yes?"

"Swedish?"

"Perhaps Danish," she said. "The words were muffled, but the sounds quite clear at such volume."

"I—"

"Throw them out of the hotel!"

Percy looked past the giantess to see an old man in a silk bathrobe peering from an open doorway across the hall, his moustache bristling with indignation.

"Please return to your room," the Waldorf security woman said. The old man jabbed a finger at Percy.

"I don't care what you fairies do in your own home, but decent people are trying to sleep in this hotel."

The woman winced and Percy felt a moment of sympathy, wondering how many entitled assholes she put up with on a daily basis. The TV abruptly roared to life behind Percy and he jumped. The woman flinched back.

The noise was immediate and huge. Guttural shouts banged against Percy's ears and he sprang across the room in one great stride to slap his hand against the power button on the TV. The cacophony stopped as suddenly as it had started.

The room was spinning and he pressed his hands to his temples to steady himself before returning to the door.

"I— I'm sorry, I didn't know it was so loud."

Eyes as grey and cold as the North Sea studied him for a long moment before she offered a curt nod.

Percy shook his head, unable to explain. "We'll keep it down, I promise."

"Thank you." She offered another crisp nod and Percy pulled the door closed.

"How could it be so loud?" Percy turned to Leslie.

"Who was that?" Leslie asked.

"Security. There was a noise complaint."

"But we weren't making much noise."

"It was pretty loud when it just came on behind me."

Leslie looked at the TV and his mouth moved like a fish trying to breathe air. "I didn't hear it."

The curtains were no longer dancing and Percy thought to ask a question but held his tongue.

"I don't know what happened," Leslie said. "I was trying to rewind it when you went to the door. I want to watch the entire video with you. But I didn't hear anything."

5.

Leslie blew out a cloud of cigarette smoke. "Something really strange just happened, right? I mean, a Japanese kid didn't crawl out of the TV, but we can't write that off as just two drunk guys."

They were huddled in their coats, chain smoking on the sidewalk below the front steps of the hotel. Percy coughed and pounded a fist against his chest, unused to smoking after years without a coffin nail. They were afraid to look at each other, both men keeping their gaze focused on the dark tangle of Central Park across the quiet width of 59th Street. The air carried an earthy reek of old horse dung and Leslie was touched by a memory of crossing this very street past the carriages...

"You said you saw a dog with my arrow in it," Leslie said through a billowing cloud of white smoke, his unkempt hair a mess of jackstraws. "I didn't see a dog on that video."

Percy stared at the orange cherry of his cigarette. "What did you see?"

"A person."

"That's not what I filmed, man. It was a dog."

A cab cruised past, slowing as the driver caught sight of them. Percy shook his head and the taxi roared off, red taillights glowing in the night.

"Right at the end of the clip," Leslie said. "Was something coming out toward us?"

"Out of the TV?" Percy was picturing the Japanese horror movie but couldn't remember the title.

"On screen. From inside the thing?"

"The bower?"

"Right. Was something coming toward you when you were filming?"

"I didn't see anything when I was out there."

"But on screen I saw something. It was tall. It had antlers."

Percy flicked the cigarette away in a burning arc that struck the grey sidewalk and bounced, scattering sparks. "I saw...something pale, like a man's chest, or a person's chest. Wearing some kind of deer horns on his head."

"Antlers."

"Whatever." Percy thumped the back of his hand against Leslie's shoulder and the smaller man shook a fresh cigarette from his crumpled pack.

"I hate these things," Percy said, inhaling.

"Yeah." Leslie blew out a smoke ring that expanded and broke apart as it drifted over the street. "Something stranger to tell you. Gonna blow your mind."

"Great."

"I didn't start walking from Stone's Throw. I drove maybe thirty miles away. Toward Franconia Notch. No way you could've wandered across a dog with my arrow in it. I was nowhere near the cabin when they got me."

"I fuckin' walked there. I saw it."

"How?"

"With these." Percy waved the cigarette at his own eyes and flinched back from the bright tip. "Shit."

Leslie tried to stifle a chuckle but Percy was infected by his mirth. Soon both men were laughing. It wasn't a long spell, but it was cleansing while it lasted.

"So we're agreed then," Percy said, resting a hand on Leslie's shoulder. "Something weird happened. Maybe is still happening?"

"Yeah, man, something is happening."

Leslie's face clouded and he averted his gaze, hiding his wounded eye. Seeing this, Percy said, "What?"

Leslie dropped his cigarette and ground it out beneath his heel. "I think I hurt someone."

CHAPTER TWENTY FOUR

1.

Argyle winced at the heat from the steaming cup of coffee as he held up three dollars to the man behind the high counter.

"Thanks, Sheriff," the man said, bright teeth flashing in his dark face. He slid four quarters back across the counter.

"See you tomorrow, Fouad," Argyle said. He stopped by the glass gumball machine at the door and fed in a pair of quarters, turning the crank until two colored gumballs tumbled down the chute.

Outside, 9th Avenue was a sea of honking vehicles, construction at 25th Street making a mess of the morning commute. Argyle tried to sip as he fumbled out his buzzing phone, managing to burn his lip and nearly drop the phone in the process.

"Shit."

"What?" a cop named Yakut asked over the phone.

"Not you. What's up?"

"That Ward thing, you wanted anything hinky connected to the guy." Gorkem Yakut was a big Turk with two gold eyeteeth who liked to put on an accent so people would think he just got off the boat. He was a sergeant at Midtown South, liked to fight, and was Argyle's friend.

"You got something?" Argyle stepped out of the flow of foot traffic into the lee of a scratched blue mailbox with *DOPE DICKS* spray-painted on the side.

"Something, might be nothing, but something."

Argyle rolled his eyes. "What is it?"

"How about Ward's ex-wife's boyfriend turns up dead out in Brownsville? Chester Waters."

Argyle balanced his coffee on the curved top of the mailbox. He shivered, wishing he'd remembered to put the lining back inside his raincoat.

"Dead heart attack or dead shot?"

"Dead eaten."

"What?"

"Something ate him."

A UPS truck was grinding past and Argyle turned away from the noise, stabbing a finger into his exposed ear.

"Eaten?" Argyle said.

"Si."

"No way."

"Way. He's at the morgue, First and 32nd."

"On my way."

Argyle disconnected and reached for his coffee, accidentally brushing it from its precarious perch. It struck the sidewalk and detonated in a dark brown splash.

"Watch it!" an orthodox man snarled as he danced away from the spill.

"Shit," Argyle said.

2.

As if to prove he didn't belong, Argyle's body launched a competing series of involuntary actions. His nose wrinkled and the roof of his mouth dried even as a shiver tickled its way up his ribs. He crunched a gumball between his molars in defiance.

Argyle hated the morgue.

Cruel fluorescent lights buzzed on the ceiling, scouring away shadows in the basement facility as surely as the strong chemical cleaners scoured away bacteria. White boards and equipment cabinets lined three walls; the fourth was gleaming stainless steel and held thirty-two body drawers.

Argyle raised a loosely closed fist in front of his mouth as if to muffle a sneeze. The normal musky locker room smell of the morgue was overpowered by something sickly sweet. The stink of bowels and rot.

"Stinks, huh?" the morgue technician said, blue scrubs making a *swiff-swiff* sound as he emerged from an office and waved to Argyle.

"Yeah."

The technician was a kid with glasses and curly hair, his soft cheeks darkened by rosacea. "Two weeks ago we got a drop-off without paperwork and it's still in there." He waved vaguely at a tall white refrigerator with one large door.

"What's in there?" Argyle drifted toward the fridge despite the smell.

"The infant."

Argyle gave him a look. "You put a baby in the fridge?"

The technician crossed his arms. "We put corpses in the refrigerator. Infant corpses. Most of them premies." He waited for Argyle to say something, and when nothing was forthcoming, pointed at the wall of body drawers. "Your guy is over here, Lieutenant."

Argyle followed the kid to the wall and stood back as he crouched, knees popping, to yank open the latch. He half-expected to see the blue-toned corpse of an infant when the drawer rolled out with a metal clatter, but the plastic body bag was stretched over something man-sized.

The technician pinched the zipper between two fingers and tugged it steadily down. Argyle twitched as if the tech were unzipping his spine.

"Jesus," Argyle said as the ravaged face was revealed.

"Massive external trauma to the face, torso, and forearms, the latter being defensive wounds. Significant internal trauma as well, with several organs completely removed, including the stomach, liver, spleen, and a good portion of the small intestine."

"It looks like he fell into a meat grinder," Argyle said.

"Or the lion pit at the zoo."

"A lion did this?"

"No, I was just— But teeth did do this. Big teeth. A canine."

"He was killed by a dog?"

The technician lifted a clipboard that was attached to the drawer by a cord. "He had recent injuries to his ankles and knee that suggested some kind of fall and had drugs in his system. Marijuana and cocaine. But he was killed by teeth."

"Alright, put him back, please," Argyle said and looked away, seeking relief. Instead his gaze landed on the refrigerator for dead babies and he felt light-headed.

The drawer closed with a hollow bang and the kid said behind him, "Your guy said this was connected to Leslie Ward?"

Argyle turned quickly, cursing Yakut's loose lips. "What about it?"

The technician cocked his head and met Argyle's stare. "Ward's kind of a freak."

"What do you mean he's a freak?"

"I mean he writes this Oprah Book Club shit under his own name, but just came out as Buddy Paretsky."

"I don't know what that means."

"Buddy Paretsky wrote some really fucked up books that kicked off a really fucked up underground film scene, Teatro Orrendo. The audience acts out sexual shit during screenings to enhance the depravity on screen."

"Why do you know this?"

The kid flushed. "I caught a basement screening in Bushwick three years ago."

Argyle ducked his head. "These movies—"

"And books."

Argyle lifted a hand. "And books. Any of them got cannibalism in them?"

3.

Up on the sidewalk Argyle spat out gum that tasted like embalming fluid and gave himself a minute to breathe the crisp air until a delivery truck groaned past billowing grey smoke from its exhaust. Something splashed on his face and he wiped his palm across his cheek, seeing a smear of clear liquid.

His phone buzzed and Argyle snatched it from his pocket. "Something dripped on me," he said without preamble.

"Just air conditioner juice," Yakut said.

"In the fall?" Argyle wiped his face again. "Why you calling?"

"You're gonna love this." Yakut's voice was laced with strange humor. "Four more guys died the same way as your boy, right around the same time."

"Why didn't you tell me?"

"They came in on a different call and their bodies are out in Brooklyn. All torn up just like Waters."

"Fuck."

"Yeah."

A hollow-faced white man in an army coat with his blond hair clumped in dreadlocks stopped beside Argyle, who shot him a narrow-eyed glare.

"What?" Argyle spat.

"Got a light?"

"No." Argyle turned away but dreadlocks didn't move, so he snarled, "Fuck off."

The man shuffled away muttering, "Chill, baby."

"Sorry," he said back into the phone. "Morgue tech said they were bite wounds on Waters. These other guys got bite wounds?"

"Bites and some other wounds..." Yakut sounded like he was reading. "Long scoring marks that suggest claws."

"Who are these guys?"

"Dealers."

"Waters had coke and weed in his system," Argyle said.

"Now we know why Mr. Soho was out in Brownsville." Yakut paused. "I'm gonna forward some crime scene photos to your email. It's a real fucking mess, man. Blood on the walls. Parts just..."

"Sounds like a bomb went off."

"Sounds like the American werewolf in Brooklyn."

Yakut hung up and Argyle stared at the empty screen on his phone, wondering what the hell he had stepped into.

CHAPTER TWENTY FIVE

1.

"I remember I was on the train. An L train. But I can't remember what happened after that," Leslie spoke as they moved through a horde of morning commuters in the underground maze of Union Square Station. The tiled floor, walls, and support columns seemed designed to amplify every step, bump, and curse to create a sea of deafening noise.

They split around an arguing couple and came back together. "Were you drinking?"

"No. It's just lost. A gap like when I was out in the woods."

"I think we need to find out what happened in the woods."

Leslie could have hugged him for saying "we." Instead, he said, "Let's find out what happened in Brownsville first."

Percy looked over the milling crowd for the grey signs leading to the L train. "There's another reason to take a train and not a cab."

"Shit." Leslie cursed the wall of people surrounding a solo guitarist busking for money. "What reason?"

"If something did happen, if you did something," Percy continued. "I don't think we want a driver to know we went back out there."

2.

It was a long, rattling ride on the L train out to Brownsville, with the passengers changing in appearance and economic status during the trip. A voice crackled from the overhead speakers and the train screeched to a stop where two teenage boys got off, joking and shoving.

When the train pulled out, Percy and Leslie were the only two people in the train car. Without the noise of other human beings, the lights seemed dimmer, the gnash of wheels hungrier.

"Is it ominous that no one else is on the train?" Percy asked.

On the opposite wall was a skincare advertisement for Doctor Zizmore. Percy focused on it as a distraction until something bumped his foot and a glance revealed a sloshing Snapple bottle. "Don't even remember the last time I had a Snapple."

"Yeah, that's probably full of pee."

"Shit." Percy kicked it away and it tumbled under the opposing bench. "I'm spooked, man. I thought it would fade, you know? But something really weird happened and it was happening back at Stone's Throw too. Those birds that came in and crapped all over the floor."

Leslie smiled. "You're our philosopher metaphysician. You'll figure it out."

"We're screwed."

The train shrieked and slowed, juddering into a dimly lit station with broken tiles on the walls and a stained cement platform.

"This is us." Leslie stood.

3.

Percy had his eyes on a boarded-up tenement building when he inadvertently kicked some trash on the sidewalk. He twitched at the sudden shock of sound. The streets were empty but more derelict than any he'd seen in the city. The few storefronts were boarded up save for a corner bodega where young men stood outside laughing and drinking from cans in paper bags. Music leaked from a parked car with a door hanging open.

"Should we be out here?" Percy asked.

"Don't be so fucking suburban," Leslie replied.

But it was murkier in Brownsville, overcast where it had been clear-skied in Manhattan. They crossed diagonally through an intersection that looked as if it saw little use, potholes in the asphalt, a dozen seagulls filling the air with shrill cries.

"Very DuMaurier," Percy said.

They stepped onto the sidewalk behind a white van with four flat tires and Leslie stopped so abruptly that Percy walked into him.

"I know that building."

It was six stories, the NYCHA signs marking it as low-income housing. Spanish music leaked from open windows.

"Why were you in the projects?" Percy asked.

Leslie shook his head and led them down the cracked sidewalk around a spray of broken blue glass. Two youngbloods were smoking cigarettes outside the steel and glass front doors. They sauntered off at the sight of two white men and the words, "Po-po," drifted to Percy's ears.

Leslie stopped in front of the double doors, wire mesh security glass marked with swirls of graffiti. "I was hoping they'd get us inside."

Percy tried the front door, which opened at his tug. "Don't be so fucking suburban."

4.

Their footsteps echoed in the cement-lined stairwell as they ascended through a miasma of cigarette smoke, food smells, and urine. They were a percussive duo, the slap-slap of Leslie's shoes beating in quadruple time against the rhythmic bass thud of Percy's boots.

The grey walls of the stairwell were sweating and Percy's palm came away greasy. "It's hard to believe we're in the same city."

"Enough to make you hate people, huh?"

"No." But Percy thought about what drugs were poisoning this neighborhood, so close to the elegance of midtown Manhattan, and felt a trickle of anger. He wondered if he could do some good here. His first thought about a personal future since he was suspended by Dartmouth and discharged from White Heart.

The ugly, utilitarian stairs bent several times at sharp angles, a windowless ascent that filled Percy with the uneasy sensation that they were actually traveling down, deep into a subterranean place they were not meant to see. Unthinking, he slowed as he mused. Leslie extended his lead, turning the corner above.

This was the very moment, he would understand later, where the world split in two and he saw from both versions of himself. That it confused and terrified him in the moment was understandable. That he relished the broadening of his perception was understandable.

Would it have made a difference if Percy had shared that dislocated feeling with his friend? Or if Leslie had not been in the lead, his face hidden from Percy as it clenched into a fist, teeth grinding together with an unnamable emotion. Would Percy have dragged his friend out of the smothering damp of the staircase and into the light of day, mysteries be damned? Would he have fled on his own?

This is what happened.

"I..." Percy stopped on a dark stairwell where a lamp buzzed without offering light. He covered his nose at a smell and took in small yellow flames dancing atop three candles arrayed on the steps leading up. The flames had blown out in Leslie's passage, but the wicks hissed back to life like trick birthday candles.

That just happened, he thought. That was real.

Leslie's voice trickled down the stairs. "There are people in there." Up above and out of sight, a door creaked open.

5.

It was the stuff of movies. It was the stuff of acid trips.

The hallway was in chaos. Running shadows and dancing firelight.

Metal trashcans placed along the hall spat streamers of fire and the ceiling coiled with smoke as people coughed and screamed and fled.

"Leslie!"

Percy struggled to make out the form of his friend in the stuttering orange light, throwing an arm across his nose and mouth as he coughed against the smoke. A door at the far end of the corridor opened and he saw the stick-like figures of fleeing men.

A gunshot! No. A trashcan had exploded, scattering flaming garbage. The stink was tremendous and the light flared brighter so that he beheld symbols written in great, red streaks on the wall—

The floor tilted and Percy fell against an apartment door. Blinked his eyes as if he'd stared into a spotlight. He remembered the kaleidoscopic chaos of rock concerts, smoke and light and noise and—

"Leslie!"

He flinched away from a burst of sparks and saw his friend, saw the white shirt, saw arms spread wide.

Jaw hanging open, Percy witnessed two scenes playing out simultaneously, one layered over the top of the other.

In the first, Leslie had his arms spread wide, and in the other...

Leslie's dimensions were wrong. A funhouse distortion. Arms stretched across the entire width of the hall. His head scraped the ceiling.

Both scenes happening. Both real.

Percy's throat choked with sand, his belly filled with ice. He shrank back, his muscles not his own to command as fear, unreasoning animal fear, took hold.

He fled, abandoning his friend to the crazed, tilting corridor. The Percy of lost jobs and suicidal girlfriends was not prepared to witness that other reality. Was barely equipped to confront his own.

Failure (that most-Percy of notions) dogged his heels as he thundered back the way he had come and ripped open the door, lunging into the dim stairwell.

It was the dead girl who saved him.

Kristi Sugar hovering in the air

(a terrified Hispanic woman on the staircase above him)

rotating in her noose

(turning to flee from the wild-eyed madman)

And his boots skidded on grimy cement. He fell hard, jarring his tailbone, biting his tongue so that the hot taste of pennies filled his mouth.

All the madness crashed down upon him, the carefully constructed barriers against his own failures caving as the runner in him, the coward, revealed himself.

And yet he couldn't stop seeing from that other perspective.

The one who saw into both planes at once. As a student he would have described it as *spirit*, looking down on the meat of his cowering body. Some power in the atmosphere around Leslie liberating his essential being. Enabling him to become his own guardian angel and reach down, uniting itself with the cowering man.

Percy rolled to his knees and stood, pulling open the doorway to enter the mad hatter's hallway. Through the prism of tears he saw the strange writing on the walls, smelled the incense and powders that burned in the blazing trash barrels, and recognized the trap for what it was.

"Leslie!" He pounded up the corridor, absently noting that the fire was not spreading to the rug or walls, that this trap had been carefully prepared by people who understood what was happening.

"Where are you?"

A door stood open, yellow streamers of police tape fluttering in the heat.

His only framework for the sight that met him was television. But Hollywood couldn't convey the horrid stink of a murder scene. The heat boiling against his back. The smoke bringing water to his eyes.

"Leslie!" He pulled out his phone and brought the camera to life without looking as he strode past shattered furniture and brown stains on the apartment walls. It smelled like a dumpster behind a butcher shop, left too long in the summer sun. Nauseating rot. The palpable stink of fear.

Tell-tale human shapes were marked by white tape on the floor. Other shapes were unidentifiable until he imagined arms and legs torn free.

"Where are you?" The weight of the place smothered his voice as he took a long step over shredded couch cushions.

Leslie stood unmoving in the bedroom, staring at the window where more liquid had dried to brown on the sill. Shards of glass lined the frame like shimmering teeth and ragged curtains flapped inside.

Percy put a big hand on Leslie's shoulder and the smaller man turned to look up at him. "I..."

"We need to leave."

Percy took his hand and led him as he would a child.

6.

Out in the hall.

The fat man threw a snake at Percy and he caught it in surprise, crying out in revulsion as the thin, strangely dry thing twisted in his fist.

Words banged against him, guttural and old, mixed with Spanish. When they were echoed by the clustered congregation behind the fat man, he recognized the words for what they were as the mass of people repeated Latin shaped by Puerto Rican accents.

Santeria. Liberating their own secondary vision, their own access to a power beyond the flesh and blood world.

The crowd clutched candles as if they were torches and the man who had thrown the snake made the sign of the cross at Percy. He dipped his hand into the sack at his waist to draw forth another wiry snake.

Red thoughts danced in Percy's imagination, an infestation of fire ants crawling across his mind.

And because the One-Eyed gaze was fixed on him across the centuries, Percy understood the effort invoked against him, his second sight now the primary, an ancient reality overlaying the mundane.

He rose to his full height and tossed the serpent into a blazing trashcan, the weight of his eyes pushing back the huddled mass of people, a wind pushing their candle flames over and setting the trash fires to leaping as the hallway became a flowing river of the wyrd.

The fat priest in his work pants and white t-shirt fell back a step and the snake in his fist twisted, biting him on the meat of the thumb. He yelped and shook his hand until the small snake dropped away.

Percy laughed and specks of blood coated his lips.

The fat man fell back a step as Percy advanced, the words booming from his throat leaving blood in their wake, his long-forgotten Latin returning in a rush to crash like thunder. In this second reality he was a giant. Urges both alien and vengeful consumed Percy and he kicked over the nearest trashcan, flaming debris scattering the congregation. They shrieked as they pelted down the corridor toward the red glow of an EXIT sign visible through black clouds.

Percy bit his tongue to stop the words. Tasted blood. He feared the language bubbling up along his spine

(so old)

something beyond Latin, something he had never studied

(so vast)

The silent boom of a door closing in his mind dropped him to his knees, a punctured balloon. The THING rushed forth from his belly, scouring him not as a cleansing wind but as a crawling (_____) that left a slimy trail in his guts

(an oily fast-food wrapper)

he was flaccid and discarded

(a used condom)

unworthy of regard by—

"Stop!" spat out on a spray of blood. Blood roared in his ears as the THING flew from his body.

And like that, the hall was just a hall again, the smoke just smoke. Percy was just Percy and he crawled to his friend, urging him to rise, ignoring the screaming voice in his mind that demanded to know what had just happened.

CHAPTER TWENTY SIX

1.

The pain behind his missing eye grew, a round, fluid-filled thing the size of a blueberry, then a grape. Only Percy's hand on his shoulder kept Leslie moving forward in a stumbling run through the falling rain.

Images danced through his mind, red streaked with pain and blood. He saw the room torn asunder. The crime scene tape on the floor. The drying blood and shredded cushions. The sharp breakage of window glass.

And teeth. Teeth filled his world as snarling echoed in his soul.

Down steps, slippery with gritty moisture. Percy's grip painful as it kept Leslie on his feet. He hit a subway turnstile, doubling over the metal bar, but Percy manhandled him over the barrier as the MTA attendant shouted from her bulletproof booth.

On a train, the floor moving beneath his feet. He was propelled into a seat as spasms shook him. The pain behind his empty eye socket now plum-sized, ripe and ready to burst.

He felt the shouting around him. The imprecations and hatred. Stomping feet and gnashing teeth.

From the swaying sea of bodies, a hag emerged, wet eyes oozing anger, liverish lips pulled back to reveal blocky dentures. Loose, spotted skin dangled from her wrists as she stretched her hands toward him and clambered up over him, her musty skirt rising over sagging support hose. Feeble white hairs curled from shins on either side of his head as she planted her feet on the bench as if to straddle him, to fuck him, to consume him...

2.

"Hold him down!"

"Fuck!"

"I got blood on me!"

"He got the AIDS!"

Leslie bucked against the hard plastic bench, clawing at the empty socket of his eye as the subway car shuddered to a halt with an ear-shattering squeal of brakes in a dark tunnel deep beneath Brooklyn. The lights strobed overhead. Shouts of panic and Leslie's screams of pain drowned out the garbled announcement over the PA.

Percy rose from one knee on the floor and nearly fell atop his friend, peeling Leslie's hands down from the wounded eye. The puckered flesh of the socket bulged as if a pencil were poking at it from inside Leslie's skull.

"Oh my God!"

"Fuckin' gross!"

It burst like a blood blister and scalding beads of liquid spattered Percy's cheeks.

The train was rocking from side to side as something tried to claw its way out from the ruin of Leslie's eye.

"Help me!" Percy cried out and was stunned to feel the sharp toe of a boot strike his ass.

"Fuck you!"

"Got the AIDS, motherfucker!"

"HE IS DISEASED." The voice huge, inside his head, issuing from many mouths in unison.

Leslie spasmed and smacked his head back into the big NYC subway map behind the bench.

The lights browned down and the air conditioning shut off with an audible snap, the atmosphere thickening into pudding. The air was as foul as a fox's den.

A wild hand pawed at the back of Percy's head. He hunched his shoulders as a handbag flew past to splat against the big window, raining its contents down on his tormented friend. Percy looked around wildly, not understanding, the scene stuttering in and out of reality like a TV with an interrupted signal. Pale faces. Brown faces. Sunglasses. Teeth.

They swarmed.

The circle of passengers closed like antibodies collapsing against a cancer cell, slipping past and around as Percy pushed and pulled and pleaded.

An old woman hiked a blue skirt up over her knees to clambered atop Leslie, her feet on the bench to either side.

Percy's strong fingers raked her back, bunching her slick blouse, feeling the elastic strap of her brassiere.

She flew.

There was a pause when the old woman toppled two men as if they were bowling pins. A dozen sets of eyes met his.

The train went dark and passengers fell on him.

3.

During the wild melee, the crowd bore him back into a metal pole as if to bind him like a witch for burning and Percy experienced a savage glee.

His big right fist crushed a Rastafarian's nose and his splayed left hand caught the tumbling beard of a Hassid to whipsaw the grey-hair off his feet. He kicked a skinhead covered in serpent tattoos, his boot connecting with the man's shin. Bone snapped and the snake man fell.

Their individual stinks erupted into the air as he struck and slammed. This woman was an overflowing ashtray. That man reeked of unhealthy bowels.

A quick-footed blonde girl ducked beneath Percy's arm to lunge for Leslie but he palmed her face like a basketball and threw her, one-handed, at an approaching trio of youths.

He roared.

The passengers that could stand fell back. The wounded tumbled to the floor.

Percy was aware of sweat falling from him, drops spattering the floor like rain. He lifted his twitching friend from the bench.

The crowd parted around a big man and Percy felt the muscles in his thighs bunch. The man was enormous, wide and tall, taller than Percy himself, his dark brown skull shining with perspiration, nearly brushing the ceiling as he strode through the whispering passengers like Moses through the Red Sea.

"Brother," the giant said.

Percy's white teeth bared themselves through the tangle of his beard.

The big man pulled his damp guyabarra shirt away from his rounded belly. "The train moves now, you will arrive safely." The accent a Caribbean mélange.

Indeed the train *was* moving, and Percy grabbed the bar over Leslie's bench, risking a glance out the window to behold the incredible sight of the red and green traffic lights, the green lamp blazing. The train roared into the station a moment later and the giant stepped to the door while the passengers, confused and rubbing at their wounds, looked about them in wonder.

Somewhere in the crowd a man sobbed.

The doors hissed open and the giant stepped out. Percy snatched his friend off the seat, feeling the warmth in the wiry body. In three booming steps he was off the train and onto the platform behind the man, following the vast yellow shirt as their rescuer moved to the stairs with the implacable power of a ship breasting heavy seas.

A woman with a stroller dragged her infant's conveyance to the side as Percy threw a hip at the turnstile, carrying his precious burden up into the cleansing wash of the sun.

4.

His name was Sala and he was impervious to the cold. He told Percy he was calling his cousin on an old flip-phone. "He drives a taxi," Sala said.

Percy slumped against a wall, grit mixing with the sweat on his neck, his t-shirt collar white with salt. The crisp fall air chilled him. He licked his lips, tasting salt in his moustache, chest working like a bellows. "Can you stand?" he asked, but received no response from Leslie.

They were on a block of warehouses and loading bays. The sun turned a broken bottle into a spray of diamonds and the nearest street corner had a pole bereft of signs. They could have emerged in Chicago for all that he recognized the place.

"I don't know where we are," Percy said, and Sala waved him quiet, spitting French into the phone as if threatening to flay his cousin alive.

Sala snapped the phone shut and made it disappear beneath his shirt, that tremendous shirt. Percy promised to buy himself a dozen such magnificent shirts as soon as the world made sense.

He flicked an apprehensive glance back at the dark opening to the subway but sensed that the moment had passed. Whatever had caused the crowd of passengers to attack

(he remembered the train rocking like a ship at sea)

whatever had caused his own berserkergang

(he remembered throwing an old woman across the car)

was passed.

Heat prickled behind his eyes and he let the tears flow. Sala, misunderstanding, hurried close.

"Evens drives like a madman, we will get your friend to the hospital," Sala said.

"Should we call an ambulance?"

Sala shook his head. "Evens will be faster."

The noise of an engine swelled and a green Boro Taxi skidded to a stop, kicking up rocks that spattered the sidewalk and thwacked off a parked car. Sala ran at the cab waving his arms and shouting as if Evens had committed a crime, but Percy didn't care. The back door was open, Sala's doing, and he dove across the back seat as if across a goal line, clutching Leslie to his chest.

CHAPTER TWENTY SEVEN

1.

Leafless trees and mourners alike bowed their heads as Chess was lowered into the ground on the eastern bank of the Hudson River. Morning drizzle beaded on the shining mahogany coffin, and the green Astroturf around the grave was gaudy with false promises.

"I'm a friend of— I was seeing Chess," Jordan said, wiping rain drops from the lenses of her overlarge sunglasses.

"He never mentioned you." The hunched matron had banished Jordan to the small group of people who weren't family.

The plot was in Sleepy Hollow, north of the city, an expensive stretch of hillside overlooking the river, with an ornate marble headstone. Chess had been so proud to hail from the legendary town, certain it afforded him a sense of mystery. Of something. Jordan wondered if he was excited to be buried there.

She mimicked the drooping, skeletal branches of nearby maples and dipped her head, blinking against the moody rain and muttering vaguely remembered prayers along with the preacher man. The grave was a violation on the hillside, and Jordan's flat-soled shoes slipped on the sopping grass every time she shifted her feet. She wasn't sure why she had come to the funeral, but was certain it was inappropriate to think about another man while her erstwhile boyfriend was sent below.

She flicked a glance toward the family, clustered beneath rounded umbrellas like an outbreak of black mushrooms.

A foghorn sounded from a passing riverboat and she glanced up to see a tug pushing a barge up stream. As if the horn was a signal, the small crowd shuffled and scattered. So many leaves in a breeze. She stared at the dark rectangular hole, mildly offended by the bright green Astroturf that had been placed around the burial site like... Like what? Something tasteless. She didn't care.

Leslie.

When she heard her name, Jordan half-thought it would be Leslie striding up the hillside between the tombstones. What would she say?

But it was a squat man in a belted raincoat with a bald, brown head, and even before he showed her his badge she knew he was city and knew he was cop.

"Jordan Ward?"

She flinched at the name and her lips pressed together, compressing her response. "Samatar."

"What?" the cop said, only now walking uphill a few steps to close the distance.

"I returned to Samatar after the divorce."

She walked past him, wondering if he would grab her arm. Instead he matched her pace as she picked her way down slope between the plaques and cenotaphs. She was pleased that he slipped once or twice while she maintained her footing on the treacherous hillside.

On the sidewalk he gestured down the row of cars, lights blazing and engines rumbling. "Give you a ride back to the city?"

"I'm taking the train."

"Ride to the station?"

"I enjoy walking."

"In this?"

She looked at him, down at him, and let her brown eyes darken. He didn't look away.

"What do you want?" She was a journalist then, not a mourner. Not Leslie's ex.

His face shifted as his mind worked, examining and discarding approaches until he shrugged and the tips of his teeth showed themselves in a smile.

"Know how your friend died?"

"He was attacked. In Brooklyn."

"Yeah, in Brownsville. Know what he was doing there?"

She walked away and he paced her as the rain picked up and the river continued its endless flow.

"Buying drugs," the cop continued. "He dealt from his gallery."

"I don't have to listen to this." Jordan lengthened her stride. Her stockings were sopping and squelched inside the expensive shoes. Already rubbing against her heels. The low brick buildings of town loomed ahead and she knew it was over a mile to the train station.

The cop caught up, struggling in vain to light a cigarette against the storm. "Hey, will you cup your hands—"

"Go fuck yourself." Jordan knew where this was going even if she didn't know why.

"Sure, but how 'bout you tell me first about your husband's relationship with the dearly departed?"

Jordan stopped, wiping sodden bangs from her forehead. "Ex-husband," she snapped and cursed herself silently, knowing he'd planted a hook.

"How well did Leslie know Chess?" The damp cigarette bobbed in his mouth when he spoke.

"What's your name?"

"Detective Argyle. Now answer my question."

"Am I being detained?"

"Jesus."

"Am I?"

"You want me to detain you?"

They were speaking quietly over the rustle of the downpour, faces maybe a foot apart.

"Answer my question," she shot back, and he smiled.

"No." His eyes twinkled. She wanted to punch him and he knew it.

"Hands up, don't shoot," she snarked and backed away, hands raised, gaping in mock fear. His smirk sickened to a frown and she added a point on her side of the scoreboard.

"Should I contact you at home or at the offices of the *New Yorker*?" he said, humor replaced by a quiet threat.

"Contact me at the law offices of David Evans," she threw over her shoulder and stalked away, spine straight, chin lifted against the spattering downpour.

Why were the police talking to her? Why were they asking about Leslie?

Cars cruising past splashed through puddles. A few of them held people she and Chess knew from the city. When the black length of the empty hearse slowed, she thought they meant to offer her a ride and wondered, strangely, how it would smell inside. Of death? Did they burn incense? Perhaps they hung pine air fresheners in the vehicle.

A belch of black smoke emerged from the tailpipe and the hearse sped off, eager to pick up the next corpse.

Good enough. Jordan was in no mood for conversation.

She sat by herself on the train as the conveyance rattled south with the grey expanse of the Hudson outside the streaked windows on the right side of the train car. It was a loud ride; the rain drumming on the metal roof sounded like a faucet pounding on a tin can. It had already snowed farther north and she wondered if the rain was harbinger of

New York's new norm...a colorless winter of freezing drizzle and hacking coughs.

Her raincoat had given up the fight somewhere during the walk and she shrugged it off her shoulders to pool around her hips. The black funeral dress clung to her shoulders and breasts and her dark hair was molded into a wet helmet against her skull.Her eye shadow had run in clownish streaks down her cheeks, but she didn't have the energy to care.

Kicking off her shoes, she rubbed at the new blisters on her heels and realized she had no idea what she would say to Leslie if she saw him. When she saw him.

I'll wing it, she thought and tittered nervously.

Two rows behind her, a hedge fund trader congratulated himself on not sitting beside the Morticia Addams lookalike who cackled to herself like a half-drowned witch.

Jordan threw back her head and laughed.

2.

Because she was scared, Jordan went to the bathroom three times during her brief stop at the Upper West Side apartment. She dumped her wet clothes into a sopping pile on the bedroom floor and pulled on blue jeans, black Doc Martens, and a blood red sweatshirt with *FASTER PUSSYCAT, KILL, KILL* scrawled across the front. Her wet tangle of hair was yanked back into a ruthless ponytail and she slapped a Yankees cap on her head.

The TV was blaring from the living room and she caught the words *Buddy Paretsky, screening,* and *Norris Chapin* before dashing in to catch the end of a NY1 segment. Cameras showed the IFC Theater on 6th Avenue, police tape blocking the sidewalk. The image cut to a close-up of Leslie in his recent televised interview saying, "I am Buddy Paretsky."

"There you have it, in his own words," a brunette TV reporter cut in, speaking to a camera outside the theater. "The cult icon is back...and so are the public displays associated with his films."

"They're not his films," Jordan snapped at the screen.

When her phone rang, she scooped it up from the charger, wondering if it was *him*. But it was a 917 number she didn't recognize. A New York cell. She thought of the cop and let it ring until it died.

She called into work, and when Maury picked up she said, "I need to take the rest of the day."

After a few more words, Maury coughed and said, "Want I should come over later, Face?" That was his name for her, short for Dollface. During her divorce he took her out every night and bought rounds of Kir Royals while cabarets and comedians allowed her the fiction of pleasure. He called himself her Mama Bear and she loved him dearly.

"I'm just gonna drink wine and watch *Bridget Jones*," she lied. They both blurted "Hugh Grant" into the phone and she ceded the bad boy to Maury this time. They shared a taste for rascals.

"You need, you call. Right?"

"I will."

"Alright, Face," he said and hung up, a big fan of having the last word.

She looked at herself in the mirror and tried to summon up her inner Riot Grrrl, but felt like a kid from Dickens.

Was she really going to just show up on Leslie's doorstep?

Yes.

The door banged shut behind her.

CHAPTER TWENTY EIGHT

1.

The metal gate in front of Leslie's building was slimy to the touch and Percy wiped his hand against his damp jeans. He felt the weight of eyes and paused to stare at the dark windows above, seeing no one, wondering if the building itself was watching—

Pale. Round. It was in the window and then it was gone.

A third-floor window. Leslie's floor.

The dog? That was no animal face.

He placed one foot on the steps, then the other. Exhausted after leaving the hospital where Leslie remained under observation. Exhausted after retrieving his meager luggage from the Waldorf, the bags beneath his eyes so much heavier than those in his hands. Seven steps to the door, aware of a growing smell. A garbage smell. A glance at the trashcans showed nothing amiss, and when he used Leslie's keys to unlock the door, he was horrified to discover that the stink grew more pronounced when he stepped inside and set down his bags.

Flies buzzed about the dank foyer. A wary look at the first-floor apartment told him nothing, so he carried his bags up the steps, forgetting about the railing until it wobbled beneath his grip. He remembered Leslie's mirth on discovering that the stairs were crooked and the railing unsteady. How he loved the odd details of life.

Was the corrupt stink dissipating? He wasn't sure, only that the ashy scent from the top floor was growing. On the second story he waved away a fly and looked back at the watery boot prints marking his trail. He wondered if the second-floor apartment was occupied and readied an explanation for his presence, but no one emerged from that apartment and he hurried past, the thighs of his jeans whispering against each other as beads of rain slid from his motorcycle jacket.

The third floor, Leslie's floor. His eyes drifted between the apartment door and the dark stairs at the end of the hallway that climbed to the fourth floor. The carpet was thin and shiny, worn to threads in patches. Dust bunnies and cobwebs littered the corners.

"Alright," he spoke to the void and wiped damp hair from his eyes, a sniper taking aim. He strode to the door with no attempt at quiet and knocked with enough force that his knuckles hurt.

He waited, pulse thundering in his ears. The musty hallway invaded his nose and he sneezed.

"Is anyone there?" He knocked again. Wondering if Leslie had a woman. Someone he hadn't mentioned.

"I know you're in there." Then, "Wotan?"

The door stood mute.

"Well, shit."

What would happen if he just let himself in? Burst in on—

Something moved overhead.

Percy lifted his chin, studying the ceiling for clues.

"Hello? I'm Percy, Leslie's friend." Thinking they might be afraid of him. Gordon was apparently a full-time drunk these days and there was always the chance a squatter had snuck inside.

He walked hesitantly to the far stairs, touched the newel post with two fingers, and peered up toward the shadowy fourth floor, half-expecting to see him sitting there, teeth bared in a sardonic grin.

The stairs were empty and he was most of the way up before he realized what he was doing.

The illumination from below was reluctant to follow him and the fourth-floor hallway light was out of commission. He could just make out a standing lamp that had been dragged into the hall and hurried to it, hands fumbling quick as beetles beneath the shade until he found the knob and turned it.

Vaporous yellow light drifted down the corridor, lacking enough weight to push back the darkness. In its feeble glow he made out vague details of chipped molding, peeling paint, and the fluttering strands of cobwebs. It was dingier than he remembered, the carpet more ragged.

The lamp's cord traveled under the fourth-floor door and Percy wondered what Leslie had been doing with this light in the hall, as if establishing a base camp.

Was he exploring the fifth floor?

"Leslie?" Quieter this time, as if he knew on some level that he didn't want to be heard. Tiny hairs on the back of his neck stiffened as an uglier scent crept in beneath the reek of the long-ago fire.

The kind of stink that drifted from metal dumpsters squatting behind restaurants. Filled with food scraps, attracting rats and mice and roaches—

Flattening his palm, Percy pressed down against the air to reign in his imagination before lifting his eyes to study the surface above, trying to see through the chipped paint on the ceiling into the suicide apartment.

He wrapped fingers around the standing lamp and carried it a few feet farther toward the final set of stairs, as far as the cord would allow.

His shadow splashed against the far wall, shrinking as he moved toward it. His boot crunched something underfoot and he felt his stomach turn, fairly convinced it was a roach.

His phone chose that moment to buzz and he nearly jumped out of his skin.

I NEED TO SPEAK WITH YOU.

"Fuck off," he said with feeling, jamming the phone back into his pocket. He snorted and took a step back toward the lamp when he heard a furtive sound from above, from behind the final door.

The stairs groaned beneath his weight as he climbed warily, wondering what he would do when he reached the locked door—

A Master Lock hung from the door latch.

Unfastened.

He swallowed through a thickening throat and felt a runnel of perspiration trickle from beneath his hairline, chilling his neck as the silent menace of the building reintroduced itself as a grinning spider, happy to invite the fly deeper into its web.

Roots sprouted from the soles of his boots and he froze on the steps, imagining a yellow gas drifting down toward him, heavier than air. Mustard gas, which he had never seen except in movies. A pure, physical ugliness that was visible to the naked eye, the yellow of bile and putrescence. Tendrils like strings of poisonous saliva seeping beneath the door of the suicide apartment, drifting down to coat the lungs of all who breathed it in on the floors below.

The reek of barbecued rot jammed into the back of his throat.

The phone buzzed again and he twitched. The toe of his boot caught on the lip of the next step and he fell, barking his shin.

"Crap."

He pulled the phone out and checked the message automatically.

GET OUT OF THERE!

"Who the fuck are you?"

His hand was a pale starfish splayed against the black door and he leaned his weight against the wood. The door scraped inward, rusty hinges moaning with disuse, and his gaze fell into darkness as deep and uncaring as a mineshaft.

2.

The dark had a mass all its own, and in the interminable period between the pad of his thumb pressing the button and the light flashing into being, Percy felt the weight of a mountain atop him, a miner in the moments before a cave-in when the tiny hairs on the back of the neck detect the first tiny tremors and send screaming klaxons of alarm racing through ganglia and cortex. Flee! Escape! Survive!

The light incandescing from his phone was built for reading menus, not combating the impenetrable blackness of the space between stars. The suicide apartment devoured it greedily.

As the heavy sole of his boot made contact with the ashy floor, a grinding step that set his nerves on edge, Percy lifted the phone high to cast its meager glow farther. Whatever relief he felt at the ability to see his own arm and hand before his eyes was smothered by the knowledge that his feet had disappeared. He had ceased to exist below the waist.

A cough against the charred air. He took a step, boot squishing something that released the rank odor of feces.

Another step forward, imagining charcoal clouds of dust rising, hoping that his tiny sphere of white energy didn't make him a target. His hearing was muffled by the dense atmosphere and the faint drumming of rain on the roof overhead. Without the ability to see walls, it was too easy to imagine there was no end to this place, that it existed in its own realm, a jet-black room that extended beyond the foundations of the building below.

He had never spent the night in this building and had never set foot on the fifth floor, but he knew the story. The tenant, despairing over a lover, had injected heroin after fashioning a noose in the living room and securing it over an exposed beam overhead.

The man stood on a chair and stepped off, but the fall was insufficient to break his neck. Strangling, he tried to escape, clawing at the rope cutting into his windpipe, but the heroin reduced his efforts to weak, pawing things. The cigarette tumbled free and set fire to refuse on the floor.

(He waved a free hand before him, fingers disappearing into the inky murk)

The coroner's report indicated lung damage and surmised that the rope had weakened in the fire and he fell to the floor, still alive, only to burn to death.

"Is anyone here? I won't hurt you."

What a stupid thing to say. But his feet had locked in place and he was unable to press forward, as if his courage were a tether that was stretched as far as it would allow.

He crouched to play his light across the floor, seeing the ashy planks, curled and separating. He fought the urge to remain in the crouch, his entire body safe within the illuminated sphere, and turned to make out a nearby wall. A step in that direction revealed the limp curls of peeling wallpaper, as if the wall had sprouted hair.

Aiming his light up revealed a blackened beam. *The* beam, he felt the certainty in his bones. Arm stretched overhead, he followed it across the dead space, tongue beading with saliva, pained where he'd bitten it, taken with a macabre fascination, boots crunching in denial of stealth. He made out the ugly curl of a rope looped three times around the wood and followed the dangling, burned bit, maybe three inches, to its frayed end.

Kristi's suicide followed him like cans tied to a dog's tail. Or maybe it was Leslie's hanging, the aborted attempt that triggered the rope's hunger. Hunger that would never be satisfied.

Percy wiped tears from his eyes and fought down another cough, noticing then the corner of a table at the edge of the light. And it was only a few steps farther, so he brought his light closer and made out the heavy wood of what might have been an antique, too heavy to be destroyed by the fire though it was scarred beyond usability.

A woman's shoe rested on the table.

New.

Unburned.

Percy moved around the table and bumped the edge with his hip. Flakes of ash fluttered away.

A barrier loomed ahead, clenched around a deeper blackness. It took him a moment to realize he faced a wall with an open doorway.

On the floor was a rumpled pile of cloth, half in his world, half lost to the unknown space beyond the doorway. Something lumpy and unrecognizable was beneath the cloth.

A woman's dress?

He heard a scuff against wood and his heart leapt into his throat.

Easing backward, his heel scraped the floor and was answered by a strange, breathy sound from the room ahead.

Chuff.

The dress was snatched from sight.

A strangled squeal of terror escaped from his throat and Percy bolted, holding the light straight ahead like a broken-field runner ready to stiff-arm a defender. His boots were rolling thunder, his wheezing breath a hurricane, and he only had a moment to correct course when he reached the doorway, missed, and slammed a shoulder into the unyielding frame to spin himself through. He heard his phone clattering down the stairs as he caught the doorway and arrested his own fall, crushed by the coal-black emptiness all around as he flailed for and caught the door, dragging it shut with a bang. He felt a fingernail bend back and snap, the pain sharp as he found the hasp and lock and slapped the metal pieces together in that intricate puzzle that would keep death on the other side of the door.

He backed away, useless eyes straining, feeling his way down the steps as he waited for a heavy impact against the flimsy wood.

An eternity of crabbing backward in the sinister gloom brought his foot into contact with the hall carpet and, hands braced on the stairs as if preparing for push-ups, he stretched his other foot down until it, too, reached the carpet.

He turned—

—a wild-eyed face lunged at him.

CHAPTER TWENTY NINE

1.

"You scared the shit out of me," Percy said into the dampness of Jordan's hat, the only coherent sentence he had managed since she startled him in the hall upstairs. The fountain of tension erupted inside him and he fought back tears. He pushed her back to arm's length. "What are you doing here?"

Jordan crushed the big man in an embrace, needing the contact as much as he did. Her leather jacket creaked along with her ribs when he returned the hug. She led him down to the third floor and had her keys in hand before he realized it.

"Don't— We have to get out of here!" Percy reached to stop her but she was already turning the key and pushing open the door.

A wave of putrescent stink washed over them and Jordan paled. It smelled like a meat freezer after a week without power. Bands of murky light clawed through the dusty air and dragged the standing antler from the darkness, a pagan shrine standing foully erect on Leslie's table. Percy shivered as if a cold hand had caressed the small of his back.

He snatched the door closed. "We have to go. You can't be here."

"Wait a minute—" Jordan was cut off when he pushed her toward the stairs with more force than he intended. "Hey!"

Of all the ways she had imagined seeing Percy again, the friend she had let go when she left Leslie, this was not one of them. His eyes blazed and his beard bristled, and she was reminded of how large he was. His huge hands lifted to grab her again and she was suddenly afraid of him, a concept that would have been laughable up until that very moment. Percy? Loving, gentle, hilarious Percy? "Stop it!"

He stopped with a great effort, struck by the fear on her face. "Jordan, we have to get outside right now. Please!"

"Fuck you," she said, stifling a sob of frustration as she thundered down the stairs, her fear catching fire, smoldering into anger by the time she pushed through the windowed door into the vestibule and opened the outer door. A wash of rain swept inside, and while Percy didn't push her out into the storm, he did pull the inner door closed behind him with a frightened look over his shoulder.

"I'm scared and Leslie is in trouble," Percy said, his lips set in a grim line that unsettled Jordan.

"What are you talking about?"

"There's weird stuff going on, really weird. And you showing up..."

"Hey—"

"I said *wait*." Percy's tone shocked Jordan, his Yankee accent hardening. "You can't be here. You can't be near Leslie."

Jordan heard the rush of blood in her ears and saw black spots gathering at the edge of her vision. She braced her hand on the doorframe and leaned out, letting the rain have its way with her face while she breathed.

"If Leslie is in there—"

"He's not. I don't know what's in there."

"What?" She noticed the swell of a shiner beneath his left eye. Long red scratches marring his neck.

"What happened to you?" Jordan hated that the tears started, but she was pinned beneath Percy's stare.

"Go home." Percy's big hand clasped her shoulder hard enough to bruise. "You need to leave now."

"The fuck are you talking about?"

"I'm talking about trouble. Real trouble. Leslie is in the middle of it."

"Then I'm—"

"No you're not!"

She stabbed a finger into his chest. "You don't have any say."

"The hell I don't."

"Fuck you, Percy." She crowded into his space but he didn't back up. "I'll stay right here until Leslie comes home—"

"He won't. He's in the hospital."

"No he's not," said a new voice.

They turned in surprise to see Argyle at the bottom of the steps, a black town car idling at the curb behind him. He raised his voice to carry over the sound of passing motorcycles. "Ward left the hospital."

"What?" Percy said.

"What happened?" Jordan found the right questions with greater speed.

"He left without checking out." Argyle raised a hand to forestall questions. "Slipped out without anyone seeing."

"Where is he?" Jordan snapped.

"I don't know," Argyle said. "We have units out looking for him—"

"What do you mean?"

"In case he's hurt." Argyle held both hands up to placate. "We just want to find him and make sure he's okay."

"Where should we look?" Percy said.

"We should stay here," Jordan said.

"I'll stay here," Argyle interjected. "You need to go back to Manhattan in case he tries to go to the condo."

"The hell I will," Jordan snapped, and Percy kept her from going down the stairs at Argyle. "This prick has been harassing me about Leslie," she told the big man, who turned hard eyes toward the detective.

"Easy," Argyle said. "I need you to listen to someone, Percy. A phone call, just a phone call." He pulled a phone from his pocket and hit speed dial. "She's been trying to reach you."

"Who?"

"Please." Argyle ascended several steps with the phone held out like an offering.

Percy took it as if Argyle was holding a banana peel plucked from the trash. His imagination was full of crashing waves and dark thoughts as he said into the phone, "What do you want?"

The woman's voice was weakened from fatigue yet driven like a marathoner in the twenty fifth mile. "My name is Catherine Van Horn, your friend saved my life on the subway. I must speak with you. He is in danger, which you already suspect, but you and Jordan Samatar are in danger as well, which you do not realize or you would not have gone upstairs."

The lines were comical in their melodrama, but Percy was chilled by their sincerity.

"How did you know where I went?"

"What's more important is that I know what happened to your friend in New Hampshire."

"It was in the papers."

A rattling carried over the phone. "After what you saw at Stone's Throw, do you really believe it was a hunting accident?"

Catherine continued in the stunned silence. "Detective Argyle will remain behind to wait for Leslie. Miss Samatar should not become involved further. She should return home. She must avoid contact with Leslie. I promise you that neither Detective Argyle nor I mean Leslie any harm, we only wish to help." A sigh whispered from the phone. "I can tell you what is happening."

"I don't believe you."

"I can't compel you. But if you decide to come, bring the totem." The energy leached from her voice. "I can help."

Percy handed the phone back to Argyle and glanced into the building uneasily.

"It's raining," Argyle said, holding out a palm to catch some of the downpour. "Can I come in?"

2.

Windshield wipers struggled against the downpour as the town car ground west through traffic on Fulton Street. People slogged along the sidewalks outside, shoulders hunched beneath the sheeting rain. It was a world of muted grey, where bright banners hung limp before storefronts and neon signs made only half-hearted attempts to pierce the gloom.

Inside the vehicle was a different world of rich maroon and shining black where heat blasted from unseen vents and the air smelled of spices. A contained world where piano jazz danced quietly from unseen speakers, bottled water awaited his thirst, and a box of Kleenex was ready for use.

It was a different world from Leslie's apartment, where Percy found the antler—the *totem*, Catherine called it—sprouting up from the old Remington typewriter as if it had been planted like a tree.

The antler was warm when he grabbed hold of it below the points. It resisted his efforts until he wrenched it free with a great tearing sound (and the incongruous ring of the carriage return), the antler bleeding and trailing long threads that resembled the nerves of a tooth.

Towels from Leslie's bathroom were wrapped around it and the bundle currently rested on the floor between Percy's boots.

The driver handed a roll of paper towels back to Percy and said, "Help you dry off."

"Thanks," Percy said from the back seat and tore off a few sheets.

"Yes, hello," he said into his phone. "My name is Percy Cronk, I'm calling to check on the status of Leslie Ward. I'm told he left the hospital." He mopped his wet beard. His eyes shifted as he was transferred. "Yes, I'm, Percy—" He stopped speaking, eyes narrowing. "I see." He hung up and picked up the paper towels to wipe his face dry. Argyle wasn't lying.

"Leslie Ward?" the driver said, his eyes finding Percy's in the rearview mirror. He was a bald man with big shoulders and three days' growth of dark beard. "Isn't he the guy who wrote those pervy books? You know, with a different name?"

"You read a lot?"

"I drive a car so I can't—"

"Right, right. You know where you're going?"

"Upper East Side. I'll take the Williamsburg Bridge, then the FDR up to—"

"Good enough." Percy slumped back into the seat and felt his sopping clothes grow clingy with the warmth. He cracked the window and leaned his head into the thin stream of cooler air. Water trickled from his hairline, and in the glare of oncoming headlights, his strained countenance gave him an unhealthy look.

He glanced down at the odd bundle between his feet.

"You a cop?" Percy said.

"No," Yakut said, meeting his eyes in the mirror and holding his stare.

"Sure you are." Jazz piano lilted from the speakers.

3.

The inner door lock was child's play. Argyle's only problem was drying his fingers enough to manipulate the picks. His coat was wet and so were his pants, so he resorted to wiping his palms on the walls, leaving smeared streaks across the dusty white surface. When his hands were as dry as he could get them, the picks came out and the lock waved a white flag.

He waited a few extra minutes to make sure the town car didn't return before pushing into the damp rot smell of the foyer.

Damp rot and something else.

The chamber was a colorless wash of brown and grey, a dispiriting palette designed to refuse welcome. A single light cast a cone of illumination down from the ceiling.

Argyle scuffed his shoes to dry them. The light flickered and shadows stirred at the far end of the hall.

He eyed the walnut-colored staircase, rationalizing his nerves. Jordan Samatar was a cop hater and definitely a litigious bitch. And Ward himself had the money to hire the kind of lawyer who loved to go after the department.

But he'd be damned if he was going to wait in the doorway.

He eased down the hall, raindrops dripping from the hem of his coat, socks squelching inside his shoes. He wanted nothing more than to go home and sit in a tub of hot water with a scotch balanced on the toilet seat beside him and a Count Basie record spinning in the living room.

Even when he reached the back of the hall, shadows conspired to conceal a door. When Argyle leaned on it, a cold draft slipped from the crack and he thought he'd found the basement.

He waved away a buzzing fly and imagined it down there. Low and cramped, maybe an old light bulb hanging from a wire. Stacks of musty boxes. Spider webs and rat traps.

"Fuck that."

He straightened up, straining his ears. Was someone upstairs?

Moving quickly but quietly to the base of the staircase, he started up, cursing when the risers groaned beneath his weight. The banister wobbled in his hand and he jerked away. Why the hell did a rich guy live in this place?

Ascending several more steps, he thought of announcing himself as a police officer, but he heard another sound. A furtive sound. The roof of his mouth went dry.

He glanced down the stairs, the weight of his gaze resting on the dark wooden door of the first-floor apartment. He imagined someone watching him through the peephole. If there was a fisheye lens, the watcher would be able to see Argyle even now.

Pursing his lips, he shooed away another fly. A blow fly? Blow flies laid their eggs in carcasses.

Corpses.

Several more flies darted about the staircase.

"Probable cause," he muttered and continued up the stairs. He considered calling Yakut for back-up but dismissed the notion. He needed Yakut where he was, keeping an eye on the big guy.

The second floor was quiet and he scuffed his way to the apartment door. There wasn't supposed to be anybody living there, but he listened with his ear against the wood for several long seconds, holding his breath. He gave the knob a gentle turn, stopped by a lock. Felt the dust of disuse on his fingers.

And there were no flies.

He grunted as he climbed, legs already tired. Wet shoe prints were visible in the dim lighting of the third floor and his lips thinned as he heard the tell-tale buzzing.

A glance at his cell phone brought a frown. The power bar was down to 2%. He thought he'd charged it before leaving in the morning but...

But the smell was growing stronger as he approached the door to Leslie Ward's apartment.

Fingertips grazed against the scarred wooden door and Argyle saw there was no spy hole. A fly crawled across the rough surface and he flicked his hand in its direction.

The door creaked open.

4.

Argyle snapped on a penlight and played the beam around Ward's vast and cluttered apartment. He slid his beam back across a long wooden table and the ugly shrine atop it.

The hair on his forearms tried to rise against the weight of his sleeves. Water dripped from the hem of his coat. Flies buzzed.

The blood-spattered typewriter sat beside a disheveled stack of papers. A manuscript. Argyle was drawn toward it, instinct guiding him to play his light over the befouled Remington before he extended a finger toward the stack.

The top sheet was marred by small brown smears, aligned in the formation of a title with the author's name below it, but unreadable. As if the ink had dissolved and spread, corrupting each letter from the inside out.

He flicked the lead paper aside and several slid off the table, stuck together.

The sheet revealed beneath was organized into paragraphs, though the words were not words. Instead of letters, the sheet was marked with rows of smeared shapes. None quite the same but all similar and naggingly familiar...

He pushed aside another sticky clump of papers and encountered more of the same.

Then again.

Page after page. Row after row.

He turned back to the old Remington and leaned closer, playing his light over the keys and into the mechanism of the thing. He tapped a key and the typebar thwacked against the cylindrical platen.

"Holy shit." A whisper. Trying to discredit what he had seen with his own eyes. He tapped another letter, a Q, and saw the typebar rise to slap its white, bony tip against the platen.

An R. An F. An O. Each time the typebar lifted and smacked home into the platen he told himself, "It can't be," until he saw the silver flash of a filling.

They were teeth. The typebars had been tipped with human teeth.

Leslie Ward was a madman.

The phone was in Argyle's hand, but even as he thumbed the call button, the screen dimmed and died. His smile was sickly, the atmosphere of the place already playing on his nerves.

He could see evidence of the man living here. Food containers. Bottles. The blanket on a couch. The typewriter. But the rest...

Furniture and stacked boxes draped in sheets like so many misshapen ghosts. Easy chairs and kitchen chairs. Another couch. Dressers and cabinets. Ward had raided the entire linens department of a store to cover this eclectic mess.

Dust motes were thick in the atmosphere and he sneezed. Saw the wet spray in his light. Sneezed again and wondered what he was awakening with all his racket.

"Hello?" His voice was reedy and timid, even with his hand inside his coat, fingers touching the butt of his .38 revolver. Old School, the younger guys called him. A stupid affectation. He wished he had a machine gun. "Hello?"

His traitorous light reached across the jumbled space to reveal a narrow staircase and he groaned, knowing that he would go upstairs.

The gun emerged from its holster with a leathery hiss that sounded like "Yesssss" as he moved to the bottom of the staircase.

The penlight didn't reveal jackshit. He needed one of those big, two-foot-long jobs. A million lumens. The weak circle of his light crawled across a cobwebby second-floor ceiling.

The gun went away and his free hand fished in a deep coat pocket to produce a slightly sticky gumball covered with lint. Held it in the light and saw it was blue. He tossed it underhand and it struck the top step, only to bounce back down toward him. *Tock-tock-tock.*

He got his body behind it and stopped it with a shoe when it reached the bottom. Swallowed against the thickness in his throat.

This is stupid. Go up the stairs.

He tossed the blue gumball again, this time with greater force. It arced up over the staircase and into the unseen space above. His ears told him it struck a wall and he heard it roll across a wooden floor, tense against the expected scrabble of claws. The howl of

(something)

but heard nothing, eyes tracking across the ceiling until the sound of the rolling gumball stopped somewhere above.

"New York City Police!" he said with more force.

A foot then, on the first stair. His free hand was pressed against the wall for balance. A lawsuit waiting to happen, that's what the staircase was. He should go back downstairs and call—

A second step. A third. The risers sang their age, groaning and creaking in mockery of his attempts at quiet. Why was he being quiet? His shouting had surely awakened whomever

(whatever)

waited upstairs.

"Stop it." This out loud, to himself.

Run. Leave.

A fourth step. A fifth.

He hoped whatever it was liked gum. Would be nice—

Argyle dragged a wet sleeve across his sweat-dampened brow to little effect. He was quite simply terrified. It made no sense at all, but between the third-floor hallway and half the distance up these stairs, his nerve endings were exploding in a fireworks display of fear. He leaned his shoulder into the wall, fabric shushing against plaster as he left a wet streak upon climbing the sixth step and the seventh.

Three to go. He could see a rickety wooden banister to his right, darkness beyond. On the eighth step, he lifted his penlight and pivoted carefully. Saw nothing but a confusion of shapes as the beam danced across the space.

He took the ninth and tenth steps in a rush and placed his back to the wall beside an open doorway. He risked turning his back on the dark, open space to aim his flashlight into the small bedroom with its slanting ceiling. He saw the crumpled air mattress. Blankets. Books.

"A fucking madman."

He pushed into the main room, half-expecting to see that horrible antler grown huge, springing forth from the floor like a tree. Instead he saw more stacks and unused furniture. His light picked out the tall, looming shape awaiting him. The hint of a pale face behind thin cloth.

Oily beads of sweat squeezed from his pores and he aimed his .38 at the ghost. "That's not funny!" he shouted. Childish in his fear. Flies buzzed and clocks ticked. He waved a hand in front of his face, the smell thicker now. Thumbed back the hammer as he wove amongst the clutter. His heartbeat thudded in his chest and he snatched the white sheet from atop the man's head—

A grandfather clock, face round and white. "Oh, fuck you."

His eyes closed in relief and he missed the movement as the tall, thin door set into the tower of the clock swung open. His eyes sprang wide as a tide of ripped and bloody fur spilled out across his shins.

An inarticulate cry sprang from his throat and Argyle backpedaled away from the feline carcasses. He staggered behind his penlight beam through the open doorway, the flood coming. Cursed the stack of books balanced atop the closed toilet seat and dropped his gun into the sink

(which thankfully did not fire)

wrenching down his zipper to release urine into the moldy bathtub even as he swallowed against a rising gorge.

He shoved aside the books with his hip and sat on the toilet lid, panting. Plucked his gun from the sink and washed the piss from his right hand. Shook it as dry as he could.

He'd go downstairs. Get to the bodega on the corner. Use their phone to call in some units—

A sound. Not in the apartment. Outside in the hall.

A cough.

5.

Argyle's penlight threw just enough light to create movements at the corner of his vision. Webs dangling from the hallway ceiling. Strips of paint fluttering like flakes of skin on the walls.

The odd, burnt odor was stronger in the fourth-floor hallway and he wondered what had happened. A fire, obviously, but when? Was Ward burning

(evidence)

something?

Beads of moisture flickered like tiny jewels as he followed the wet footprints down the chewed carpeting to the end of the hall and a final, blackened staircase.

"Enough."

Who was the madman? He was the one talking to himself. About to climb the staircase to the fifth floor.

He shivered in the cold and damp.

And sealed his fate by placing his foot on the step.

Then the next.

A strangled laugh escaped him when he saw the padlock laying on the top step and the unfastened hasp on the door. As if Ward had been locking something inside. Something now free to wander—

The door opened under the pressure of his fingertips, hinges screeching in protest.

A black and choking space awaited him, swatting his light into insignificance. He tried to call out and coughed against the disturbed ash in the air.

The fifth floor.

Argyle stepped inside. Heard the grit beneath his shoes. Saw the charred wood on walls and floor with his meager penlight.

Rope hanging from a cross beam...

And that was as far as he could go.

He worked his dry mouth and spat. Fished in his coat pocket, fingers pressing past the stiff fold of a movie ticket. A paper clip. Found the round, sticky object and held it in the light.

A red gumball, faded almost pink.

He tossed it into the impenetrable murk and it was swallowed by the dark. Heard a muffled bump as it struck something and walked carefully toward the sound, playing his light around until he saw the table and, on the table, a woman's shoe.

It was clunky. Funky in the way young white women liked them these days. Heavy in the way immigrant women used to wear them, not because they liked them, but because they were solid. Cheap.

He pushed it over and it plopped on its side atop the table.

Argyle continued toward where he thought the gumball had landed and finally saw a glimmer of red, the round object dusted with ash.

He sniffed and wished he hadn't. Spat and froze when his light slid through an open doorway. Spotted the edge of cloth on the floor.

A careful underhand toss sent the gumball into the mysterious space beyond the doorway and he heard the faint thump and roll. Stepped forward—

The crash and bang of noise sent him reeling backward so that he struck the table and it fell over with a clatter. He heard bells and bongs and that goddamned grandfather clock going off downstairs in Ward's apartment.

"Oh fuck," he said, straightening up—

The darkness in the room beyond came alive.

Argyle shrieked and turned, tumbling over the table with a horrendous crash. He hit the ground even as a weight struck the table from the other side and the wood slammed against him.

He fled in a simian scramble on hands and knees. Desperate to turn and see what pursued him but knowing that to do so would be fatal. His eyes focused on the dim rectangle of the open door and he lurched through, clawing it closed behind him.

Not a moment later it shuddered beneath an impact. Argyle jerked his pistol free and fired, the report deafening as he lost his footing and fell.

His shoulder blades slammed against the stairs and his head snapped back. Lights flashed behind his eyes as he slid to the floor where he piled in a heap of coat and limbs.

The gun was still in his hand and he fired twice up the stairs, chunks of wood exploding from the door. He heard a wail of pain and rage and claws digging into wood. Something powerful and angry

(fangs)

and Argyle forced himself to his knees. Fought down a screech of pain from his left arm when he tried to lever himself upright.

He fled down the hall and darted into Ward's apartment as howls rang out on the floor above. He slammed the door, stuffing the .38 in a deep pocket as he shoved boxes and furniture against the entrance.

He touched his head and the blood was as black as oil on his fingers.

He remembered the pale, chewed face of Chester Waters.

Yakut said he'd been eaten.

Voices! Voices below!

"Help!"

Argyle stumbled for the narrow staircase leading down to the third floor of Ward's apartment. Whomever it was had to get out. They all had to get out!

151

Reeling like a drunk, he made it to the stairs, stumbling, crying out when his injured arm struck the wall. He missed the last step and sprawled on the floor.

Thick, dull light drifted through the windows and collected around the hideous typewriter on the table. A gathering nimbus dirty with motes, as if the air were water mucked with silt.

Pressing his wounded arm to his belly, Argyle pushed himself up to his knees, staring past sheet-draped shapes to study the door to the hall.

Had he closed it?

On his feet then, and he tripped in the gloom, sending a stack of books crashing to the floor.

Voices again and he lurched toward the table, toward an old black rotary phone. The receiver was off the hook and he heard the susurrus of conversation crackling from it.

He plucked the receiver from the table and held it to his ear, only to hear the click of a hang up followed by a dial tone.

The receiver clattered to the table and his vision blurred through tears of pain. He took a step back and his heel struck an obstacle. There was a brief moment when he thought he would regain his balance, and then he was falling back onto an unseen chair covered in a flowered bed linen.

He came down on something soft beneath the draped sheet. There was a rush of foul gas and a ripping, flatulent noise as he slid forward and off, tangled in the linens.

A woman leaned forward from the chair as if to stand. Her hair was stiff and wild, her face a savage mask of wounds.

Argyle shrieked as Lavinia fell on top of him.

He pushed desperately with both hands. The bloated corpse toppled aside like a manikin. Flies were buzzing like angry dive bombers and a hideous spill of white rice—

Argyle crawled away on three limbs, whimpering. Mind receding as shock overwhelmed him. He reached up to open the door and pulled himself into the hall.

From two floors above, he heard the crack of breaking wood and the loud, chaotic descent of the thing from the fifth floor.

Argyle found himself on his feet and sprinting without conscious volition. He reached the staircase leading down and leapt, screeching as his ankle turned upon landing. Saliva sprayed from his mouth with every grunting breath as he hobbled for the final staircase, the crash and snarl of pursuit gaining. It was on the third floor, right above him.

The stairs. He hobbled down as quickly as he could, losing ground but knowing that to injure his ankle further was to die.

He could see the first floor. The dingy carpet leading to the door and escape—

Too slow. It was above him. He heard the canine grunt of effort and a tremendous impact spun him into the banister, which gave way under his weight.

Argyle landed on the ragged carpeting. He heard as much as saw his pursuer reach the first floor, carried into the door by momentum. Glass shattered from the collision and then the fearsome pitbull was on its feet, great ropes of drool swaying from its jaws.

A single, golden eye blazed from the white scar tissue of its face as it lurched toward him on three legs, momentarily stunned.

It was between Argyle and the exit. He pulled himself across the hallway to the door leading into the first-floor apartment.

If it's locked, I'm dead. The thought was surprising in its clarity.

The knob turned beneath his sweaty palm and he shouldered his way inside. He slammed the door behind him just as claws raked the other side. Snarls and teeth held back by a mere inch of wood. Deep throated barking roused him to his feet and he blundered in the gloom into an enormous edifice of stacked magazines, toppling the mess and sliding over the top.

He blinked in the gloom, the floor grimy beneath him as he found himself in a narrow passage between piles of

(hoarder)

magazines and boards and boxes and kitchenware and canned goods

(as a uniformed rookie he had been called to a hoarder's apartment)

He stood, listing on his bad ankle. He could see the oasis cleared for chair and television and tray table. He angled down the passage and cut through another that led to the chair and beside it a table lamp with a moth-eaten shade.

(Thank God)

Weak effulgence revealed the extent of the mess. A maze of waist-high piles, snakelike passages constructed through the mass of unidentifiable stuff.

He limped down a winding path to the nearest windows and yanked aside the threadbare curtains. The window lifted with a screech and he reached through to grasp the security bars over the window. He shouted, "Help!" into the rain. Shouted again and again until a noise caused him to turn and he saw a ripple in one of the stacks. His frantic mind imagined a movie screen. A shark skimming just below the surface of the ocean.

Cans clinked as something brushed a tall pyramid.

He was being hunted.

Argyle stepped away from the window and drew his gun, doing his best to understand the passages, wondering if he could—

He heard a rumbling growl and heaved his weight against a tower of newspapers, so old they had grown together into something nearer to tree than pulp.

It toppled and he climbed over it into the next passage, bulling his way toward the darkened hallway as his pursuer sprang high over a barrier and landed in the twisting passage behind him.

It was huge and black, much larger than the dog in the hall. Blunt of muzzle and dense of shoulder. Argyle fired twice, shouting as he saw the bullets pulp meat and bone. The dog yelped piteously and fell, but Argyle was already moving into the hall. It was divided into two separate passages with a waist-high wall of—

Movement from a doorway up ahead. Low. Darting into the righthand passage.

Argyle fell into the lefthand passage, teeth bared in terror as the dog rose high, paws planted, barking and snarling and pushing at the barrier between them.

A door! He pressed against the thin wood and muscled it open. Rushed inside the black and windowless cell, slamming the door behind him—

His shin struck something hard. Porcelain. Arms windmilling as he tripped into a slick shower curtain. Heard rings popping and dragged it down with him as he fell into the bathtub.

Slime and stink. Hard, long objects and slippery things. He squirmed and forced his head up but could see nothing. Hoped his phone had enough power left and pressed the button to activate the flashlight application.

The light blazed bright and clear and he found himself in a red stew of gore where white bones peeked from crimson flesh. Shreds of cloth and meat dripped from his hand and he recoiled from the grinning countenance of Gordon's skull, mounted on the showerhead.

The door rattled in its frame and he wondered how many dogs were out there. How long the weak particle board barrier would hold.

The light winked out and he shrieked.

As it turned out, the door didn't hold long at all.

CHAPTER THIRTY

1.

Percy planted his boots in the flowing gutter beside the curb. The town car had let him out in the Upper East Side, cars and people alike crawling through stone canyons beneath imposing towers, no bigger than insects to those who lived above.

Barely a drop of rain had touched his head when a uniformed doorman appeared with an enormous umbrella, big enough to shield them both until they stepped into the safety of the awning. He had googled Catherine Van Horn on the drive over and wondered what a "society dame with loads of money" wanted with him.

"This way, please," the mustachioed doorman said, holding open the glass door so that they could pass into the cavernous lobby of the high-rise. Percy stared as if they'd accidentally wandered onto a movie set, taking in the elegant art deco wall sconces and aqua-toned furniture. It was a future vision from long ago. Metropolis. Alphaville. The high ceilings encouraged footsteps to echo, emphasizing the insignificance of visitors. He expected that those who lived above felt that much larger in comparison.

A stiff-looking fellow in a starched uniform cleared his throat from behind a counter. "Mr. Cronk?"

"Yeah?"

"Miss Van Horn is sending someone down to collect you."

Percy twitched at the metallic scrape of a door opening in a row of brass elevators. An old-fashioned iron gate was opened by one white-gloved hand and a sepulchral man in a black suit stepped out. A gust of cool air rolled forth from the open elevator in his wake, as if the shaft led to a deep subcellar walled in ice. Percy studied the man's milky skin and narrow fringe of gray hair and wondered what he did for Van Horn.

"Miss Van Horn extends her welcome," the man said, voice terribly quiet. "If you'll come with me."

He stepped back into the elevator like a wind-up toy returning to its box.

"Twentieth floor," the man said and closed the gate.

2.

They were delivered to a round windowless room with high ceilings. A single door faced the elevator across a parquet floor. The door was a massive thing, nearly eight feet tall and built of dark wood that gleamed from frequent polishing of its ornately carved surface. The lighting in the room came from partially hidden sconces made to resemble torches hanging on the walls, as if they stood in the antechamber of a medieval lord.

The tall man moved in an effortless glide across the checkered floor, a menacing chess piece belonging to the black queen. Not a knight or a pawn, he resembled a ruthless bishop.

"This way," the bishop said. The great door whispered as he pulled it open and stepped aside.

3.

The sound changed as they stepped through the door, shoes scuffing on a smoother surface. It was as dark as a mine shaft but as airy as a football stadium and Percy could feel a breeze.

The door shut behind him with a muffled crump. The click of the locking mechanism was threatening in its finality.

"My name is Percy Cronk," his voice boomed. "You called..." He had no idea what to say and finished weakly. "Where are you?"

He had the sense that he was not alone.

"You said you'd tell me what happened in the woods." His words rolled against the black as if he could push it aside through force of will.

"Your friend woke a spirit." It was a voice without a body.

"Bullshit."

"He woke a spirit and fled." The voice rippled around him as if emerging from hidden speakers. "You stumbled across echoes of the awakened spirit yourself."

There was a pale shift in the emptiness, the distance impossible to guess.

"What do you have to do with it?" Percy called out toward the shimmering white thing.

"It touched me with tooth and claw, but Leslie held it back." The sound came from the direction of an approaching alabaster form. "When it comes again, it will own him and destroy those it has touched."

"Turn on a light," he said, voice breaking like a child's.

"Do you love him?" The question emerged from the swaying pillar of white, closer but too far to touch.

"Turn on the lights or I'm out of here."

"Do you love him?"

"Last time." Percy lifted his phone and thumbed the light, but found himself alone in the small circle of radiance.

"Do you love him?" The woman displayed none of the fatigue heard over the phone. This was a voice of power and it grabbed him like a giant's hand.

"Yes!"

A click heralded the glow from a crystal chandelier, casting radiance over a living room the size of a ballroom, the furnishings immaculate and elaborate as if the past had been trapped under glass. Percy threw a glance over his shoulder and saw the sepulchral bishop standing beside the door, his hand raised to a bank of light switches on the wall.

The woman in flowing white approached. Pale of face and hair, the only element of contrast were her large, black sunglasses.

"Come with me," she beckoned. "He hasn't much time."

4.

Their steps were muffled as Catherine led Percy along a carpeted pathway winding between outgrowths of furniture, social stations devoid of life like so many deserted islands.

Passing an elevated stage with a grand piano, he saw they had arrived at a wall where velvet curtains of shimmering burgundy covered towering windows.

The comfort at discovering that there were boundaries to the opulent expanse was dashed when the chandelier (now far behind them) dimmed and they were plunged into sudden night.

After an uncomfortable pause during which he was unable to walk farther, a series of lights fashioned in the manner of old sidewalk gas lamps glowed to life up ahead. He detected a scent and studied the dancing blue flames with greater attention, realizing that they were actual gas lamps liberated from some long-ago street.

Catherine led him through an archway into a passage large enough to accommodate a truck, where similarly fashioned lamps hung from black iron hooks on the wall.

Wide doorways lined the great hall, and while most were closed, others opened to reveal different realms of indulgence. A carpeted bar colored in deep red and shining brass. A wooden floor beneath a glimmering disco ball. A luxurious screening room, an elegant dining area, a tiled Grecian bath. It was a passageway between worlds that took them nowhere near Van Horn's private self.

Shades of Norma Desmond, Percy thought.

"This way," Catherine said as she descended two slate steps off to the right into a stone-floored room where towering ferns dripped moisture and small trees were hung with delicate cages. Brightly colored songbirds came and went as they willed, trilling greetings to the people below, secure in the knowledge that no predators existed in their world of leaf and feather.

They crossed a gurgling stream on a short wooden bridge and Catherine paused, offering her first smile. "This is the portal between the public and private realms. Welcome to my home."

Catherine continued to the base of a black spiral stair that rose from a copse of trees.

"Watch your step," Catherine said and began to climb. She paused once and the left side of her mouth twisted in the same wry smile that once graced magazine spreads. "Norma Desmond my ass."

5.

"The Hopi used peyote and the hippies took mescaline." Catherine rattled ice cubes in a stainless-steel martini shaker. "I like gin."

They were in a cluttered library where conversation was muffled by the long-haired carpet and endless shelves of books. It was a room of comforting browns and blues, and several reading chairs were scattered about, each accompanied by a fringed lamp suited for a bordello.

Catherine seated her guest at a scarred oaken table beneath the large window and turned on the nearest lamp, a leggy purple number with Chinese ideograms inked on the shade. The table was covered in familiar lettering and adorned with the type of gewgaws favored by carnival fortune tellers.

Percy watched in admiration as she poured two perfect martinis without spilling a drop. "I hope you like them dirty," she said as she lifted them from the drink trolley onto a round tray and carried them to the table, sliding aside one of two malformed candles to set the load down before placing a tall-stemmed cocktail before each of them.

"Salud." She sipped. "Trust me, a drink will make this easier."

"This is an interesting table, Miss—"

"Cat."

"Cat." Percy sipped the martini and closed his eyes as the cold gin slid down his throat. "Like I was saying," he continued, "these letters—"

"You mean my Ouija table? Doesn't inspire much confidence, does it?" Cat chewed an olive plucked from her drink.

Percy tapped two fingers on a waiting deck of cards before cutting them. He grew still at the sight of the Hanged Man. "Tarot is mostly bullshit," Cat chimed in, taking the cards and shuffling quickly. She set them down with a card shark's snap. "Cut the deck."

He shrugged and cut the deck, turning over the top card.

The Hanged Man.

"It's a card trick," Cat said.

"I saw someone hanged recently."

Cat tilted her head in surprise and said, "Did you now?" She pursed her lips. "I'm going to cut to the chase, because we have work to do and my pills are wearing off. You." She aimed a long finger. "The first time you had sex was the summer after your sophomore year in high school. You were so excited that you ejaculated prematurely and spent your junior year praying that Tory Dillon would transfer to Holyoke Academy."

Percy twitched and spilled a little of his cocktail.

She set her drink down. "Now how would I know that?"

He opened his mouth and closed it, face hot with embarrassment.

"Something else," Cat said. "I asked you to bring the totem, where is it?"

Percy stiffened and confusion washed over his features. A door across the room opened quietly and the bishop carried the towel-wrapped item to the table. He brought with him the aroma of exotic spices, which departed along with the man in black.

"You left it in the car," Cat said. "It's not your fault. It doesn't want to be here."

Percy nodded and tugged aside the wrappings so that the antler lay exposed atop the table. "I can't believe I forgot about this thing. Just looking at it feels like a toothache in my mind."

Cat dragged a fingernail along the curve of sharp bone. It rocked on the table with the sound of dead branches clattering in the wind.

Percy pulled out his phone. "You should see this," he said before catching himself.

"It's alright," Cat said. "Describe it to me. Share what you see."

"But first, faites-noue un autre martini," Cat said, tipping back her glass to finish the dregs before scooting her chair closer to his. "Make another batch, dirty as sin," she said as he took the delicate glass in his large hand. "After this video I want you to tell me everything that's happened."

He pushed back his chair and stood, his large shadow looming over her.

"Open your mind, Percy."

6.

"Light me up," Cat said, the long black cigarette holder touching her red lips. Percy finished lighting the second candle and held the wooden match across the table as Cat rose and leaned in, her cheeks hollowing as she pulled the flame from Percy to herself. Twin spirals of smoke drifted from her nostrils as Percy turned off the lamp and returned to her seat. "Some things are better done by candlelight."

Cat waited for him to sit. "Quite a story, Percy." She gestured with her cigarette. "What do you think, hon? Are you crazy?"

"No."

"You believe these things happened?"

"I lived through it and still don't know how to deal." He looked at his hands. "But I can see the marks. Those people on the train...all of it happened."

"Maybe it will help to give it a name." Cat pushed back from the table and retrieved a couple of thick books stacked on a chair. The first volume thumped on the table and the candle flames jumped, their firelight picking out the gold tracery on the brown leather cover. Woven among ornate runes, the face of an old man peered from a filigree of leaves and berries. Long of hair and beard, he wore a patch over one eye. "Wotan, also called Odin. The All Father. He appeared in different guises throughout Northern and Western Europe before the Christians put paid to the old religions."

She blew smoke across the cover and the lines of the face shifted subtly, as if to regard Percy.

"These candles smell funny."

"Rendered goat fat." Cat revealed her perfect teeth. "Always makes me hungry." She lifted the second book and let it thump down beside the first. The candle flames fled sideways before resuming their tall dance.

This book was uglier, the cracked bindings made from some kind of hide and stitched rudely along the spine. "Tell me what you see."

"Antlers, deer antlers," Percy said, flicking a glance at the jagged deer horn on the table. "And a man's face. His eyes are empty."

"Because he has given up his soul and is no longer a man." Cat paused. "In your studies, you have heard the word *divine*."

"You're saying this is God?"

"Not in the Biblical meaning. Older." Cat steadied her voice with another mouthful of gin. "More akin to the Neolithic Death Mother of Malta or Aganju, who cultivated cities in the Nigerian desert. Leshy, who lived in the forests of Eastern Europe."

"Are they gods?"

"It's a working term." Cat touched the leatherbound tome and drew her hand back. "If the spirit Leslie awakened is anima, a spirit, its focus is simpler. The Hunt. While it cannot be reasoned with—"

"What if it's more than an anima?"

"You know the answer." Her laugh was hollow and she set her drink down to place both hands on the table, fingers spread. "Avoiding it is best. If you can't, placate it. Give it what it wants and avert your eyes."

"And what's that?"

"You tell me."

"Worship? Ritual?"

"Yes, and from the little we know, what is its ritual?"

"The Hunt. Like it did with Leslie." Twin spirals of flame rose as the candles crackled. Light played along the hard lines of Percy's face, and glinted orange in his eyes. "The Wild Hunt."

162

"Yes," Cat said. "The elemental concept of the hunt, the chase, and the kill, incarnate and real. The same people who spoke of Wotan knew of the Wild Hunt and sometimes told their stories as one. Older, crueler folk called him the Great God Pan."

Percy's eyes locked on the shining lenses of Van Horn's opaque glasses. "I've read other things said about Pan and what he represented."

"Christians borrowed from older faiths." Cat nodded. "Let's hope they were wrong."

"You said Leslie woke up a spirit. This?"

She picked up his hand, her grip stronger than expected. She placed his fingers atop the hide-bound tome and the cover crawled beneath his touch.

"I have studied the smoke and the leaves and the coals," she said. "I have followed the blood trail on stone and seen it written, the Wild Hunt never fails to run down its prey. The Hunter and his pack of hellhounds can never lose the track, can never be dissuaded. Once marked, a man is doomed."

"And it's after Leslie?"

"No, child." Cat lowered her cigarette. "It caught him in the wilds of New Hampshire." She tapped a length of grey ash onto the table and blew gently so that it spread into designs. "He is becoming the Hunter."

"What is he hunting?"

Her fingers stretched out toward the book of the Hunter again but stopped short of the binding. "What would Leslie hunt? What does he want most of all?"

Percy stared at the Hunter's empty eyes on the book cover. "You're talking about Jordan." He shook his head. "If anything happened to her, it would kill him."

Her laugh was ugly. The croaking of a bird. "Him, her, and anyone who gets in his way."

"Can we stop it?"

Catherine leaned back in her chair, removing her sunglasses. The play of light and shadow made dark caverns of her eyes. "We can try."

A gust of wind blew out the candles as the door opened. The bishop entered with an unlit lantern in each hand.

7.

The bishop closed the metal gate of the elevator and said, "Sub-basement," before turning the brass crank on the wall. The small elevator was crowded with the three of them and uncomfortably warm. Cat carried a small, pearl-studded purse and Percy carried a lantern as well as the totem, wrapped once more in dishtowels.

"This spirit does not belong in North America," Cat said.

They heard an audible thud and the elevator lights flickered as they passed each floor.

"The dolmen in your video was not built by people indigenous to the northeast. Without seeing it I can't be sure, but it could have been built by Vikings as far back as the year one thousand, when they landed nearby in Newfoundland. Or it could have been carried over from Europe by a wealthy settler in later years."

"Why is that important?"

"The White Mountains are old and have their own spirits, genius loci," Cat continued. "The existence of this nature spirit is *unnatural* in North America. Simply being on this side of the Atlantic weakens it. New York City," she waved her hand at the gleaming confines of the elevator, "is toxic on a metaphysical level. As the fabric of reality grows thinner in its presence, people near Leslie will experience strange events. He will draw the ire of others, even violence, as the land seeks to drive him out as a body would drive out disease."

"That's what happened on the subway," Percy said.

"Yes." Cat pulled out her cigarettes and tapped a finger against the cellophane. "Think of it as a spiritual malady." Seeing that meant nothing, she added, "He's like lead in the water, sickening everything around him. That's why he has drawn these assaults from people, as if they were antibodies. The places he has been living, the lake cabin and Brooklyn, will be deeply poisoned wells, rooted to his energy." She turned her blind gaze toward him. "Do not go back to the building in Brooklyn."

He had a thought and she plucked it from the air. "Burn it down? You might set the whole block on fire. How many people will you kill to give him a hotfoot?"

"What can we do?"

The elevator rang as if struck from the outside. Percy's eyes darted to the wrapped antler in his fist. "It just moved in my hand."

"Do we have your attention?" Cat murmured to the bundle.

"Are you saying that Leslie can escape even though he's marked?" Percy asked.

Cat remained silent as the floor indicator passed ONE and settled on BASEMENT when it came to a shuddering stop. The bishop produced a dull skeleton key and inserted it into a slot, turning it to the right until it produced an audible click of tumblers. The elevator resumed its descent.

"Are we supposed to be down here?" Percy asked.

"I'm very rich," Cat said with a twist of her lips.

"Sub-basement," the bishop announced as the elevator juddered to a halt. "Light your lantern, please."

Cat added, "No electric light from this point forward. Man-made electricity is a disruptive element."

The bishop slid open the gate as Percy opened the small glass door on his lantern and lit the wick. The familiar scent of goat fat filled the air.

Cat placed a hand on his shoulder. "If you'll guide me."

"Of course."

"Thank you. Watch out for rat traps." Cat led them from the sanctuary of the elevator into the mineshaft blackness of the sub-basement, shoes scraping on the floor. The ceiling overhead was lined with rust-caked pipes from which dangling streamers of cobweb swayed like hag's hair. Metal clanked in the distance and they heard deep and liquid gurgling, as if they had stumbled into the mechanical gut of an enormous machine. Percy's nostrils were clogged with the scent of dirt and he wondered if this was what Kristi Sugar smelled when they lowered her casket into the ground.

The elevator door closed behind them and they were left with only the uneven yellow glow of the lanterns. "Why are we down here?" Percy asked, raising his light overhead. He could make out a dirt pathway between walls of chain link fencing, the spaces beyond hulked with shrouded shapes and he had no idea how far back they went.

"Holy shit, don't tell me this is a morgue?"

Cat shook her head as his light picked out square metal doors set into a cement wall behind fresh new fencing. "No," she laughed, a rich contralto. "Wine lockers."

She turned to him in that eerie way of the blind. "You asked why we are down here. I believe that Leslie was attacked on the subway because he was surrounded by bedrock, where the land's power is amplified and it could activate the other passengers against the intruder."

"Why didn't it activate me?" Percy asked.

"You know the answer."

Percy dipped his shaggy head before fixing her with hard eyes. "He calls it *pack*."

He saw a tic in the old woman's cheek at the word *pack*.

"We're bringing the Hunter's totem into the embrace of Manhattan Island to convey a message."

"What message?"

Cat turned her blind eyes to the wrapped bundle.

"Get lost."

8.

The ceiling dropped enough that Percy had to duck to avoid rubbing his hair against the corroded pipes. The fencing was rusted and sagging from its frame, the stacked boxes inside crumbled into piles of rotting boards and mysterious debris.

There were rat traps aplenty now, some empty, some clutching the mummified remains of rodents. Still others were splintered as if the rat in question had torn its way free.

He dragged his gaze forward, seeking to distract himself from the unshakable feeling of being followed. He surprised himself by saying, "This is its own place."

Catherine stopped. "Yes, priest."

"I'm not a priest."

Reflections of Percy's lantern shone like twin fireflies in the lenses of Cat's sunglasses. "A church does not make a man a priest, Percy. Study does. You are what you are, and you are here for a purpose."

Percy waved the lantern from side to side to brush away dangling strands, the illumination swinging wildly from left to right to reveal glimpses of ancient shapes moldering in the gloom and give them the illusion of movement. Their path was a winding one and he was grateful for their footprints in the dirt. It was too easy to imagine wandering lost through the narrow passages until the lantern ran out of fuel.

Despite his efforts, grey strands clung to his hair and shoulders and he imagined crawling things beneath his clothes.

"How much—"

"Here." Catherine's hand tightened painfully on his arm.

Faint threads draped the older woman's hair and drifted from the flow of her pale garments so that she seemed to float beside him. A thick strand of webbing clung to a corner of her upper lip, affixing to the lower and moving as she spoke as if skin had flaked away to reveal the mummified tendons beneath.

She extended a finger at the ground. "Percy."

The big man twitched at his name and set down his lantern. The light stabbed up from below to draw cruel lines across his face, aging him, as if the stale subterranean air were leeching away his vitality. He lowered into a squat and beads of sweat pattered onto the thirsty earth. His fingers dug under the edge of a tarp covered in dirt.

He grunted as he stood. Grit rattled off his shins as he tossed the stiff cloth aside to expose a thick wooden door set into the ground, the planks petrified and blackened by age, banded by iron strips orange with rust.

"Open it," Cat ordered.

"Where does it go?"

"Down."

9.

Down and down.

It sounded like they were descending into a gargantuan shower room, a gymnasium built for giants beneath New York City. Water, huge and slamming below. The air thick and wet. Percy shivered in the damp even as beads of perspiration emerged from the skin of his forehead. The atmosphere was thick with spores. Full of tuberculoid intent.

Down and down in the warm glow of the lantern held overhead in his left hand, Catherine following with a hand on his shoulder.

The tiled wall might once have been white. He focused on the tiles as much as he could, torn between unraveling the mystery of their color and watching his feet on the stairs.

It didn't pay to look left.

To the left was the void. A dark world without definition or detail. To fall over the open edge of the stairs was to fall forever. Or to slam into a crippling floor. It was to blow sideways on an endless loop beneath the earth's crust or crash with immediate and jarring force into another tiled wall. It was a dark of tar pits, of lightless caves that fed on eyesight.

"Don't trust the railing," Cat told him when they ventured down through the trapdoor eons ago. Trust it? He wouldn't look at it.

"How are you doing?" Catherine's voice drifted down from above and he wanted to look but was afraid to turn too much, his neck rigid.

A hundred million stairs down into the Shower of the Gods. Where the fuck were they?

The bottom was shocking. Rushing up at him. Was it over? He picked up speed, clattering, his lantern shook and his light danced with nightclub abandon.

"Percy?"

Catherine's cry ignored as he landed hard on both heels, feet skidding on a film of muck.

This will leave a bruise, he thought when his left buttock smacked into the merciless solidity of the floor and his head snapped on his neck, banging his teeth together.

"Shit." He set down his lantern and labored to his feet.

"Don't go squirrelly on me." Catherine's voice preceded her from the darkness as she drifted down the stairs and toward the light, an amorphous white shape gaining detail as she materialized.

"Where are we?" Percy asked.

"1912." Cat grinned.

"What? Why do I hear water?"

"Rain sluicing down from the city above, far above," Cat said, flicking her fingers out into the darkness. "Somewhere out there."

How far was it falling? How far below ground were they? Below curbside gutters choked with rainwater and trash? Five stories below ground? Ten? He imagined a churning column of water as thick around as he was. Objects below would be hammered flat by Thor's waterbolts.

Percy picked up the lantern and crossed the chipped cement of the platform until he reached the cracked edge. Flickers of movement danced below and he heard the gurgle and splash of a stream, the train tracks transformed into a canal. He sensed a greater density to the void beyond, as if there was a wall out there.

"I had no idea this was down here," Percy said, awed, trying to use his ears to figure out the dimensions of the space. Enormous. A man-made cave the size of a stadium with its own rainfall and river.

He turned away from the platform's edge and his lantern light found distant cousins in a row of display cases. Signal lamps more than a century old, four-sided with colored lenses, their sarcophagus a case without glass, the glass now only shards that crunched beneath his heels as he dragged the yellow glow over them. Additional displays were visible farther down the platform, some with dusty glass intact, most broken by time.

"The first underground railroad went operational in New York around 1904. Before my time," Cat said sotto voce. "They were private then, the subways."

Percy crouched beside a toppled case and lifted the lantern over the model of an antique subway car sprawled on the floor. He brushed grit from the side and saw writing too faded to read. A glance down the platform revealed more display cases disappearing into gloom, toward the crash of the waterfall. How long was the platform? He stood, knees popping.

"A herd of cattle barons out west pooled their money and decided to buy a piece of the city for themselves, underground, as it were." Cat continued, stretching fingers toward a wall. "These ranchers set to digging, employing local contractors of course, greasing municipal palms. They broke ground and built a grand platform with some notion of western railroads in mind. Held a big to-do with fiddles and dancing on the platform, made the papers, and found out their project was dead before it began. Maybe two hundred feet of tunnel bored out before their coffers were looted and their machinery hauled away." She felt along the wall and waved Percy over.

He lifted his lantern to reveal an enormous X carved into the wall. "Those boys were not ready for New York. I mean, they wanted to name the subway line after one of their ranches, the Bar X." Her laugh was sharp-edged glass. "Can you imagine the X train?"

"How is all this stuff still here?" Inside a glass case was a largely intact crystal chandelier easily six feet in diameter, shaped like a wagon wheel. He shook his head and wiped a palm along the plaque, long since faded. He imagined that the cattlemen meant to light their rail with such extravagances and thought that Catherine was right. These men were not ready for New York.

"Used to be preserved by a historical society. Ran tours in through an entrance down there." Cat pointed toward the rumble of water. "The city decided it wasn't safe and sealed it off back in the 70s."

"Anything live here?" Percy cast his eyes around, a little too much of the whites showing.

Cat shrugged. "Just whatever lives below the city."

He imagined albino rats the size of cars.

"New York is a jealous bitch, like me." The old socialite slapped the wall with a hard crack. "She'll let an outsider in for a quickie, but they'd better leave their money on the dresser and be gone by morning or *she'll* have her way with them."

Percy dragged a sleeve across his sweaty forehead, smearing dirt. "That's why you wanted to come down here."

Cat nodded. "Give this spirit the bum's rush."

"What if it's..." He couldn't say *god*. "What if it's more than a spirit?"

"I expect we'll piss it off." Catherine cocked her head toward the flooded tracks. "Hadn't counted on the water."

"What does that mean?"

She patted his chest. "You're getting wet."

10.

It was loud.

Water, huge and enormous, more felt than seen. Mist in the air radiating from the shimmery translucence at the end of the platform, the column of water falling from the world above.

"Farther down the platform, where the walls are weaker," was Cat's only direction as she guided him toward the waterfall. Away from the stairs.

Away from the path to the surface.

Percy's big hands twisted on the haft of the pickaxe, a batter choking up on his Louisville Slugger. He'd found a display of tools bundled against a wall, most of them corroded, wood rotted through and metal pitted with rust. But the pickaxe was one of many wrapped in oilcloth inside a great box on wheels.

His eyes bored into the water and he tossed the pick from hand to hand as if it weighed nothing, terror writ large in the forest and canyons of his face. The lantern was at his feet and threw his great shadow over the sparkling froth below.

"That stuff about the alligators is bunk. Great blind beasts, albinos with white skin and pink eyes," Catherine said, pitching her voice to carry over the watery thunder. "Urban legend."

His head whipped toward her too quickly. She showed white of her teeth in a smile.

He picked up one of the antique signal lamps piled behind him. He balanced it for a moment and then heaved it like a fastball out over the stream.

The lamp smashed against something lost to darkness.

"Just getting an idea of width," Percy said. "And scaring away the reptiles." He strode to the ladder connecting the platform to the tracks and gave the upper curve of metal a brisk shake before wiping flakes of rust onto his pants.

"How big can an alligator get?" Catherine asked.

He descended the ladder, wincing as water sloshed over the top of his boots. "Cold."

"Is the current fast?" Catherine called out.

"Nope." He descended another rung, knees disappearing into the subterranean river over the tracks.

"If I'm wrong and this isn't rainwater, it could mean a sewer ruptured."

"Cat!" Warning her.

"And that water could be full of—"

He was snatched into the water before she could finish.

"PERCY!" Catherine screamed.

"Blaaargh!" Percy erupted from the surface, shaking glittering droplets from his hair.

"What happened?" she cried, dropping to her knees as if to drag him out.

"Rung snapped." Percy was hip-deep in oily water, looking around with wary disgust. He dragged a wrist over a madman's grin. "This better not be sewage."

11.

What happened then could have been a coincidence.

Percy reached the far wall of the subway tunnel. A smear of substance existed before him, and by hand he found the crevices and gaps in the tiles. The tips of his boots, having grown sensitive after tripping over invisible train tracks, felt the mounds of silt and debris that had leaked from wounds in the wall.

Occupied, he didn't notice that Catherine had fallen into a deep meditation where she stood guard over the totem.

It could have been a coincidence that Argyle was breathing his last, bubbling breath at that very moment in the world above. That a backed-up gutter far overhead reached a point of critical mass just then, the water stronger than the blockage so that it surged below where rusting pipes gave way.

The path of the water was toward weakness, and the weakness beneath Manhattan led ever downward until the spill encountered a vast, empty cavity. It erupted into a spray more than a hundred feet above the doomed platform of the Bar X subway line.

The cascade of water struck the platform and detonated like an explosive, bowling Catherine off her feet and dousing the lamp. She sprawled atop the totem and the tines dug into the meat of her hip, gripping as if it were a claw.

The old woman filled the dark with shrieks as instinct propelled her, tripping and stumbling, toward the stairs. She climbed on all fours like a woman gone mad.

It could have been a coincidence, or it could have been the spirit of the Hunt, who counted among its many selves the cornered animal, a being of fang and claw and fury. It could have been the Hunter drawing strength from killing Argyle to defend itself from the witch who sought to do it harm. Its presence weakened the nature around it, digging invisible fingers into seams in the reality of Manhattan Island.

It could have been a coincidence, but it was not.

CHAPTER THIRTY ONE

1.

Galaxies exploded across the black expanse of his vision as gravity was upended and Percy tumbled through liquid, drowning, dying, and sinking beneath the weight of his heavy leather jacket and boots.

He shimmied free of the garment, banging his shoulder off iron tracks. Stabbed out with fingers to clutch at the unmoving metal even as the current gripped his legs and flung them over his head.

Bubbles flooded from his mouth as he screamed, as upside down as the Hanged Man of the Tarot.

It's a rare moment when one is afforded a glimpse into the essential being of another, let alone oneself. Firefighters experience it, as do soldiers. The patient swimming up toward consciousness during surgery can see with such eyes, as can the passenger in a crashing car.

Percy regarded his own essential nature in that moment of splashing blindness. Knew why the addicts and the forlorn clung to him as if he were a stone pier rising from a tumultuous sea. Knew why Leslie clung to his friendship so desperately even when he pushed everyone else away.

Having fallen within his ability to shape the world, there was no chance, none whatsoever, that Percy would not pull Leslie back from the edge.

And that meant surviving.

He rose from the river, feet planted and fists upthrust as if against an opponent. Water flew from his beard as he cast about in the subterranean darkness.

"CATHERINE!"

He needed light. Struggled to slip fingers into a wet pocket and extract his phone. He smeared a finger over the button.

The sharp white glow sprang into being and Percy gasped at the sight of the tide streaming from the platform.

"Catherine!"

Panic threatened and he forced himself to perform a cold triage. Catherine either got out or died, and he could not escape the way he had come.

The voice was clear in his head. His own voice. His own choice.

He marched away with the current.

2.

The cold triage had continued after Percy found his escape route. The untenable reality of his position. Deep beneath the surface with a woman of tremendous wealth. An old, blind woman who died in his company. Who would believe his story? The cop, Argyle?

He was so tired, his feet shuffling. Recent events were too large to comprehend and he had never been so aware of his own insignificance.

The old woman was gone. One minute so confident, the next, just gone.

Spirits and gods?

He was tired.

He trudged toward the red glow of an EXIT sign. Located a door with a small, inset window, the glass threaded with security mesh. A padlocked chain stood between him and escape.

A deep breath. Two.

He reared back, stomping hard near the lock plate. The chain was no match and the padlock bounced off the wall as the door swung open and rain lashed in. He lurched outside and sagged against the wall, sliding down to sit on the sidewalk. His failures. Kristi Sugar. Catherine Van Horn. Leslie caught up in a nightmare from which there was no waking.

A man wearing a hefty bag for a raincoat splashed past on the sidewalk, a truck horn bleated, and a shout rang out. The city coming alive around him. It had never felt larger or more hostile.

3.

Jordan surged awake and gasped, "Leslie!"

The pursuing footsteps in her dream becoming a pounding fist against her door. She was in her own living room, the TV screen flickering with the volume muted, a half-empty bottle of cheap Merlot on a coffee table marred by sticky rings from her glass.

She remembered running, dodging around trees. Central Park, but not the park. Behind her—

"Open the door!"

The voice hoarse and anguished beyond recognition, muffled through the wood. A concern about waking her neighbors struck her as embarrassingly middle class, which struck her as embarrassingly classist—she realized she was still high as she stumbled in sweatpants and a hoodie to the door, her fuzzy socks generating static electricity.

A blue SNAP shocked her as she turned the deadbolt and she stuck her finger in her mouth as she pulled open the door, too late to ask who it was.

He filled the doorway, spittle flying from his mouth as he grabbed her shoulders in a powerful grip and hissed, "Jordan!"

CHAPTER THIRTY TWO

1.

Leslie's last clear thought was of Jordan.

Immense pressure collapsed inward around his bones and his muscles spasmed, hurling him to the ground. Pain. His chin struck the sidewalk. Heat. Blood from a bitten tongue filled his mouth. Agony. Tearing. Stretching. Screaming. Thoughts shredded like so much gauze in a hurricane.

Rain drops erupted into steam when they struck his naked back. Deep, wet thumps heralded the breaking of bones as his tibia cracked and a plafond was ground to meal. The medial malleolus slid beneath Leslie's skin like a moving bubble and the distal most aspect of the fibula, the lateral malleolus, was pushed down toward his toes where the nails thickened and grew.

Had Leslie still been himself and aware, the man of words would have been unable to describe the nature of the pain that sang from his spine as the nerves stretched and vertebrae altered. *White* was how his invaded mind perceived it.

A wail of terror was wrenched into a series of bestial coughs as his vocal cords shortened and melded into the pink meat of his throat. Teeth, bigger and blockier, the canines extending, set his mandibular nerves aflame.

All sensation was swept aside by the tidal wave of FEELING that exploded from his empty eye socket. Great scraping movements rippled beneath his scalp as the new form stole bone from his narrowing skull and thrust it forward in a sharp point to puncture the scar tissue covering his eye socket. The bony emergence of antler thrummed like a tuning fork and a streetlight exploded in a shower of sparks.

2.

"Just say no," M'lese said before he sucked lovingly on the pipe like it was the dick of a king, or maybe a motherfucker gonna pay him beaucoup bucks.

The downpour on their tarp added an upbeat rhythm section to the slow Gladys Knight tracks as M'lese handed the pipe past the battered boombox—more electrical tape than machine—and Shawn said, "Two lighters, one pipe."

"Sheeit," M'lese laughed and the smoke curled away from his mouth as Shawn flicked his own lighter to life and applied flame to bowl.

Sure, thirty people had fried their brains near the Myrtle J train stop by smoking K2. And yeah, it wasn't putting food in their bellies or money in their wallets, but ain't no one cruising on a rainy night looking to insert cock A into mouth B.

"Am I right?" Shawn said through billows of white fog, certain that M'lese had picked up his thoughts.

"Too right," M'lese drawled, mascara running down his cheeks because the tarp was leaking. He leaned forward and waved heat from the coffee can fire toward his face.

"Fuck it. This is the only way to fly." One of them said it and the other one heard it, but neither could say who did what.

"What the fuck that?"

"What?"

"That's what I said."

The two men stirred from their cocoon of packing blankets and their bodies took form, thin limbs extending as they each assumed a crouch.

Screaming.

"That ain't no dog." M'lese stretched out a hand and pushed aside the tarp as Shawn picked up the Folgers can containing their small fire.

They slipped from their alleyway fort like hunters from a cave, Shawn protecting the can of fire with a fold of blanket as M'lese slid a kitchen knife from the homemade sheath along his calf.

Guttural sounds drifted toward them. Somewhere between animal bleating and a giant's cough.

The junkies drifted toward piles of debris on either side of the alley and slipped forward toward the construction scaffolding at the front of the building. White eyes met white eyes before M'lese stuck his head around the corner.

His shriek sent an electric jolt through Shawn, who hurled aside the Folgers can and clapped hands to his ears. "What is it? What is it?"

M'lese backpedaled saying the same thing. "What is it?"

The scattered flames from their small fire landed on a remarkably dry cluster of thick paper used to wrap cement mix, carelessly tossed aside by the construction crew. The flames spread and uneven light sprang up beneath the scaffolding.

"Lord..." Shawn said as a thing—all he could say later was it was a *thing*—stalked into the mouth of the alley.

"Tall, too tall," M'lese would add after he came down from his high. "Manute Bol tall. Skinny like a starvin' man."

It was indeed tall on its weirdly delicate and oddly articulated legs. The great ribcage heaved as it breathed, xylophone ribs dancing beneath pale skin. It towered over the two men, mouth stretching wide over a terrifying jumble of teeth, the one eye huge and black and without humanity.

The other...

"Didn't have no other eye," M'lese would say through chattering teeth in that puke-green interrogation room. "Was a great big horn stickin' out, all white like a tangle of branches. Like a briar patch. Huge. Big as a cloud!"

"You mean an antler? Like a deer?" a cop would ask.

"I mean a horn big as a cloud!"

The two men fell together with identical cries of terror as the sparking fire hurled waves of orange light over the monster. It regarded them, disturbingly human nostrils flaring as it consumed their unsavory odor. Tree branch arms stretched out to either side and great fingers spread, big enough to palm a beer keg.

It howled, a primordial sound that froze the blood in their veins and locked their muscles into immobility.

A long arm swept low and M'lese was snatched off his feet. He wailed as the great head lowered toward his face, nostrils flaring. M'lese was scoured, tasted by the olfactory probing. The thing's singular eye was a universe of blackness streaked with red stars. M'lese felt himself tumbling into the gaze and wrenched his stare away only to cry out in greater terror.

The great, twisting antler had punched through the second eye socket from within the thing's long skull, and oozed pus where flesh met bone. Small white grains of rice wriggled in the yellow mass of coagulating grue. Maggots, M'lese realized, clapping his hands over his eyes and compressing his lips against the rain of larvae.

Flight was sudden and unexpected, cut short by a plywood barrier. Wood cracked at the impact and he fell to the cement, limp as a ragdoll.

A wash of bright white light froze the scene as an Escalade with bright halogen headlights whooshed toward the terrifying confrontation.

The gangling thing took two steps into the street to confront the intruder in its territory. The Escalade's horn blared and it skidded toward impact—

And the monstrous creature *leaped over* the sliding vehicle.

Shawn and M'lese were startled by the loud crash as the SUV slammed into a fire hydrant. The resulting geyser of water made Shawn cackle through tears as the street threw a middle finger at the rain clouds.

But M'lese couldn't fall back into the protective haze of the drug, adrenaline clearing what little mind he had. He heard the rapid slap of feet, but the thing was too fast to see clearly. He caught a pale flash as the nightmare accelerated around a corner and out of sight.

"Help!" the driver of the Escalade cried through his broken window.

"Heeeelp!" M'lese cried to the night.

"Heeeeelp!" Shawn howled and wept, his drug-addled mind succumbing beneath the weight of chemicals and fear.

The Hunter was loose in Brooklyn.

3.

Yakut rested one scarred hand on the wheel; the other held a thermos of cold coffee as he waited in the town car half a block down from 269 Macon Street.

Crummy neighborhood and pounding rain. Dead of night. Waiting for Ward to come home. Waiting for Argyle to show up.

An hour into his surveillance, his bladder was swollen like a melon and he pushed open the door, cursing as a gust blew a fucking tidal wave of water inside. The car was parked beside an empty lot and Yakut pissed through the chain link fence. He was holding his hands out to let the rain wash them clean when he noticed a slight shift in the darkness beyond the fence.

"Hold it," he shouted in reflex and slapped his right hand to the pistol at his belt. The left plucked a mini-flash free from the pocket of his windbreaker and threw a beam into the lot. Fat drops of rain made mincemeat of the light, but enough radiance pushed forward to reveal a hulking black shape, eyes flashing when the beam swept over them.

It was a dog. Big. A Rottweiler or something like it.

"Fuck."

Yakut glanced to his left and right to make sure there were no holes in the fence, expecting the animal to have fled when he looked back.

It sat there unperturbed by light or rain, staring at Yakut from inside the empty lot. Yakut ducked back into the car.

It wasn't long after that Yakut spotted another mutt trotting along the flowing gutter, weaving in and out of parked cars. He thought about calling it in but didn't want the Animal Control guys to have to go out on such a shitty night.

He tried Argyle's phone again and left another message. Thought he saw movement in a downstairs window of 269. Imagined Argyle inside sipping a cold beer in a warm apartment while he shivered in his car.

Yakut glanced in the rearview mirror and imagined eyes that flashed with reflected light.

Devil eyes on a goddamned dog.

The next time he felt the urge to piss, Yakut dug the pickle jar out from under his seat and took care of business inside the car.

Devil eyes.

"Fuck you," he snarled at the memory. The memory stared back silently, just like the dog.

Music blasted as a van roared past. Yakut flinched. In the rearview mirror he could see red veins threading the sclera of his eyes.

"Fuckyoufuckyoufuckyou."

He lifted his chin to scratch the beard on his neck. Fucking dog really got under his skin. He was pissed off. Pissed because it was late, pissed because he had to take a shit, pissed that he couldn't put in for overtime because this wasn't official business, pissed because he was worried about his partner, and pissed because he was scared.

That's what it really came down to: Yakut was scared. Scared by a fucking dog like a fucking little girl.

180

Was that movement behind the window again? Even through the rain he saw a curtain dropping back into place.

"Fuck it." He pushed the door open and splashed across the street, ducking his head against the rain as he mounted the steps leading up to the front door and raised a fist to bang on the wood.

It lurched open a foot and he staggered, surprised and off balance. The door hadn't been fully shut.

"Argyle? Yo!" He stepped into the vestibule and left the door open behind him so he could plausibly deny any kind of attempt at illegal entry. It was open, see?

He pressed his nose against the glass window of the inside door. Saw that the door to an apartment on the first floor was open. "Hello?"

He tried the knob on the off chance—the door swung inward.

"What?" His face wrinkled as the ugly smell struck him like a blow, and while he was blinking his eyes against the unexpected stink, several shapes darted out of the first-floor apartment, low and snarling. Something else was hurtling down the stairs from above in a thunder of claws.

Yakut made no conscious decision to flee. In fact, his first coherent thought didn't take shape until he was flying off the front step of the stoop in an athletic leap toward the iron gate.

That thought was: *Close the gate behind me.*

He slammed chest-first into the iron barrier and felt it shake. Grunted an explosion of breath even as he moved fast, so fast, and wrenched open the gate to spin through with all the dexterity of a running back...

But his snatching hand missed the iron bars as he passed and knew they-it-they-something was after him as he sprinted across the street and lunged for the driver's side door of the town car. He dragged it open a split second before something slammed into his spine and he fell, twisting, back against the car as his hands dug into fur and he smashed the yellow dog against the road.

Howls and snarls drew his gaze and he saw a pack of wild dogs rushing across the asphalt. He dropped to his belly on the pavement, crabbing sideways beneath the car into the frigid flow of water in the gutter.

Foaming, snapping muzzles thrust after him and he swung his fist at them, clumsy in the cramped space. Two muzzles. Three. He scrabbled away from them into the grey deluge of the gutter and thanked God that his parking was sloppy enough to leave plenty of space between his car and the curb. Ignoring the metal tearing, ripping his jacket, Yakut dragged himself onto the sidewalk.

He heard a howl of rage from the other side of the car and knew he had mere moments. Praying that his luck would hold and that the—

The unlocked passenger door opened and he threw himself across the front seat to drag the driver's side door closed. Twisting desperately, he moaned with fear as he pulled the door closed behind him.

Panting, desperate. He twisted his knees painfully to get them into position in the footwell. Getting the keys from the pocket of his wet jeans was a herculean effort but he managed it, eyes wide and staring as he jammed the key into the ignition on the third try and cranked the big car to life.

His hand was orange in the glow of the dashboard as he found the knob for the headlights and twisted it, bathing the street ahead of him with brilliant yellow light.

The windshield was fogged with breath and he couldn't see to drive. Yakut wiped at the fogged glass before the thought struck him.

He felt the hot wash of breath against his neck.

"Don't!"

Teeth closed on the back of his head, the jaws closing with immense force. Fangs punched through skin and into his skull with bone-crushing force.

Yakut shrieked as he was dragged into the back seat.

CHAPTER THIRTY THREE

1.

"What the fuck?"

He'd use phrases like "So there I was" and "naked as a jaybird" if he was telling the story in a bar. If he were *writing* about the moment, he'd never use "naked as a jaybird" because he didn't know what a jaybird was. But in a bar he'd say, "So there I was, naked as a jaybird, the rain falling like cats and dogs." Some wit would interrupt with a crack about shrinkage (it being that kind of bar) to which he might retort with the words "giant boner." He'd never write "giant boner" unless it was dialogue. He'd employ words like *massively erect* (Buddy Paretsky might write *boner*, but not him). Then again, if he were writing, no wise ass would be around to chime in about shrinkage.

"So there I was, naked as a jaybird, the rain falling like cats and dogs and me with a giant boner in the middle of the park." Which park was it?

He padded on bare feet through the rain until he reached a muddy path and splashed through puddles.

"So there I was, naked as a jaybird, the rain falling like cats and dogs and me with a giant boner in the middle of *Prospect* Park in the dead of night, no idea how I got there, and you know what?"

"What?" He added the dialogue of the wise ass next to him at the imaginary bar.

"I felt incredible."

The warbling cry of an ambulance siren drifted across the park and he slowed to a walk, aware of the tap of individual drops against leaves, the scrape of branches already stripped for winter, and singular grains of sand shifting beneath his heel.

His nostrils flared at the stink of exhaust and lights sparkled ahead.

Ribs heaving, he wasn't cold. His skin was electric, wildly alive under the peppering of a thousand icy needles. He caught water on his outstretched tongue and wetted his mouth before laughing at the absurdity of the moment. The circumstances should have bothered him, but they didn't. That lack of bother should have bothered him. But it didn't.

"What the fuck?"

2.

The dark bar was dimly lit by flickering light.

"Is it still—"

"You got about four more minutes."

"Another Jack and Coke then." The man was hunched over the bar, a narrow guy with bony shoulders protruding from a long spill of hair. He slid four crumpled dollar bills through wet rings on the wood.

Norris Chapin planted an elbow next to the long-hair, a regular named Chip or Chet, he didn't remember or really care, and said, "Check this out." He gestured at the screen. "I had to use a dolly made from..."

But Chip or Chet didn't care. He came in for the screenings to drink discounted booze, not to watch movies.

Every night at midnight and at three in the ay-em Gods and Monsters showed a half-hour from one of Chapin's films, offering half-price drinks while the black and white projections danced across a beer-splattered screen mounted on the wall between the two bathrooms. The projector was up in the office, a low-ceilinged loft overlooking the bar. He kept a futon and a hot plate up there along with his film equipment and had, for the last several months, called it home.

Chapin renamed the bar Gods and Monsters after his fiancée left it to him, the fiancée in question succumbing to illness and leaving his worldly possessions to Mrs. Chapin's little boy.

He was nice like that.

"One more." The long-hair dragged a wrist over his mouth and shoved the glass at Chapin, who was already reaching for the bottle of Jack Daniel's. When his back was to the room—not that anyone would care—Chapin slipped a chocolate-covered mushroom beneath his tongue and felt it begin to melt.

Purists would say he was whoring his work with these nightly screenings, but Chapin believed in attracting followers any way he could. It was his place and his movie and—

A naked man strolled into the bar as a scream blasted from the speakers.

"Dude..." Chip or Chet perked up from his stupor and tossed back his drink, flashing brown teeth in a grin.

Rivulets of rainwater rippled over the man's bare skin as he padded past the few occupied tables and mounted a rickety stool at the bar.

"Hey, princess," was all Chip or Chet managed to say before the newcomer fixed him with a one-eyed stare. It was as if the ruined socket of his missing eye vacuumed up Chip or Chet's next words. His vitality. The long-hair mumbled what might have been, "Sorry," and stumbled toward the exit.

"A whiskey and some pants." The voice a smile and a snarl. A single eye was aimed toward Chapin, who felt the stare like a physical blow.

"Leslie?"

3.

Chapin scuttled around the empty bar waiting for the mushroom to kick in, collecting glasses and shooing the stragglers out the door. Small Christmas lights on a string added their red and green glow to the dance of light from the movie projector. Emptied of drinkers, Gods and Monsters smelled like booze and popcorn, with a soupcon of urine from the restrooms.

"Turn off the volume," Leslie said from his stool, head wreathed in a cloud of marijuana smoke. Chapin obeyed and the shrieking soundtrack was replaced by the steady *clack-clack* of the film reels.

Leslie was wearing a pair of borrowed chinos, unbothered by the cold, leaning regally against the bar as if he were overseeing his manor, a goblet in his hand instead of a tumbler of cheap liquor. The tip of a joint glowed orange as he placed it to his lips and inhaled.

Peter Lorre, Leslie thought as he blew out the smoke. That's who the Leech resembled. Peter Lorre in *Casablanca*.

The Leech set the cameras on the bar, hanging on every word as Leslie quietly outlined an idea. A brilliant, avant-garde idea wilder than any collaboration he had ever imagined with Buddy Paretsky.

"I can put cameras around the venue and catch just about everything," Chapin said. "And I'll have a pinhead camera on my hat."

"You will film everything."

"You'll let me use it in the new movie?"

"Yes."

"What I want to do is a story within a story. Telling *All the Teeth in the World* at the same time we flash back to the real world and writing in the cabin, the divorce, the incident in the woods, everything."

"Cool."

Chapin felt a tingle in his fingertips and couldn't suppress a grin that was equal part hero worship and psychedelics. "Can't you tell me more about it?"

"Pick up a camera."

Chapin snatched a video camera from the bar and hurried to face Leslie, who was a flickering silhouette in front of the movie screen. Chapin thumbed the record button and dropped to one knee to film his idol.

"Watch this." Leslie sprang atop the bar and threw wide his arms.

Tingling suffused Chapin and the spit dried in his mouth. He felt the mushrooms kick in hard and he saw...

"My god."

CHAPTER THIRTY FOUR

From www.BrooklynPaper.com.

POLICE BLOTTER

Police: Drunk Woman Slaps Straphanger on C Train, Williamsburg

Homeless Hijinks as Tripping Duo Wake Neighborhood, Bushwick

Crown Heights Animal Shelter Vandalized, Animals on the Loose

Prospect Park Zoo Vandalized, Wild Dogs Freed

Police: Shots Fired in 200 Block of Macon Street, BedStuy

Police: Rottweiler Rips Revelers Outside Good Time Tavern, BedStuy

CHAPTER THIRTY FIVE

The yellow cab raced over a bridge of stone toward a city of jewels with the rear window down, Leslie's hair whipping in the cold breeze.

The storm had broken during the night and gifted New York with a stunning morning, the apotheosis of fall with bright blue skies and light clear enough that a man could see for miles. A confident sun bathed the skyscrapers of downtown Manhattan with brilliant white and yellow light that capered across a million tiny windows in elemental glee.

He closed his eye and widened his nostrils to drink in the city, the passage of living things, the path to his heart's desire. He was relaxed in the way an animal is relaxed, a pulse in his neck still throbbing visibly, muscles ready for movement.

Leslie gave directions to the driver and they whipped north along the FDR. He draped his right elbow out the open window to watch the East River sparkling as if lit with a galaxy of chandeliers.

He felt like a time traveler in his clothes, a brown leather jacket with wide lapels that once belonged to Chapin's fiancé. Pants that flared around ankle-high boots and sunglasses large enough for a decade when cars had fins.

He was a time traveler in his skin, in his body, in this city, a proto-man ripped from the whispering savannah and dropped into a stone jungle.

Slowing down as they pushed west on 82nd Street, gagging on the fumes of a garbage truck that blocked the narrow passage, choked with parked cars on either side.

"This is it," he told the driver.

Outside the towering pillar of wealth that housed his rival, Leslie waited for a uniformed doorman to open his door. When the older man said, "How are you this morning?" Leslie said, "I'm awake as fuck!" and slipped a folded twenty into the man's breast pocket as he stepped past, lord of all he surveyed.

The doorman, used to the cocaine habits of the rich and famous, tipped his hat.

At the desk in the stunningly rendered foyer, Leslie paused to gawk like a tourist before turning to the grey-haired man in a matching uniform waiting behind the counter.

"Leslie Ward for Catherine Van Horn."

The grey-hair tilted his head as if he'd seen something amiss and asked, "Is she expecting you?"

"I think she is." Leslie leaned an elbow on the counter and split his lips apart to introduce every one of his teeth.

"You're not on the list."

"Call her, boy."

The older man flinched. Leslie lowered his shades and offered a wink with his good eye as a pair of maggots wriggled in the weeping socket of the other.

Placing one hand on the phone, the grey-hair narrowed his eyes. "I'll call the pol—" The phone rang beneath his hand and the uniformed man flinched.

Leslie covered a laugh by pushing his sunglasses back up the bridge of his nose.

The uniformed man looked a decade older after he set the phone back on the receiver. Mustering what dignity he could, he gestured toward the lobby. "The elevators are this way, sir."

"Thanks." Leslie tapped his palms on the countertop in a quick drum beat before making his way to the lobby, shaking his head at the things money could buy. As his boots tapped down smooth marble steps into the wide space, his gaze sought out dead branches that might break beneath his feet, drifts of wet leaves that could muffle a step. He sought movement in the shadows behind high-backed guest chairs where furred things might crouch. The tiny hairs on the back of his neck lifted beneath the leather collar, as if to sense shifting air caused by the movement of other predators.

These functions were as autonomous as the expansion and constriction of the grape-like alveoli in his lungs. The notion that a lobby like this would ever allow a litter of sticks or furred things beneath chairs never entered the equation. As Leslie moved, he breathed. As Leslie breathed, he probed with his senses. This was who he was.

At the endocrine level, glands swelled ripe, ready to release Greek fire into the riverwork of his veins.

As smooth machinery tumbled and clicked below the limbic level, his active mind was delighted by the ostentatious wealth and outdated style of the building. It reminded him of the world's gaudiest game show, this great octagonal chamber with a separate elevator on each facet. What prize would he win were he to open the door at the farthest left? At the right? How beautiful would the women be? Enough to satisfy his appetite?

Musings were cut short by the parting of golden doors, the elevator splitting apart with a gentle whoosh of welcome. He pushed aside the iron security gate and accepted the invitation with a step.

As the doors sealed him inside the ascending tomb, Leslie wondered how Catherine Van Horn planned to kill him.

CHAPTER THIRTY SIX

1.

The chime was quiet, as if a glass were delicately struck by a Zen master with a talent for music.

The twentieth floor.

Gold elevator doors split down the middle, replaced by a widening blackness until Leslie faced the unlit room beyond.

Cute.

He slid aside the iron safety gate and stepped onto the hard tile floor, immediately gliding to his left to avoid being silhouetted against the elevator light. He had the faint impression of a parquet floor of black and white squares before the elevator doors closed and took the light with them.

He was in a crouch without realizing it, nostrils quivering, pulling scents from the air over the lemony tang of floor wax. He knew that Percy had been here and was gone but...

IT was here.

He licked his lips and made out the lesser dark in the artificial night. Scuttled toward it across the floor, the arteries in his neck pulsing, saliva rimming his lips, a river of drool trailing from one corner of his mouth.

A door stood half-open. Vague, shifting light existed beyond.

He lowered himself and slithered through, cursing the squeak of leather as he snaked around the door frame and resumed a crouch with his back against the wall.

Vast and gloom-shrouded, no real sense of size save *enormous*. A ballroom. Factory. Stadium. This last idea brought to life by the arena-in-miniature he saw ahead, the image suggested by standing lamps in a rough circle, aimed to cast cones of light upon a central...

MINE.

Between the light and himself, the only light in the great symphonic space, a dozen or more humped islands loomed, indefinable in the dark. He slid the sunglasses up on his head and felt the tickle of a maggot tumbling from his eye socket. His smile trembled.

A sound? Keen ears detected quiet strains of music but he ignored it, breaking into a trot toward that which was his.

There were five standing lamps with bulbs like berry clusters. The lamps were positioned around a low table at the center. The divans and couches the rich and famous had once reclined on (this island was encircled by a velvet rope on brass poles) were discarded to the tender mercies of shadow while the glass table shone with a near blinding brilliance, the object atop it ugly and twisted and beautiful.

The totem.

The antler.

MINE.

2.

Leslie unzipped his fly to release a hissing stream of urine on the carpet.

"...can make it here, you can make it anywhere..."

A distant archway filled with shimmering light. His keen nose picked up the trace of gas. The music was louder, drifting to him from beyond the arch, crackling as if from a phonograph.

"New York, New Yoooork."

His lips twisted in a grin as he made his way to the arch and smelled the tang of alcohol. After a brief pause to ensure that Van Horn hadn't conscripted a hypo-allergenic, scent-free sniper, he stepped through the arch and into the strange indoor Victorian street with its flaming ranks of gas lamps. The atmosphere was perfect, positively cinematic. Dean Martin began crooning "Everybody Loves Somebody" and added to the sense of an alternate reality.

He sauntered past the opening for an elaborate Roman bath as well as an elegant library where shelves of books stretched away into infinity.

"Never spin Sinatra alongside Dean Martin," Leslie said as he stepped through the next doorway onto the shining hardwood floor of a bar, his bare feet making sucking sounds against the varnish.

She was standing behind the bar in loose white robes, her face, hands, and the exposed skin of her forearms wrapped in white gauze, spotted here and there with fresh blood.

"Catherine Van Horn?"

She nodded but held up a hand while raising a bottle of Vermouth. "Lift the bottle and nod in the direction of France." He heard the effort in her voice and saw through the projection of strength. "Then set the bottle down."

She raised the metal martini shaker and shook it three times, ice inside banging against metal. The lid was removed and replaced with a small strainer designed for the task and she poured perfect martinis into two waiting glasses.

Leslie stepped closer, winding through half a dozen small tables to place a hand on the marble countertop, a body-length or so away from her. The bar was lit by gas lamps in the four corners and from subdued, golden light glowing from behind a wall of liquor bottles rising up toward the ceiling.

"I had this at home, I'd never leave," he said.

"Some days I don't," she replied, sipping carefully to avoid a spill. She nodded at the second drink. "I'm buying."

Leslie eased toward her, pausing when she stepped away. But she was only lowering herself into a wheelchair.

"You look like the mummy," he said, lifting his glass. "Wait—Claude Rains in *The Invisible Man*."

She grinned and a fresh blot of red spotted the gauze. "Your missing eye looks like a mossy hole in dead wood."

"You're blind."

"Then you have nothing to worry about. You're beautiful."

She used her toes to pull the wheelchair closer to a table and set her drink atop it. "By now Jordan is long gone."

He lifted his nose and made a show of sniffing the air. "I don't think so." He sipped his drink and found it dry and excellent.

"Would you prefer wine?" she asked. "Pipes in the forest? I have a room with trees and birds, just like home."

"You a virgin?"

"Not so much." She shrugged. "Is the Goat-Legged God so picky?"

"Is that who you think I am?"

She grunted and lifted a book from the table, ancient and leatherbound. He shivered as an indefinable sense of recognition washed over him. Ice-cold gin ran across his wrist.

"The people that knew you best weren't much for writing," she said.

"I'm Leslie Ward."

"Not anymore, and I'm sorry for that. Sorry for Jordan's sake and for Percy's."

His grin soured and he set his drink on the bar. He could see the rise and fall of her chest as her breath quickened, hear the rasp of paper-thin lungs.

"If you know who I am, you know what I like."

She tilted her head as if to look up at him when he moved behind her chair. "What's tha—"

He jolted the back of her chair with his hip and she knocked the table forward, her glass toppling.

"I like a chase." He grabbed the handles of the wheelchair and shoved. The chair rolled several feet. "Run, bitch." He shoved her wheelchair again and she knocked a cocktail table over with a clatter.

She turned her wheelchair with great effort and fought back a moan of pain. "Tell me, Hunter, are you weeping maggots?"

He was at her side with the speed of thought, one hand over her mouth. She struggled under his grip and he lowered his face to her ear. "You're not worthy of the chase."

She struck with all the speed an old woman could muster, producing the weapon from beneath her bandages. She thrust a sharpened silver knife into his lower abdomen, the tip gouging his hip bone.

He roared and lifted her from the chair with a single hand, iron fingers below her jaw. She worked her mouth and forced out, "Maggots!"

She sailed over the bar and collided with the wall of bottles and the mirror to fall in a rain of glass. He was after her in a second, vaulting the bar to land in a crouch over her twitching form.

"Mag—"

Stiffened fingers smashed in between her teeth and caught her tongue. She bucked as he braced his other hand against her forehead and pulled the meat free. A gout of black blood geysered past his face.

"Choke on it." He dropped the aged chunk of muscle.

Leslie caught sight of himself in a section of mirror still clinging to the wall. He was dark with gore, his good eye wide and white amidst the red. Leaning closer, he studied the reflection of his eye socket while Catherine Van Horn gurgled at his feet.

"No maggots."

4.

The boots were loud as Leslie strode across the freshly waxed lobby floor. Heavy biker boots of the sort Percy favored. He'd found the bishop's private quarters and got the sense from his wardrobe that the man liked to spend his off-hours cruising leather bars. Still, Leslie had been able to find some jeans to roll up at the cuff, a black shirt, and a motorcycle jacket with a lot of zippers. The wound in his abdomen seeped but was not deep. He'd found bandages and medical tape to seal it closed. His hair was damp from a shower.

He'd gone to the colossal effort of putting the blood-clotted antler in a pillowcase, but that was as far as his subterfuge went.

"Thanks for your help." He touched finger to forelock as he passed Captain Stick-up-the-ass at the front desk. He figured the old busybody would discover the carnage in short order. The police would come. The press would buzz about like flies.

"Can I get you a cab, sir?" the uniformed man at the curb asked and Leslie shook his head.

"Think I'll walk."

"It's a beautiful day for it."

Leslie zipped up the jacket against a clean, crisp breeze and tilted his head back, running his gaze up the side of the building until he found the twentieth floor.

Oh, they'd find out what happened and who did it. He was certain he'd been picked up by several security cameras. He didn't care.

By nightfall, it would all be over but the screaming.

"You're right, it is a beautiful day."

CHAPTER THIRTY SEVEN

1.

The memory of Horton shouting, "There's another one," would haunt Officer Delgado for weeks. The call had come into Brooklyn's 79th Precinct during the night, but between the darkness and the storm, it took the responding unit a while to arrive. They radioed, "Officer down," and units from the 79th and 81st precincts swarmed the scene.

One officer emerged weeping.

By the time the rain stopped, the crime scene crew had arrived and yellow police tape was blocking off both ends of Macon Street.

"I need the overtime," Delgado said, cigarette bobbing in his lips as he spoke, standing on the stoop for 269 to protect the scene from curious bystanders and media alike. They kept trying to do that. Make light of what they'd seen. But no matter what they said, they couldn't forget what they saw inside.

"Why would they arrange the bodies like that?" Delgado finally asked. Horton shook his head. Neither of them was sure who Delgado meant by "they."

2.

Like most organizations, the primary objective of the NYPD was protection of self, and it reacted to incursions against its officers with ruthless speed. Tremendously efficient when focused, the department quickly drew a connection between the bizarre arrangement of corpses in Brooklyn and the vicious displays on the Upper East Side.

A name was produced.

The hunt for Leslie Ward was set in motion.

CHAPTER THIRTY EIGHT

"Buddy Paretsky put me on the list and I'm putting you on the list," Norris Chapin huffed into a lapel microphone as he trod over a sidewalk grate bellowing steam, pushing through tourist throngs. He thrust out both hands to push through the heavy swinging doors into Grand Central Station, enveloped in a sudden stink of cotton candy. "Even now they're getting ready. Stars. Directors. New York glitterati. Ready to slide through the crowds to the madman's ball just beyond the sight—no—the comprehension of mortal men."

He shoved down the echoing passage past glass-fronted stores. Tiffany's. Swatch. Vineyard Vines. Caught a whiff of bagels from Financier and then he was through, spat out like a salmon from a river into the wide lake of the main terminal.

Chapin stopped and turned his face slowly from left to right, panning the camera mounted on his hatband across the bustling atrium of the most famous train station in America, a towering chamber clamoring with voices and the stomp of a thousand feet. Travelers and tourists—

"Hey!"

"Watch it!"

Chapin cursed as he was buffeted by businessmen in grey pinstripes. He steadied the Stetson on his head.

A shrill voice. "Are you blind?"

He nearly tripped over a woman's suitcase and shoved out his hands to either side like a referee. "Alright!"

The camera picked up faces, zooming in on eyes, nostrils, fleshy lips, and bouncing hair. He was using a filter to distort colors and enhance shine. It made mouths wetter and skin oilier.

The camera followed Chapin's pointing finger to a wide staircase that descended to the lower level of the station.

"That's where it's all gonna go down, people. The Henley Apartment. If a martini turned into a venue, it'd be the Henley Apartment." The area was already cordoned with velvet ropes and massive burgundy curtains obscured the doorway. Two doormen the size of linebackers turned away the curious. "That's where it's happening, friends. Buddy put me on the list and I'm putting you on the list."

He panned the camera over to focus on the standing clock towering over the atrium, its bright face visible above the crowd. "It kicks off in two hours, people. Who wants to crash the party?"

He tapped the button on the camera to stop recording and slid the phone from his pocket, connected to the camera by a whisper-thin wire. He was licking his lips when he uploaded the video.

CHAPTER THIRTY NINE

1.

Naked and in pain.

Percy opened crusted eyes and stirred, agony blazing along the length of his body. He closed his eyes and drifted as waves of warmth returned to blanket the pain.

He heard the word, "Sleep," and obeyed.

2.

Naked and in pain.

Percy opened crusted eyes and stirred for a second time, pain coursing through his limbs. His back ached and his arms and shoulders were leaden.

He was on a couch. A weak glow sketched the hazy outline of furniture. Coffee table. Chairs. Bookshelves. Familiar. Sunlight drifting in through half-closed blinds.

He sat up with a groan and held his stiff neck. Massaged the muscles, a thin blanket pooling around his waist.

Brandy waited on the coffee table. A glass. His glass. A bottle of Tylenol stood beside a plastic cup filled with water.

Water first. He drowned his tongue with the stuff, room temperature ambrosia. Coughed. Felt his stomach rebel and closed his eyes to fight back the nausea.

"Jordan?"

He remembered shouting. Her wide eyes, refusing to listen.

The bottle of Tylenol found its way into his hand and he popped the cap, tipping a few pills onto the table. He leaned forward, belly on his thighs, and read the word VALIUM printed on the blue pills.

"She slipped me a goddamned mickey."

His phone was placed conspicuously on the coffee table, and he picked it up out of habit to see a message waiting. It was Jordan, tension audible in every word.

"I hope you're feeling better this morning. You frightened me last night. You weren't making much sense. I put Valium in your drink to calm you down. I'm sorry, I didn't know what else to do. Please stay until I get home so we can talk. Please stay calm. He sent me an invitation to an event tonight. I forwarded the email to you. I'll be home soon with Leslie."

"What the hell?" Percy lurched to his feet and swayed, pressing fingers to his head. He staggered into the bathroom guided by vague memories and found his wet clothes hanging over the shower rod. Noticed his phone had shut down and pressed the power button to no effect.

He cast about the slightly messy bathroom in search of a power cord when he spied a waterproof digital clock mounted near the showerhead and saw the time.

3:53pm

"Holy shit!"

The doorbell rang.

3.

Percy stumbled to the door with a towel around his waist. "Who is it?"

A voice from outside said, "I'm Ali Patel and you're in trouble."

"What?" Percy unfastened the deadbolt and yanked open the door. A short man with a combover and a grey raincoat was waiting with a briefcase by his side.

When he smiled, it was as if shark teeth had slipped from sheaths in his gums to replace the friendly human variety.

"I can't talk in the fucking hall, let me in."

4.

"Catherine Van Horn said that if certain events occurred, I should bring this to you. Those events have occurred," Patel said, bracing his elbows on his knees to face Percy, who was perched on the couch in the living room.

"But she—" Percy blurted, but Patel cut him off.

"Don't talk, just listen. I don't know what shit you're into and I don't wanna know." He popped out of his chair and snatched open the liquor cabinet, retrieving a glass and a crystal decanter. He poured a finger of scotch and downed it with a slug, hiss, and smile. "Gotta be 9:00am somewhere in the world, right?"

"Help yourself," Percy growled.

"Your towel's coming loose." Patel shook his head. "Take this." He shoved his briefcase across the carpet with his foot and Percy picked it up with the hand not holding his towel.

"Don't fuckin' open it yet."

Patel yanked his raincoat tight and tied the belt around his waist before hurrying to the door. "Go straight to the airport," he said and left, slamming the door shut.

That just happened, Percy thought.

Placing the briefcase on the coffee table, he popped the brass clasps.

A matte black semi-automatic pistol rested in a holster along with several magazines of ammunition. It was squared off and ungainly, with the word GLOCK stamped on the barrel.

"Huh."

He ran his fingers over two envelopes stuffed with cash before picking up a sharpened silver table knife. He lifted a single sheet of paper wrapped in a tube, tied with a length of red ribbon.

Movement caught his eye and he heard the tock of bone against wood. A small, angular length of bone tumbled across the table. Roughly an inch long, it was sharp at one end like a tooth.

Blood roared in his ears and the floor rippled beneath his feet—and though the effect passed in less than a second, he knew what the object was.

The totem. A piece of the antler had been concealed inside the note. He flattened the paper on the table.

PERCY,

YOU MUST TAKE JORDAN FROM THE CITY IMMEDIATELY. THE HUNT HAS BEGUN AND SHE IS THE HART. GO TO THE AIRPORT. PUT AN OCEAN IN BETWEEN YOU AND THE HUNTER. CONTACT ALI PATEL WHEN YOU ARRIVE AND HE WILL WIRE ADDITIONAL FUNDS.

LESLIE IS NO MORE. THE HUNTER WILL COME FOR JORDAN, HIS CHOSEN PREY. SILVER MAY WOUND HIM BUT THE TOTEM IS THE KEY. USE IT AS A PRIEST. HE CANNOT LET YOU HAVE IT.

I WILL STOP HIM IF I CAN.

GOOD LUCK,
CAT

Percy rose on unsteady legs, towel falling away, brandishing the ridiculous silver knife and even more ridiculous note. Go overseas? His passport was in New Hampshire...

Brandy burned his throat when he slugged it back, emptying the glass. The world steadied around him for approximately two seconds before he doubled over and threw up.

5.

After several frustrating minutes of figuring out Jordan's Keurig, Percy was sipping a cup of strong black coffee to clear away the Valium fog.

He padded naked through Jordan's home, wandering from room to room and back again, feeling the texture of rug and tile beneath his bare feet, waiting for inspiration. If Jordan came back while he was al fresco, it was only what she deserved for slipping him a Mickey.

He made a second cup of coffee with less struggle.

In the study, he sat naked in the leather chair and it took him several moments to understand why he had settled in this room.

It was still Leslie's. She had kept a piece of him—of their marriage—alive. Sticky rings on the dark desk told him that this room had been recently used and he wondered how often she sat in this same place, searching for answers when there were only questions.

How do I find Leslie?

How do I find Jordan?

What do I do if Leslie is the Hunter?

What do I do if he's a god?

WORSHIP

He had written the word with a chewed pencil on the desk blotter. WORSHIP. A god wants what it wants and what it wants from us is WORSHIP.

HOW DO I WORSHIP THE HUNTER?

He left the coffee in the study and hurried past the big picture window of the living room, vaguely aware that he should put on clothes, but something was tickling his brain stem and when that happened...

He picked up the sharpened bit of bone from the coffee table and trotted back into the study, placing it on the desk blotter alongside the question HOW DO I WORSHIP THE HUNTER?

"The totem is the key. Use it as a priest." He said the words aloud and they meant nothing, so he picked up the yellow pencil in sweaty fingers and wrote beneath the cursed object, HOW DOES A PRIEST USE IT?

The pencil tip snapped as he slashed a curving line from that sentence to the word WORSHIP. Snatching up a red Sharpie—the first writing utensil he saw—he circled the word WORSHIP.

"The hunt has begun and she is the chosen prey. She's the hart." He pictured the deer he'd hit. The animal who had provided the totem. He remembered Leslie describing his memories of the time in the woods, of shooting at the biggest deer he'd ever seen.

THE HART, he wrote in red ink.

He picked up the bone and held it before his eyes, concentrating on its greasy feel. He remembered every word of Catherine Van Horn's explanation of the Hunter. Anima, spirit, or god, there was no bargaining with such a thing. It was power with a capital P. One could not fight Power. One could surrender to it and be consumed, or one might appease Power through worship. One might direct Power, in some fashion, by becoming the object of its desire.

By becoming its desired form of worship.

The Hart.

Object of the Hunt.

BECOME THE HART. He could smell the tang of the ink rising from the words and he wrote them again. BECOME THE HART.

"Alright then," he said to the piece of antler. "Come and get me."

CHAPTER FORTY

1.

Briefcase in hand, Percy was stepping out of the elevator when a commotion across the lobby caught his attention. The doorman was speaking to two ruddy-faced police officers, one of them rubbing his hands against the chill.

Cold sweat broke out along his hairline and he pivoted as if that had been his plan all along. Walking away from the front entrance toward a plain door marked AUTHORIZED PERSONS ONLY, he turned the knob, hurrying down a carpeted hallway, narrower than the residential corridors upstairs. He heard a voice from an open doorway up ahead, as if a woman was speaking on the phone. He tried to walk quietly in his heavy boots, passing the doorway without looking, struggling to come up with an explanation for his presence if she—

The hall ended at a door marked LOADING with a glowing EXIT sign above it.

The push bar had a bright yellow sticker announcing the words ALARM WILL SOUND and he struck it without hesitating, covering SOUND with his free hand as he heard the click of the lock releasing. The door swung open into an empty loading bay as an alarm began to ring.

Four running steps took him to a metal door beside the closed garage door and he wrenched it open, taking the three cement steps outside in a leap before he fled down the alley.

2.

Jordan was in her office but facing away from the desk, looking out across the uneven Manhattan skyline as the lowering sun cast a golden light across the rooftops. She was counting the anachronistic wooden water towers, a Zen exercise not unlike a mantra, clearing her mind, seeking calm amidst the insecurity that grew with each tick of the clock.

Leslie. She was going to see Leslie in a few hours. The thought of it brought her mind to a halt. Foolish, foolish, it was an event, they would be surrounded by people and Leslie wasn't there for her, he was there to celebrate his own success, to bask in the adoration of his...

"Sweetling?" her intercom buzzed with Morry's voice.

She pressed the button. "I'm here."

"Turn on the TV. Turn on NY1."

"What—"

"Do it."

He ended the call and she picked up the remote from her desk, rotating, banging her knee with a mumbled curse as the small flatscreen on the wall sprang to life.

"Oh my god," she said. "Oh my god."

A shadow filled her doorway and she could smell his cologne. "Morry, what is this?"

"Oh, baby." He perched on the edge of her desk and shook his head at the image of a sheet-covered body being carried out of the building at 269 Macon Street.

"Leslie wouldn't— I don't understand what they're saying," Jordan said when a buzz interrupted her.

"What?" Jordan nearly shouted at the intercom.

"A call came in for you at the general number." Even through the distortion of the intercom, Jordan could hear that the receptionist knew about the news. "It's the police."

Morry shook his head and mouthed, "Call them back."

"Tell them I'm not in my office and will have to call them back."

"But—"

Jordan hit a button to cut off the conversation.

"You go to your lawyer's office right now and call from there," Morry said, standing.

"Morry?"

"Do it, Face." He circled her desk and put a kind hand on her shoulder. "Right now."

CHAPTER FORTY ONE

1.

Percy shoved a wad of bills through the opening near the bottom of the bulletproof glass protecting a glittering wall of liquor bottles behind the counter.

"Thanks," he said as the dour cashier slid his change back, followed by a plastic bag clanking with bottles.

151 proof rum. Four bottles. He expected it would be enough to scatter around Leslie's apartment, his loose plan to kill the oven's pilot light and turn on the gas before lighting several candles. The accelerant provided by the rum should spread the fire quickly and destroy the place that Leslie—that the Hunter put down roots. Give the motherfucker a hotfoot to draw his attention away from Jordan.

Focus the hunt on himself.

Become the Hart.

Run like hell.

"Gimme a dollar," a woman said sullenly as he pushed out of the liquor store to the clatter of a metal bell. She wore three jackets and torn gloves on her hands, huddled beside a shopping cart full of cast-off junk.

"Give up," Percy said.

"Fuck you!" The woman stabbed two middle fingers into the air.

The sun was setting in the west, casting an orange hand across the sky. He shivered, damp clothes drawing the chill to his skin, a perfect conductor.

Time. Not enough time. What time did the party start? When would Jordan get there?

Splashing through puddles, Percy hurried past the storefronts of Fulton Avenue, reassuring himself that Brooklyn was so wet that his fire wouldn't spread beyond Leslie's building and jeopardize the people around it.

A mother crossed the street ahead of him, yelling at the boy clinging to her hand. "Pay attention!"

The fire wouldn't spread.

It wouldn't.

2.

"Fuck me."

Percy stood on the corner of Macon Street with a small cluster of people strung along the yellow police tape, watching uniformed men and women buzz around Leslie's building as if it were a hive, the street clotted with police vehicles, lights flashing, and several ambulances with their lights dimmed.

Two emergency techs were carrying a stretcher from the building, the body covered by a sheet.

More police tape was strung up around a town car parked at the curb and several plain clothes officers were huddled beside it, as if afraid to open the door.

"What happened?" Percy asked, and a tall young man with big hair favored him with a quick glance.

"Motherfuckin' Freddy Krueger, man. Some dude tore everyone up."

"Yo, they was eaten," a woman chimed in. "Like animals."

Percy backed away as the argument spread through the crowd. A few blocks later he realized he was approaching the liquor store and spied the woman with the shopping cart, who concealed a brown bottle at his approach.

He set down the bag of rum at her feet. "All yours."

CHAPTER FORTY TWO

1.

Officer Morello heard the news. Every cop on the force did. Two detectives dead in BedStuy. Torn to pieces. There was a BOLO for Leslie Ward.

It gave the dull duty at Grand Central Station a bit of color. Brought details into focus and purpose to routine patrols.

Just like the NYPD and Metro cops at Penn Station, Port Authority, and the airports, Morello and his partner Nancy Stallings studied photos of Ward and hoped they'd be the one to get him in their sights.

2.

The ParetskyBytes message board hummed like a livewire as Buddy Paretsky fans watched the video of Grand Central Station uploaded by their high priest of deviance, EyeofGod, aka Norris Chapin.

Those that lived outside the New York City area gnashed their teeth in frustration, but those who lived in the city itself, the few, the very few who considered themselves something more than cinephiles, but true aesthetes of Teatro Orrendo, wrote down EyeofGod's instructions.

It was going to be one hell of a party.

CHAPTER FORTY THREE

1.

The office was sleeker than an attorney's office should be, with framed gold records on the walls and a Les Paul guitar mounted over the couch like a barbarian's broadsword.

The attorney himself was sixty and still rock and roll lean despite a paunch, and if his gray ponytail was thinning, at least the hair was all his.

"Alright, thanks, Detective," Tommy Gunnderson said into his desk phone. "We will. We will. Okay, I'll call you back."

Tommy hung up the phone and rubbed the bridge of his hawk-like nose before fixing his client with a sharp look.

"The remains of three people were found in the building, one of them possibly the super."

"Gordon?" Jordan said from the couch, small and hunched in on herself.

"The other a police officer, and the third..." Tommy shrugged. "Another police officer was killed in his car less than a block away. Same cause of death."

Jordan shook her head in confusion.

"Mauled to death by dogs, Jordan. There's shit and piss all over the building, especially in the apartment your ex-husband occupied."

"Leslie. You can call him Leslie."

"Your ex-husband was keeping a pack of dogs in the building. Did you know that?"

"I—"

"When were you last at the building?"

"I—"

"When did you last speak to your ex-husband?"

Jordan shook her head, stunned. Stunned but thinking. Did they not know she had been at the building only yesterday? That if the dead cop was Detective Argyle, she was one of the last people to see him?

"Leslie went off the rails." Tommy's tone softened. "Did you know about any of this?"

"No, I swear."

Outside the big window behind Tommy's head, the lights of Madison Avenue buildings burned bright against the fall of night. The leather chair creaked as Tommy leaned back, silver curls of hair peering from the open collar of his shirt.

"Okay, we have to go talk to the police."

"I don't—"

"If you don't, they get a warrant and pick you up," he said, overriding her. "I have to call them back in a minute and tell them we're coming in, but I want to run through some questions with you first. A practice run, okay?"

She could feel the color draining from her face and a live thing turning over in her guts. "I need to use the bathroom."

Tommy nodded. "You know where it is."

Jordan stood with her bag clenched in a white-knuckled fist. His voice stopped her at the door.

"Kid," he said. "This is going to be alright."

"I know," she lied, stepping through the door and closing it behind her.

She scanned the quiet bustle of the secretarial pool and located a red EXIT sign just down the hall past the restrooms.

Twenty seconds later she was clattering down the stairs, hoping to reach the sidewalk before Tommy grew worried enough to check on her.

The phone was in her hand and she tried to dial without tripping, finally pausing to tap in Percy's number.

NO SIGNAL.

2.

When Percy emerged from the subway at Columbus Circle at the southwest corner of Central Park, the heavy atmosphere below ground gave way to the cool winter night amidst towering skyscrapers.

The darkness of the park beckoned to him, but first he had an idea that was no more terrible than any other, so he turned toward the brilliantly lit towers lining the south end of the park. Stunning hotels and expensive eateries attracted crowds in ankle-length furs. It wasn't really his scene.

He cut diagonally across traffic, the headlights of passing taxis streaming by like tracers on a battlefield.

It really was a beautiful night.

Inside a shopping center, the air was thick with perfume, the chatter of voices competing with music. He asked for directions and soon found a kitchenware store where he made two purchases—envelopes full of cash were turning out to be useful—and a Starbucks where he purchased a very large and very hot recyclable cup of tea in holiday red.

Back out into the night and the lights and the roar of traffic, the car horns and screeching brakes cutting through the noise like sudden bursts of laughter.

A jog took him across the busy road and through a large plaza surrounding a statue. The delicious smells of hotdogs and roasting nuts rose from silver carts and he remembered that he still hadn't eaten...

Into the park then, trotting, a big man moving with the easy grace of a long-distance runner around brightly jacketed tourists.

Wet and slippery with fallen leaves, the trail wove and descended and warped away from people as his breath steamed and things scuttled beneath spindly bushes.

His boot heels churned up divots of rich-smelling loam as he loped off the trail and onto the grass toward a scattering of boulders.

The rock he chose was the size of a small house and he clambered up, clutching his briefcase and purchases in one hand, hot water from the tea splashing his knuckles.

The moon gifted him with a bright sliver glow and he squatted in imitation of his ancient forebears, pulling a stone mortar and pestle from the plastic shopping bag, biting off the price tags with his teeth.

The brass clasps of the briefcase snapped, loud in the sudden quiet, and a distant part of his mind observed that something more than just the park was shielding him from the city tumult.

(Was something happening?)

The night tingled on his exposed skin and tickled the inside of his nostrils.

(Was something...?)

He dropped the small bit of antler in the stone bowl.

"Hunter." He said it conversationally as he gripped the stone mortar like a dagger and smashed it down. Again and again he drove stone against bone until he heard the crack of the antler. Having taken a foot, he took a mile, shucking his jacket as he methodically ground the antler into meal, putting the weight of his shoulder into it, supported by the unyielding rock of Manhattan Island.

"Heh." A breath of satisfaction. He licked spittle from his upper lip and popped the plastic lid off the cooling tea before pouring in the lumpy powder. Deciding that hesitation might cause thinking and that his plan wasn't up to much scrutiny, he drank from the cup, tilting the bottom up and gulping it, gagging at the grit and slime but choking it all down before crushing the paper cup in his fist—

Setting it beside him, he sat and waited.

The chill settled into his bones, made its home in his hot sweat and cooled him in the icy water of *Nibi Tibik-Kizis*, which meant Moon Water in the old Algonquin tongue.

A canine howl carried across the park. Sneakers slapped against asphalt and a burst of Dominican music shattered the peace. Percy imagined seeing the world through colorblind eyes but corrected himself, because this was a world of blues, of hues, of silver ribbons of asphalt and azure lakes of grass. He imagined snow on the ground as if he were in New Hampshire, in the mountains, and thought that moonlit snow should be the subject of more poems.

He waited.

Out of some ingrained notion of manliness, Percy fought the urge before dragging his jacket around his shoulders. Down below, a couple with matching scarves walked hand in hand, oblivious to his presence. Their conversation was a velvet murmur and then they were gone.

A squirrel moved along a leafless tree limb and the moon shadow spread into something vast and frightening. The Squirrel of Doom. Percy resisted the urge to make up further names for the squirrel.

Something would be happening soon.

A low shape dashed below the rock, fast and four-legged. Too big for a cat.

Central Park was full of sounds and moving shadows.

Percy thumped his chest. Released a quiet belch.

And waited.

3.

Jordan hurried north on Madison Avenue, bumping shoulders with pedestrians heading in the other direction. Angry ad execs and office interns alike cursed her passage until she spotted an opening and skidded through, eastbound on—she didn't even know what street it was, just wanted to get off Madison Avenue so that Tommy Gunnderson wouldn't—

"Pick up the goddamned phone, Percy," she snarled into the phone mashed against her cheek, cursing Verizon, crowds, tall buildings, and—

"Hello?" His voice crackled like an AM radio station.

"It's Jordan—JORDAN!"

"I hear(static)okay?"

"What?"

"Are you okay?"

"The cops want to talk to me about Leslie. There were bodies—what do you know about—"

"What?"

"Fucking murders, Percy!" A pair of women draped in
  Hermes hustled past
Jordan with worried looks. She stepped into a doorway for some semblance of privacy. "Can you hear me?"

"What?"

"GODDAMMIT!" She grabbed the phone hard enough that the casing creaked. "Grand Central Station, the Henley Apartment. That's where Leslie will be. Meet me at Grand Central Station at the Henley Apartment."

"(static)Station!"

"Yes, Grand Central Station!" She was speaking to a dead line. "Percy? Percy?"

4.

Percy stood very still atop his boulder, looking down at the gathering below.

Four dogs of no recognizable breed stared up at him. Two had collars, one was slat-ribbed and scabrous, the other thick with fur. All of them were sitting, pink tongues lolling, waiting.

He slid his thumb over the screen of his call and cut off Jordan's incoherent words. He was afraid to move.

The slat-ribbed dog tilted his head to one side. Another dog slumped down to its belly, panting. The third raised his blunt Boxer's muzzle to Percy and planted his front paws on the base of the boulder. He was a brindle creature with black stripes slashing across his torso and seemed to draw on the insubstantial essence of the night itself.

"HUNTER!" he roared without warning.

All four animals bolted, racing off the path and out of sight.

"Holy shit." He scrambled down the rock after them. He was aware of fleeting shapes around him in the dark as howling filled Central Park. He wondered how many dogs were on the move.

Something was happening.

CHAPTER FORTY FOUR

1.

Morello tossed a handful of peanuts into his mouth and nudged Stallings, who lowered a Powerade and wiped her lips.

"What?" They were leaning against the wall next to a closed ticket window, out of the chaotic flow of foot traffic.

"There supposed to be a protest today?" He coughed, peanuts caught in his throat.

"Huh?"

Morello nodded across the busy floor to a cluster of gangly types beneath the clock tower. Androgynous in their black hoodies, they could have been men or women. Black Bloc. Antifa. Call them what you will. Morello called them assholes.

"Let's check it out," Stallings said before a boisterous herd of people with shopping bags blocked their view. When they passed, the black-clad trio was gone.

2.

Jordan was struck by the ugliness of Grand Central Station when she emerged from a taxi on 42nd Street. It was an anachronism, a gray stone pile bearing no resemblance to the skyscrapers surrounding it. Temple-like. Of a more ancient model than the synagogues and churches littering the city. Aztec. Mayan.

Standing beneath the Park Avenue Viaduct, she studied the squat absolutism of Grand Central Station and hated it. In its shadow the people were shabbier, the cement was stained with more pigeon shit, the smell of the food carts more nauseating.

The interior was little better, crowded like a football field overrun with fans.

She tensed at the sight of policemen in the crowd. Shoulders hunched and head down, she wove through the noisy throng until she reached the wide stairs leading down to the lower level and the food concourse, locating her destination by memory.

The Henley Apartment.

CHAPTER FORTY FIVE

1.

Velvet ropes restrained a short but well-dressed line of aspirants waiting for the promised debauch. A tent of burgundy curtains concealed the entrance, as promising as the entrance to Caligula's grotto.

Past the velvet ropes and thick-necked doorman who checked her name against a list, she pushed aside heavy curtains to traverse the dimly lit, curtained maze, designed to disorient, to separate the wanderer from the noise and clamor of Grand Central.

Smells of cedar smoke and mulling spices. Music. Lyrical pipes of pagan design. The buzz of conversation.

Hands took her coat, a living shadow in a black body suit whipped it away with a flourish and handed over a folded bundle. Jordan shook it open and discovered a hooded robe of lightweight material. "Really?"

"Everyone has been asked to wear one." The living shadow vanished back into the coat check room.

A thin blonde wearing a headset smiled at Jordan with vacant eyes, writing her off as unimportant.

"I'll show myself in," Jordan said, beaming at the blonde's momentary confusion.

A discreet but cleverly placed sign informed Jordan that there would be NO PHOTOGRAPHY. The open doors were wreathed in pine boughs speckled with red berries, and the lighting was dim, bulbs glowing the red of burst blood vessels, of all-consuming rage.

2.

"Oh my god."

The words slipped out sotto voce and Jordan tugged her hood up over her head, stepping out of the doorway with a New Yorker's instinct for foot traffic so she could stop and gape.

Leslie, what have you made?

It was a subterranean wonder, a dark forest conjured whole and leafy in a vast, brick-ceilinged cavern. Torches blazed from iron sconces. Smoke spiraled upward and pale tule fog rippled across the ground. Music pulsed from unseen speakers, an unsettling clamor of pipes and strings. The Gatsby elegance of the underground club (where the liquor was always top-shelf and the conversation witty) had been consumed by a forest of nightmares.

Hooded druids drank wine from jugs and ate meat from skewers. Seated in red leather banquets, they sipped from long-stemmed martini glasses while waiters in black ties circulated with trays of spirits and flutes of champagne.

This glimpse into Leslie's mind was new. Different. And it was only after she accepted the reality of this faerie underworld that she saw the familiar cruelty of Paretsky on display.

Human trees stood on pedestals above the undulating fog, branches and twigs extending from hands as if their fingers had elongated into wood. Crowns of leaves birthed pagan antlers that spread above their heads. She thought they wore the thinnest of body stockings painted white and black as if to suggest a stand of birch. The tuft of hair between a woman's legs dispelled that notion, as did the black spread of branches dangling from a penis.

Every five minutes the trees moved into new positions.

"Jesus." It came out as a breath.

Real trees had been uprooted and planted about the space to complete the faerie wood, their branches concealing crimson bulbs set to strobe in uneven cadence. It was the image of a woodland washed in fire and Jordan's cheeks flushed at a flood of memories. That she was younger then did nothing to absolve her behavior with Leslie at the long-ago event. Paretsky screened at a secret underground venue. She hadn't liked what she saw in Leslie then. What she saw in herself, if the truth be told. The books encouraged the release of urges best left buried. The films were worse.

When a waiter in a black tie passed with a tray, she selected a flute of champagne and sipped the effervescent liquid. A pair of giggling druids staggered from a doorway marked RESTROOMS, wiping at their noses in brazen display. The moneyed set had come downtown to walk on the wild side of Paretsky's forbidden id.

A bestial howl cut through the susurrus of noise and Jordan craned her neck to look up at cages dangling beneath iron chains from catwalks overhead.

The cages held living things. Animals tufted with fur. Shifting uneasily. A lucky strobe of light flashed across a snout and it jerked back with a snarl.

Coyotes. There were live coyotes dangling over their heads.

The urge to leave gripped her like a vise. Fear sickened her so that for a moment she feared vomiting. Gritting her teeth, she quelled the rebellion by downing the champagne, the liquid bubbling from the side of her mouth before she tossed the glass over her shoulder and belched.

She was not leaving without Leslie.

Jordan flowed into the swirling crowd, kicking up tufts of fog. Hoods were thrown back. Vanity on display. She recognized faces now. Mouths wide in laughter, food spilling on the floor. So different than the people they portrayed on screen, these true selves with bigger noses and red-veined eyes, thinning hair and blackened teeth. A woman tugged open her blouse as a man pulled at the strap of her bra. Druids pressed in pairs and trios against trees.

The essence of Buddy Paretsky was infecting them all.

Obscenities had been scrawled about the place in glowing paint, a disgusting graffiti that seemed intent on corrupting the fantastical forest. Her gaze was drawn to flickering screens behind bushes and benches, displaying the lurid horrors of Norris Chapin's Teatro Orrendo. A quick scan revealed the man himself capering about like a goblin in the mist, clusters of guests recoiling and shifting until he moved on.

The neatly attired bartenders were authored by a different hand and grounded Jordan. "Red Breast, neat," brought a tumbler of Irish whiskey to reassure her that some rules stilled applied.

She considered pulling a fire alarm, assuming she could find one. She considered calling Animal Control about the coyotes.

The sight of the Wicker Man derailed her plans.

It was a hunched golem of woven branches, more troll than man. A robed crowd jostled and cheered around the cruel figure, stepping in and out through a swinging door in its belly while a staff photographer snapped Polaroids with a blinding flash.

They had no idea what they were doing.

She ordered another whiskey to help her reconcile what she saw with what she had heard from Percy. Feeling Leslie's contempt even in his triumph. None of these people understood Paretsky. Tourists hoping for an illicit handjob at the coat check. Movie types trying to smear a bit of his evil excrescence on themselves in pursuit of a paycheck.

There, a face she recognized. She caught herself from calling out when she realized it was Martin McDowell, the talentless pretty boy who had cut Leslie's literary legs out from under him. She remembered arguing with Leslie about the upstart. How could he share an agent with McDowell? The argument blew up into a full-blown fight. It was near the end when everything had gone bad for them.

She shoved away the memory and turned to the bartender. "Have you seen Leslie Ward?" The balding man shook his head.

Her heart gained weight. She didn't like what she was seeing in this place. Saw in its artifice a chaos that matched the stink and disorder of his apartment in Brooklyn.

And allowed herself to believe, really believe for the first time, that what the police were saying might be true.

3.

The Hunter's expectations were absolute, and when his arrival in the dark forest failed to turn every head, black worms twisted in his gut. The corruption that had become so much a part of the Hunter's essence manifested as a rank sweat breaking out across Leslie's body. A maggot tumbled down his cheek, unseen in the dim light.

Leslie knew that among the well-heeled guests were movie stars and directors of renown and that the event, every event, was always about them, (snarls echoed through his mind) but the Hunter was unable to comprehend such a state of affairs.

When his gaze picked a rival out of the crowd, the snarl leaked out between his teeth. Martin McDowell was nothing to the Hunter, but Leslie's hatred gave him import. A reason to choose one prey animal over another.

Leslie's monocular gaze rose above the throng and took in the little hunters in their cages. The coyotes stirred in their narcotic haze and eight glittering eyes found him as noses twitched, drinking in his scent through the stinking miasma of sweat and alcohol and smoke.

Even through the swamp of body odor, the Hunter smelled Norris Chapin and several others concealed on the catwalks. He nodded and felt Chapin respond to his silent command.

Movement. White fluttering. Hatches atop the dangling coyote cages were opened.

Four muzzles lifted and four sets of lungs hurled their howling challenge over the crowd.

4.

Jordan was lifting a third whiskey to her lips when a white feather see-sawed from above to land on the bar. She picked it up with a quizzical look, her thoughts sluggish, only then detecting the change in sound, the hungry canine howls.

The cages overhead rocked as the animals inside devoured their living meals. Bloody feathers exploded between the bars to rain down on the guests as the chickens were torn limb from limb.

5.

Ramesh ignored the howling coyotes as he ignored the stares of partygoers, their comments about his physique, insults, and innuendos.

More difficult was resisting the urge to look down at his penis as the itching increased in intensity. *Time*, he said to himself and shifted atop his pedestal, a living tree in silver body paint raising his arms in a Christ-like pose, if Christ were an Indian man who posed naked for a buck.

As he reached the apex of his pose, he turned his head to the right to look down the length of his arm, past the black, jagged branches at his fingertips, to see D'Anielle finishing her movement, the pose bent toward him, her head lowered, the wide spread of fog-shrouded antlers aimed his way.

What Ramesh first took to be some kind of fog were in fact fluttering webs stretched between the antlers crowning D'Anielle's head. He squinted to make out movement in the dim, red light. Black spots skittering along the web.

Spiders?

Intense heat rose from his groin as his penis was engulfed in pain. He looked down to see a long, many-legged millipede writhing in his painted pubic hair.

He screamed.

6.

Norris Chapin ducked through the curtains obscuring the entryway and said, "Leslie needs you right now."

The event coordinator looked up with wide eyes as hurried reports shrieked from her headset. "What's happening out there?"

"Go now!" Chapin grabbed her shoulders and shoved her toward the vine-covered arch. She shot him a withering glance and ducked inside the party.

The door to the food hall had been propped open to let in fresh air. Chapin pulled it closed.

"What are you doing?" The coat check girl materialized behind him, hands on hips.

"You'll want to see this." Chapin slid a deadbolt home, locking the door. "It's all happening."

Screams from the party drowned out her reply.

7.

When the coyotes howled, the living trees screamed and scrambled from their pedestals. One sprawled full length on the floor and disappeared beneath the tule fog.

With every head turned to follow what they thought was part of the show, Leslie vaulted athletically onto the bar, a bottle of clear rum clutched in one fist, a torch in the other. Steam rose from his superheated body in waves and his hair flared in a mysterious wind.

Heads whipped around to take in what new spectacle had appeared. Cheers erupted as Leslie threw his arms wide and shrugged off his druid robes. A gust swept through the subterranean realm and torch flames leaned over as if bowing in Leslie's direction. The robes, freed from his shoulders, fanned out like wings before dropping out of sight.

He was taller. Taller than the elevation of the bar should allow. Unseen pheromones filled the air and men and women alike salivated in the clutches of primal lust.

Leslie filled his mouth from the bottle before blowing a spray of rum over the torch. A fireball exploded and the room was filled with cheers.

"My friends!" He was the lord of the manner, the center of attention, the apple of everyone's eye. He didn't see their confusion. The lack of recognition. Only their hunger for entertainment. "Welcome to Teatro Orrendo!"

Cheers and roars filled the cavernous forest as the spirit of Bacchus worked its will. All eyes were upon the Hunter. It was devotion. It was worship.

No one saw the cages rip loose from the ceiling.

CHAPTER FORTY SIX

1.

The crowded 6 train thundered to a halt at the 42nd Street platform in the bowels of Grand Central Station. After an unintelligible announcement, the doors whooshed open and Percy was carried out of the subway car by a seething tide of humanity. He was shoved and buffeted, craning his head while everyone else moved with purpose.

The dipping notes of a saxophone attracted him and he stepped into the small sphere of calm around a long-haired musician leaning against a support column, black sunglasses suggesting he was blind. Percy's entire body hummed like a tuning fork.

The Hunter was near. He could smell the psychic stink gathered in the tunnels. Breath whistled from his tortured lungs and he patted the pocket that concealed the Glock.

The musician drew his lips away from the instrument and said, "Steady, brother."

Percy nodded at the sax player who nodded back—not blind—and stared down the empty subway tunnel with a skin-crawling conviction that a deadly tide was boiling toward him at that very moment.

"Don't stay here," he said to the sax player before he was herded toward a muddy staircase and spat out into a wide, echoing corridor with white marble walls and a ceiling far overhead.

Percy found himself marching toward a set of doors leading to the sidewalk and earned curses when he reversed course, a salmon swimming upstream until he found a current of like-minded travelers and burst into the cacophony of the station proper, disoriented by blaring public address announcements and the endless array of apertures leading to train platforms.

He dragged a hand through his hair, wild-eyed and panicked. He remembered the great flood below ground when he and Catherine tried to drive away the spirit, and looked up at the swaying chandeliers of Grand Central Station, imagining the carnage if the Hunter struck the station itself.

Pulling out his phone, he dialed Jordan's number.

2.

The saxophone player froze in a crouch on the train platform, halfway to closing his instrument case. A terrifying wail swelled from the tunnel, as if the gates of Hell itself were vomiting forth legions.

Jaws slavering, eyes flashing, the dogs blasted from the dark subway tunnel and sprang in ones and twos and then dozens onto the platform. Passengers shouted and fled, many jumping onto the tracks only to find more dogs racing toward them. Blue fire crackled from the third rail as human and canine alike struck it and died. The stink of burnt meat filled the underground chamber.

In moments the enormous pack was charging up several sets of stairs toward the upper levels of Grand Central Station.

3.

Outside the Henley Apartment, Percy dragged the big doorman out of the stampede of escaping party guests. A roar rose from a thousand throats on the main floor above. It sounded like the Super Bowl. Like the Roman Coliseum.

The crack of gunfire told Percy he had to hurry.

Pulling the big man upright, Percy gave him a shove. "Get out of here!" A new sound seized his attention. It was a sound that reached back through time to trigger ancient ganglia, the reflexes of his hominid forebears. He spun toward the broad stairs that led up to the ground floor and his blood turned to ice.

A furred wall of teeth and claws spilled down the stairs into the food hall. A wave of predators howling and slavering with bloodlust.

Charging dogs met fleeing humans and a wild melee ensued. People leapt over food counters with dogs in pursuit. Glass shattered and metal crashed. The Starbucks became an abattoir, the pizza counter a battleground.

Screams filled the air.

Percy froze, torn. People needed his help, but Jordan was inside the Henley Apartment.

Inside with Leslie.

He turned his back on the chaos and rushed through the open door into the red light and fog. Keen eyes picked out the details of a metal doorframe and he spun, snatching at the nearly invisible door to yank the metal portal shut.

The heavy fire door shook as a tide of animal fury struck the other side.

CHAPTER FORTY SEVEN

1.

Norris Chapin sidestepped through the mist inside the Henley Apartment. "Piss, shit, booze, and smoke," he cooed into the audio pickup. "It smells like a porta-potty at a rock festival. The stink of body odor is thicker than an NBA locker room."

Kicking off his shoes, he lost them in the ground fog, using his toes to deftly peel off his socks. He panned the camera down to show his bare feet as they vanished into the white clouds. "The ground is wet and sticky. They left their fear behind."

Fleeing partygoers had bottlenecked at the locked door. The crowd had grown loud and violent before the door was forced and they squirted out. It was glorious. Hilarious. Chapin did all his own editing and had already decided to leave the sound of his own laughter on the audio track. Thought about speeding the film up to add to the comedy.

Climbing onto a red leather banquette for a wide shot, he kept his eye on the camera view screen and saw that someone was trapped inside the Wicker Man.

"Look who it is!" he said, zooming in on a desperate face.

The night couldn't have unfolded better if he'd scripted it himself.

2.

Martin McDowell huddled within the Wicker Man and wished himself small.

Wished himself invisible. He was drenched with sweat beneath leather pants and suede shirt, carefully coiffed hair limp with perspiration. Perhaps if he was better read he would have understood the purpose of a Wicker Man. Perhaps if he understood the purpose of a Wicker Man he wouldn't have sought safety inside the woven branches of the trollish body, pushing out the young woman who had tried to wedge herself inside with him.

Leslie Ward stared at him from atop the bar, his one eye more than a match for McDowell's two. His agent—their agent—had said if he wanted to be the next Leslie Ward, he had to show up at the party.

He hoped Angie was trampled in the stampede to escape.

"Little pig, little pig, let me in," Leslie spoke conversationally, but his voice carried across the distance.

McDowell felt as if a thousand tiny spiders were crawling beneath his clothes as his flesh broke out in goosebumps. He shrank back from the hideous grin Leslie aimed his way, the mouth too wide, the teeth too many.

When Leslie sprang from the bar, he traveled an impossible distance. Fog swirled when he landed in front of the Wicker Man. An incredible leap. Twenty feet at least. Thirty.

This is not happening!

"Not by the hair on my chinny chin chin."

McDowell couldn't ignore the leering tone and cracked open his eyelids as Leslie strolled toward him. He was tall. Too tall. McDowell had stood next to Leslie Ward at more than one event and silently reveled in towering over the veteran hack, but Leslie was looking down at him with that one shining eye.

"Then I'll huff and I'll puff..."

Leslie unzipped his fly and tugged out his swollen cock. He was excited and terrifying. McDowell feared violation of a different sort and croaked, "Stay back."

"Shhh." Leslie looked down at his cock held in one hand, the free hand patting the air in a shushing gesture. "I can't pee if you're talking."

"Ward, what the fuck are you doing?"

It was a mewling sound, weak, and Leslie's grin widened. His prick jerked and a jet of golden urine arced forth to splash against the Wicker Man.

"Stop! Stop!" McDowell shook and twisted, but the woven cage offered no shelter from the rain. He uncurled his body and raised his head when the enormous flow of piss stopped, only to freeze.

The coyotes were stalking forward, bloody muzzles twitching. White feathers still clinging to the red grue. McDowell's muscles locked painfully tight and his breath was strangled in his chest.

"You've been marked, dear boy," Leslie purred. "Time to run."

"Fuck you!" McDowell gripped the branches of his cage and hoped they would hold. "Get away from me!"

Leslie shrugged and spread his hands as if in surrender, but two hooded men plucked burning torches from iron sconces and circled to the rear of the Wicker Man.

All at once the strobing red bulbs scattered among the trees flared to blinding red and exploded in a series of popping flashes. Flatscreens cracked and sparks filled the air, but everything was drowned out by the cascading avalanche behind the bar when every bottle on the shelves detonated.

3.

Jordan ducked behind an overturned table as the world exploded. The air was filled with diamonds and sparks danced among the shards like fireflies, and for a moment it was the most beautiful thing she had ever seen.

When the patter of falling glass stopped, she peered around the table at the grinning madman who had replaced Leslie Ward.

The scarred, one-eyed creature bore no resemblance to the man she had married and divorced but never truly let go. The man who had defined her and destroyed her and who, childishly, she had hoped to one day marry again. A sickening bolt of electricity struck her when she saw Leslie with his cock in his hand, a flashing arc of urine striking a leather-clad man who hopped and slipped, a cloud of mist puffing up when he went down. McDowell.

"Get the fuck away!" McDowell spun about inside the Wicker Man like a trapped animal as the robed men, devotees of Chapin and Paretsky both, held their torches against the bottom of the woven prison.

Jordan heard a roaring in her ears and black spots danced across her vision. Words ran through her mind on an unending loop. *ThisishappeningThisishappeningThisishappening.*

The Wicker Man shook as it was engulfed in flames.

"Nooooo!" The scream escaped her lips before she could stop it and Leslie turned with a grin, the coyotes following suit.

McDowell seized the moment, kicking open the Wicker Man's door and running for the kitchen doors. The coyotes sprang after him with a chorus of howls. The young writer banged through the swinging barrier at a full sprint and Jordan thought for a moment that he had escaped. But even as the doors swung closed, she heard his screams.

The table she cowered behind was flung aside and Leslie threw wide his arms. "Just think, you left all this!" She was struck physically by the force of his smile. There was nothing recognizable in that expression.

When he whispered, she heard the word in her mind: "Run."

His voice grew shrill and he shrieked, head tilting back and mouth gaping as his empty eye gave birth. It was black with blood and white with bone. A branch. A tree. Growing from his head. From his face.

A great, bleeding antler.

Jordan fell back on her haunches and wailed in horror. Her body sought a final defense, to make itself unappealing by voiding bladder and bowels, but found itself empty of material.

She was going to die.

A gunshot rang out and Leslie spun away from her. Two more shots drove him into a banquette and he tumbled over the leather seatback, falling out of sight.

Percy was at her side a moment later, his big hand gripping her upper arm hard enough to bruise.

"Run." He dragged her to a glowing EXIT sign.

CHAPTER FORTY EIGHT

1.

Percy banged down the steel fire stairs, every moment limned in light and thunder yet strangely distant. Students of PTSD would recognize his mental state. His mind was like a submarine closing bulkheads when it took on water. Shutting down all non-critical functions in order to survive.

The result was reductive. Percy the man became Percy the machine. He tracked Jordan's rapid descent in his wake—distantly noted she was huffing less horribly than he—and cast his hearing up to the fire door above, waiting for the descent of

(mental static)

that which pursued them.

Percy's planning function thought in direct lines. They would emerge in the station and he would push for the nearest exit to the street, knocking people aside if necessary. They would find a cab and pile in and he would shove so much money at the driver that all questions would be waived until they were safely out of the city and reached...

The door. Unpainted steel.

"Jordan!" he huffed, crashing into the door full-force and grabbing it in both fists, fully prepared to break the lock with pure muscle if necessary and certain that he could do it.

The door flew open under his weight and rebounded against the wall as he skidded onto the cement train platform.

Smoke. The crash of metal wheels. Glaring lights. Shouting conductors.

It was an underground chamber the length of a football field with a curved, roughhewn ceiling and a long cement platform stretching away from him, deep channels to either side. Channels with tracks at the bottom instead of rivers.

A Metro North platform.

People were chasing the metal bulk of a Metro North train straining against its own weight to gain speed. Some fell, others dove through open doors on the passenger cars. It was like newsreel footage from a war. The terrified exodus before the invading army.

Howls echoed from the dark tunnels.

"C'mon!" Jordan shouted and dashed past him, faster now that he wasn't slowing her progress.

The survival machine was dumping blood into the big muscles of his thighs and feeding chemicals into his system to dull the fear and pain. His eyesight narrowed to a black tube focused on Jordan running full out, her long ponytail flying in her wake.

The shouts. He struggled to understand that a door remained open on the moving train. The blue-sleeved arm of a conductor was urging them on board. "Run! Run!"

Jordan caught the edge and flung herself through the door with the strength of her arms.

Percy dragged a hand along the vibrating steel bulk of the passenger car. Breath whistled in his lungs and his steps slowed as his circle of vision narrowed, spotted with black.

Three giant steps. One! Two! Boots kicking up mud and grit. A hand caught his and he grabbed it with bone-crushing strength. The conductor screamed and pulled as Percy lunged and Jordan cried wordlessly with effort, a human chain with her as the anchor.

Percy barreled through the door like a cannonball, bowling over his saviors and crashing into the window on the far door hard enough to crack the glass.

2.

It was a terrorist attack. There was an explosion. Every dog in Manhattan went rabid. There was a serial killer.

The rumors buzzed about the train, the blue QUIET CAR signs hanging from the ceiling ignored by everyone.

Dogs made it onto the train at the rear car. No dogs made it onto the train. A dog was killed in Business Class.

Percy and Jordan were huddled together, seeking solace in each other, realizing the pain in their bodies and minds as the adrenaline faded. They were on the west side of the train and treated to a sight of the beautiful stone of the Palisades rising across the wide, grey expanse of the Hudson River. Jordan spoke in a whisper.

"Leslie—"

"Yes."

"He—"

"Yes."

"Where are we going?"

"Leaving the city. Leading him away from the city."

Percy excused himself and rose, catching himself against the swaying motion of the train to move down the aisle between frightened passengers to reach the restroom. He yanked the door closed and turned the lock to activate the OCCUPIED sign outside and bent to assess himself in the mirror, hair wild, beard matted, eyes haunted.

He struggled to get his hands beneath the faucet in the tiny sink and settled for just his left, cupping water to splash on his face and beard, running fingers though his hair, ignoring the sign declaring that the water was NOT POTABLE to carry some to his cracked lips.

Did he really shoot Leslie?

No. He shot the Hunter...and he had no doubt that the Hunter was coming.

The chase was on. The worship had begun when Percy, high priest of the Hunt, shot his god.

How fast could Leslie run? As fast as a dog? Faster? Would he have his pack of hellhounds baying alongside?

"Fuck 'im if he can't take a joke." He grinned and didn't believe his reflection. Fought to keep tears from his eyes. He wished he could check himself into White Heart and that Kai could console him, guide him through withdrawal, promise that the madness would end, the itching would stop, that his heart would cease trip-hammering on the other side.

But there was no other side to this. No end other than appeasing his god.

He unzipped his leather jacket to check on the cash-filled envelopes and silver knife, changing pockets until he could drag the borrowed 9mm pistol from the back of his waistband and eject the slide. Three rounds remained. He reseated the slide with the heel of his hand and slipped the weapon into an interior pocket along with the extra magazine before zipping the garment closed.

When he sat heavily back down in his seat, he reflexively turned to apologize to the passenger sitting behind him, an elderly Asian man who worked his mouth as if to speak but could find no words.

Jordan gripped his shoulder. "They say the police will be interviewing everyone when we stop in Yonkers."

"Where's Yonkers?"

"Next stop."

"We'll get a car there."

A ripple of sound went through the train, a social media wave caught in real time as voices rose over the tinny, out of sequence noise from dozens of tiny speakers.

Percy was still looking around in confusion as Jordan pulled out her phone and shouted, "Where is it?"

"New York One!" a deep voice replied.

A moment later they were watching the bouncing, hand-held footage of panic inside the dark forest of the Henley Apartment, courtesy of Norris Chapin and his acolytes.

The fearful moans of the passengers were carried like prayers to the ears of the Hunter.

3.

A cold wind whistled across the Avis parking lot, blowing around a dusting of snow.

"A Kia?"

There had indeed been police waiting at the platform, but the attempt to corral passengers was disorganized and Jordan led Percy straight outside where she suggested they skip the taxi line—which was monitored by an officer wearing earmuffs—and found a green taxi with its light off in the lot amidst the minivans and SUVs.

Sixty dollars was enough to convince the aging Jamaican driver to put his lunch down on the seat and drive them to the nearest rental car office. His meter read $6.50. Not a bad deal.

"What's wrong with it?" Jordan asked.

Percy swept snow from the windshield, towering over the car. "I won't fit."

"Jesus, get in."

She slung herself behind the wheel as Percy circled to the passenger side and wedged himself into the seat. He managed to move the seat back with some effort but still looked like a giant in the cramped interior.

"Just go," he said, and Jordan drove out of the lot.

A couple turns later they accelerated south onto New York State Route 100.

They had been driving for several minutes before Jordan asked the question that had been weighing on her. "How fast can a dog run?"

Percy twisted to look at the road behind them. "Not as fast as a car."

CHAPTER FORTY NINE

Dark as Caliban, Leslie sprinted north on the tracks in the wake of the vanishing train, his ground-eating stride terrifying to behold. He was covered from head to bare feet in ash from the pursuit through the tunnel, a dun-colored being of congealed smoke with blazing coals for eyes. Around him swirled a pack of hounds with fur of charcoal, their red tongues dangling like rivers of fire.

Splinters were crushed beneath his calloused soles and his ragged jacket—a fine garment bought only the day before—streamed in his wake. Still, the pack was too slow to catch the Metro North train once it reached speed.

It would be a long chase.

The long chase favored the pack.

The long chase wore down prey until they staggered and fell.

He threw back his head with a screeching yowl and the hounds bayed in response.

Leslie slowed to a jog and then a walk, the pack ranging before and behind, yipping and barking with excitement. Tunnel Dogs. Hell Hounds. They were transformed by his presence, pet and wildling alike.

He made a coughing sound and chuffed as he veered to the side of the track to pick his way up the trash-strewn slope toward a sagging chain-link fence above. The pack followed, weaving between piles of refuse, discarded toilets, and rusting bits of machinery.

Traffic whooshed along the road beyond the fence and he grabbed the chain-link with his fingers, studying the Bronx neighborhood of two-story row houses, parked cars, blue mailboxes, and streetlights just glowing to life as dusk settled her skirts over the city.

He knew where Percy and Jordan were going.

CHAPTER FIFTY

1.

I-95 North was a slow-moving sea of headlights and Jordan shifted nervously behind the wheel, wishing Percy was awake, that she had someone to talk to, to tell her that she hadn't seen what she saw and that all of this was—

Percy snored. Exhausted. The car was choked with cigarette smoke and exhaust from the hundreds of cars around them. Her mind danced over the events of the night before, Percy's raging, crazed stories. His terrified eyes.

Slipping a Valium into his drink. God, she wished she could take that one back.

2.

The rest stop was a long white building with a Dunkin Donuts, a Subway, a McDonald's, and a Panda Express. It smelled like gasoline and sounded like car horns and voices. Noise from the nearby highway was like the scrape of a steel brush across the world.

Percy and Jordan stood beside the Kia as the car suckled from a gas pump mounted with a small screen. A safe-looking woman offered an endless loop of discounted products from the store inside. "Like chips? Why not add nacho cheese for only ninety-nine cents?" They couldn't shut her off.

No matter how many times Percy looked at the logo on the pump, he couldn't remember what kind of gas station it was. The free-standing roof overhead with the glaring lights was white, trimmed with blue, and speakers piped in an endless flow of scratchy music.

"Hot dogs are only a buck twenty-nine!"

Percy just couldn't focus.

"Four hours until we hit New Hampshire?" Jordan said, eyes fixed on the building. Percy shrugged as R&B music swelled and faded with a passing pick-up truck.

The woman on screen was suggesting that, "Your drive is smoother with a hot cuppa joe," when Percy yanked a big black pistol from inside his jacket.

Jordan blurted, "What the fuck?"

"A dog." His voice was flat and she had never seen such a ruthless expression on his face. Percy who laughed. Percy who held your hair when you puked on 7th Street after too many shots of Jim Beam.

A pregnant lady in a pink satin jacket was walking a German Shepherd, its bushy tail swishing lazily. They were separated by thirty feet of open blacktop, the pair strolling along the grassy verge alongside the building.

"Is it one of his?" Jordan whispered, her face wan in the gas station lights.

"I don't know." He racked the slide to chamber a round.

"No." She placed a hand on his forearm. "You can't just start shooting dogs, Percy."

"Fuck dogs."

"Fuck you. You want to kill that pregnant lady? You want the cops to come? That dog's not even— Look, he's pooping."

Percy thumbed the safety on the weapon and slid it back inside his jacket. "Four hours to New Hampshire and then another couple until we reach the cabin, depending on the roads."

"You're sure this is the right thing to do?"

"Hell no." Percy looked around, stepping away from the pumps. He spotted a group of people milling around a white bus with LUCKY STAR written across the side. "Getting him out of the city was right. Getting him to Moon Lake... I'm doing the best I can."

"I know." Jordan's eyes were scanning everywhere, alighting on everything except Percy. "I don't like this."

"I know."

CHAPTER FIFTY ONE

1.

The sun rose on a snowy world as the Kia followed curving roads up into the White Mountains of New Hampshire. The hip-hop radio station out of Manchester (New Hampshire's Hip Hop HQ!) had long since dissolved into static. In the last half-hour Percy had seen two cars coming from the other direction, flashes of light in the distance that grew into shining windshields until they became a sudden thunder, a shudder of wind, and were past, soon consumed by the winding wilderness.

He cracked his window to light a cigarette and shivered from more than the cold. The sense of something happening was fading. The feeling of certitude that he had felt in Central Park had grown gossamer.

"Take a left when we get to 119," Percy said from the passenger seat and Jordan grimaced behind the wheel.

"I forgot the way," she said.

"It's the only turn in the next twenty miles."

Towering snow-capped pines gave way to blasted passages of granite, the ice-coated rock revealing the bones of an older, harder earth beneath.

Eventually the Kia slowed as a white road sign indicated the intersection with 119. Her blinker was loud in the quiet and she flicked an almost embarrassed look at Percy. "Habit."

Percy stirred from his slump to look through the smeared window glass at the passing beauty as they followed the winding path of 119, which ran alongside the black band of the river down below. On the opposite side of the road the ground rose, a forested upgrade leading to Moon Lake.

They were close.

He remembered the last time he had driven this path, on his motorcycle in the snow. Close to cutting his wheel to the right and plunging deliberately into the river below. An innocent strip of water and ice that wanted no part of his suicide.

It seemed impossible that only weeks had passed since then.

Weeks in which he had grown closer to Leslie than ever before, even as he lost him. He remembered seeing Leslie in the hospital, so much smaller and less vital than before.

The Leslie Ward who went into the woods with a rope never really came back.

This understanding freed him to think of that which lay in the woods. The shifting location. The shadows inhabiting wild things. The bower, the altar where none should be.

To accept that his friend no longer wore the body that looked and acted like Leslie Ward. That it was the Hunter. Only the Hunter.

The Hunter wanted this chase to conclude in the woods where he had spread his stain.

So be it.

Percy would find this altar and commit his final act of worship. Offering himself through an act of violence against his friend. Offering his body to become the body of the Hunter.

He wiped absently at tears, vaguely aware of conversation in the front seat.

Jordan would make it through the day, but Percy would send the Hunter to its destruction. In doing so he would give Leslie the freedom of death.

Percy would follow.

2.

The occasional splatter of snow struck the windshield as branches relieved themselves on the car below. Jordan would flick on the wipers to smear it around for a minute before turning them off, made tense by the swish and click of the blades. She checked the gas and saw she had half a tank, the whining engine drinking it down faster than she liked.

"Hey." She pointed through the windshield. "See that sign? We're here."

Percy felt a tremor through his body and looked out wildly. He felt as if his throat were clutched in a fist of ice and couldn't cry out in warning even as he saw the snow on the side of the road erupt.

"Oh shit!"

The noise was huge. World filling. That it could be so sudden and all-encompassing seemed unfair as the towering pine cracked at the base and tilted toward the road, green boughs filling their windshield as the tree fell atop them.

It struck with incredible force.

The lightweight Kia rocketed left on a diagonal across the yellow lines and smashed into a snowbank. White powder exploded in a momentary blizzard and Percy hit the dashboard with his full weight.

Percy struggled to sit up, coughing, shoulder radiating pain. He rotated with difficulty onto his hands and knees and found the door handle, pushing open the door to fall face-first into the snow outside.

He tried to speak and made only wordless grunts. Stood, right foot sinking to the thigh in the snowbank so that he tripped and sprawled into the road.

The enormous tree had fallen across the road as if a giant had leaned his weight against it.

He cried out for Jordan, his own words lost to the ringing in his ears.

Percy made his way around the Kia and noticed smoke was bubbling from the tail pipe, the engine still muttering. But there was no way to get the small vehicle free without a tow truck and no time—

Howls shivered the morning air.

Percy waded through the snow and forced open Jordan's door against the underbrush, pulling with his weight. She was hanging against her seat belt, blinking and confused.

"C'mon, Jordan," he said, leaning down to unfasten her seat belt and untangle the straps from her body.

More howls echoed up from the river, raging cries from many throats.

"Fuck." Percy manhandled Jordan from her seat, and when she slumped he dragged her to the road. "C'mon! C'mon!"

"Percy?" She stood uncertainly, looking at the Kia. "Who..."

"It was Leslie." Percy looked at the scarred place where the Jeep had gone over the side. "We have to get to the cabin." Percy dragged her into a trot to the wooden sign announcing STONE'S THROW. "C'mon!"

They confronted a foot of snow on the path as it climbed up and around a sweeping curve to vanish into the towering pines. The great evergreens lowered their branches in salute, weighted with snow that blew off in cloudlike designs.

Their run slowed to a jog and then a trudge.

Uneven temperatures in recent weeks had thawed and refrozen the snow a dozen times so that it was covered by a thick crust of ice. Each step crashed through as if they were driving posts. The noise of their passage audible for miles. In the lead, Jordan began to slow and Percy noticed speckles of bright red around her footsteps.

He huffed up beside her as she was reduced to limping. "Fucking pants," she snarled. He bent to look and saw that the thin dress slacks had been frayed and that her bare ankles were streaked with red from punching through the ice.

"Can you make it?"

"Yes."

Their passage was marked by a line of blasted holes as if they were B-17s cruising low over the driveway on a bombing run. A brilliant blue jay alighted and pecked at ruby specks on the snow.

The rippling laugh of a loon sent a shock of memory through his body and Percy released his grip on Jordan.

The laugh repeated, high and shrill. Percy's head jerked to the right as if pulled on chains and he shrieked at the sight of Leslie, floating deep in shadowy spaces between trees, his body rippling and crowned with antlers. Percy landed on his backside, feeling the concrete reality of the pistol jabbing his ribs even as Leslie twisted and dropped, exploding into a cascade of white snow.

"Percy!" Jordan hissed. "Shoot it!"

He rocked back on his buttocks to unzip the jacket and dragged out the pistol, flicking the safety off and firing at the quick-moving shadow in a wild motion with little hope of a hit.

The loon trilled its derision and he surged upright, stiff-legged from cold and fearing the wrenching pull in his back as he dragged Jordan up and lumbered into a run up the road while the breath rasped through his sandpaper lungs and the tears froze into icy rivers in the seams of his face.

"We'll get into the cabin," he panted. "Board the windows. Take the weapons."

Percy could not escape the feeling that they were being watched. His gaze raked the trees for that terrible horned form, every snow-covered knot of wood Leslie's face, every cyclone of snow a charging dog.

"I'm freezing," she huffed, cheeks aflame with cold.

His radio dial was open so wide that the word was leaden with meaning, crashing down to the ground as soon as it emerged from his lips. *Spirits.*

The spirits of Stone's Throw.

He felt it, the invisible currents rippling through himself and this place.

A new and powerful will was driving him to Stone's Throw.

Moon Lake.

Leslie wanted to chase Percy into the forest.

Percy would lead him to the moon water.

"There!" Jordan's cry snapped Percy around and he fired wildly at a black shape churning through the snow. It veered back into the trees. He swung the gun to the right and glaring red eyes ducked back.

"We're here!" Jordan called out.

Frozen spit sprang from his lips as he gasped with relief, the cabin of Stone's Throw humping up out of the snowscape ahead.

A horrible chorus of baying filled the air. The terrible noise that called the pack to the kill.

Jordan never stopped moving. Faster now, stumbling up the front steps to the icy porch where she slid, tumbling in a pile of limbs against the front door.

He saw it, for a split second he saw it as clear as day. The door opening, Leslie waiting for them with a bottle in hand, cigarette in his lips.

It was all a joke that went too far, c'mon in.

"JOOOOOORDAAAAAN!"

Leslie's cry drove Percy to his knees. Snow was jarred loose from the cabin's roof, sliding to the ground in a series of muffled thumps.

He scrambled up the steps to the porch, too terrified to look at the thing that could produce such a sound. Bowling over the rocking chair with his shoulder in his haste to get at the key hooked beneath the seat.

With more luck than grace, he found the lock on the first try and twisted the knob, pushing Jordan ahead of him into the dark cold of the cabin, unaware of the lean hound that took the four steps to the porch in a single bound and flung itself through the door on their heels.

Jordan screamed as the weight sent her sprawling across the wooden floor. Claws scrabbled as the beast threw itself at her, growling like an engine at high rev.

She kicked but the dog snatched her ankle and shook its head. Her scream rose in pitch.

Percy woke from his paralysis and yanked the pistol from his waist, only to have the snow-slick grip squirt from his fingers as if it had been soaped.

He gave no more thought to the gun and simply grabbed the animal, fingers digging into fur and meat to catch on the natural hook of its hips. He lifted, and for a terrible second Jordan came up with it, her leg trapped in its vise-like jaws, blood pattering on the floor like rain.

It released and twisted, snakelike, snapping at Percy even as he shoved his arms forward in a push. The dog struck the small woodpile beside the fireplace and bounced to its feet, shaking its head.

A fatal delay.

Percy dropped his shoulder and drove low with all the power of an NFL lineman. He slammed the animal back into the brick around the fireplace hard enough to strike his own head. Red washed down over his right eye from a cut, ignored, as he grabbed a foot-long length of maple in his right hand and leaned his weight on the desperately wriggling beast.

He brought the maple club down a dozen times until the misshapen pile of fur and pink flesh stopped moving, his hands and face coated with gore, his own blood mixing with that of the dog.

The steady bang of gunshots brought him back to the moment and the battle at the open door. The door he'd left open.

Jordan stood in the portal, firing wildly as brass shell casings flew free and the air outside filled with canine barks and howls of rage.

She stepped back and slammed the door just as the glass windowpanes beside her shattered and a big-shouldered beast pushed through the window, belly stuck on the sill as its rear claws sought purchase on the outside wall.

Percy grabbed a fistful of its ear, bringing the club down in short, vicious blows as lines of red appeared like molten crevices in the fur of its skull.

He tried to shove the crippled beast back out, but some trick of anatomy and wood had it wedged, so he pulled it into the cabin with a savage jerk, dumping it on the floor in a loose pile to step over it and slam the wooden storm shutters over the broken window.

The gunshot behind him told Percy that Jordan had finished the job.

3.

With the patience of wolves they attacked the door and the windows, alternating sides of the house as Percy and Jordan slammed the wooden storm shutters closed.

They were hunters worrying a great animal, as if nipping at the heels of the house to exhaust it. Percy upended the table and broke it into boards while Jordan found the tool chest. Hammering filled the cabin as they reinforced the windows while the animals barked and howled outside to keep them hustling.

They worked in the electric glare of a Sportsman camping lantern, the sweat freezing beneath their hair and on their exposed skin, breath puffing and billowing.

"I can't feel my fingers," Jordan whispered frantically.

"Build a fire or we'll freeze."

He shouldered over the wooden bookcase containing Leslie's first edition Jack London collection and kicked the thing apart to use on the barricades.

While Jordan stuffed priceless first editions beneath kindling in the fireplace, Percy took down the shotgun and box of shells, dumping the plastic twelve-gauge cartridges on the kitchen counter to load the weapon.

Jordan screeched and scrambled back as ash shook down into the fireplace and something bulbous and grey swelled down from the flue. Percy was frozen, mouth agape, as what he first thought was a blister and then an enormous egg rasped free and tumbled across the floor in several pieces. The brain-like construction broke into several pieces and malignant insects crawled across the interior.

"Burn it," he said through his teeth.

It was a wasp nest, black hornets crawling sluggishly across the papery outer surface. Jordan kicked the pieces toward the fireplace, knocking several insects free. The *tick-tick* of their hard bodies against wood clearly and horribly audible.

Jordan struck a long match alight and held it to the nest. Blue flames licked reluctantly across the surface until she picked up the nest and stuffed the pieces into the fireplace, piling books over the top and holding another match to them.

Wasps popped like kettle corn.

Percy heard a sharp crack from the bedroom and dashed into the dimly lit space. He discharged both shotgun barrels from a distance of three feet, the flames from the muzzle scorching the wood as he blasted a fist-sized hole in the right shutter.

"Percy!" Jordan called out.

"Get more wood to board this up!"

And that was the way of it as the barricades gave way and were replaced. The smell of gunpowder filled the cabin and the store of 12-gauge shells dwindled.

4.

Rays of sunlight through gaps in the shutters told them they still had a few hours of daylight.

Several pots of water were boiling on the stove. "I saw it in a movie," Jordan said. Coffee was made by hanging the kettle over the fire.

Leslie's bow was strung and arrows laid out beside it—though neither of them had much skill—and Jordan carried a long carving knife as she moved about. The wood axe was never far from Percy's side.

"Why'd they stop?" she asked.

"Dunno."

"How many are there?"

He had tried counting, peering out through gaps as the shadows lengthened into afternoon. "More than a dozen, but they all fucking look alike."

Jordan's laugh held little humor. "Where is he?"

"He's out there somewhere."

"What's he waiting for?"

"Dunno."

5.

Percy was staring past a spray of red flowers on the snow, suggesting he'd hit at least one of the curs circling the cabin.

It was the cusp of night, darkness about to swing shut on a hinge. His gaze wandered down slope toward the flat snow-covered expanse of Moon Lake, frozen and still.

His plan was nascent and hung on a detail, so he looked around from different vantage points in the cabin, ignoring Jordan as she asked what they were going to do, familiarizing herself with the pistol though there were few bullets remaining.

"Some of them don't look like dogs," Jordan whispered from the other side of the cabin, eye pressed to a slit. She crouched beside the two stinking animals they had piled in a corner. "These are regular dogs, but the ones outside... What the fuck is happening?"

There by the lake's edge. He saw a long, low shape humped up under the snow like a lodge house built for tiny Algonquins.

"I have a plan," he said.

"Me too," Jordan said, and he turned to see her pulling the cork from a bottle of red wine. She lifted it like a Viking and drank from the bottle, red ribbons of liquid trailing from either side of her mouth.

"No way those dogs ran here all the way from New York—and they're not all dogs..." She trailed off, uncertain.

"He's calling stuff in from the woods, whatever's out there that's his to call."

He gestured her closer. "Listen." They took turns with the bottle as he quietly relayed the outline of his plan. When he finished, she pursed her lips as if the wine had gone sour.

"In the history of shitty plans, your plan is the shit-stinking crappiest shitty plan from shitsville."

"So you like it."

"It stinks. Like shit."

She upended the bottle and belched when it drained dry. With a sudden twist she hurled it against the fireplace.

"This isn't just killing." Percy waved his hand to suggest the outside. "Not even hunting. It's worship. Worship is why he lured you to the Henley Apartment. Worship is why he chased us all the way from New York before knocking us off the road. Do you think it was a coincidence that he nailed us right at the end of the driveway? He wants us running. I think he's stalling now to wait for night, to get us scared enough that we'll bolt. He wants to chase us through those fucking woods out there to that weird fucking dolmen and that bower and get his rocks off by killing us there."

He stopped and closed his eyes.

"The Hunter thinks he wants us here. What he doesn't realize is that *I* want *him* here." He looked down at the axe in his hand.

On the kitchen counter, the Sportsman lantern flared like a supernova and went out, leaving both of them blinking after images from their eyes. Percy felt the hairs rise along the back of his neck.

Someone knocked on the door.

"Guess he's here." Orange firelight drew harsh lines down Jordan's face and made black pits of her eyes.

The door rattled under heavier blows, but it was made of stout wood.

"Percy?" They heard a hissing sound and the acrid odor of urine reached them. "Jordan?"

Jordan lifted the shotgun and fired through the door. "I think we should see other people!" She laughed, gape-mouthed and loud, and Percy realized she was drunk with wine and fear.

Snarls erupted around the cabin like a dozen starting motors and an eye pressed against the buckshot hole in the door. The eye pulled back and the pink meat of a questing tongue pressed through the hole.

The shutters on the lakeside window chose that moment to cave inward, the recently nailed boards clattering free. Percy rushed at the breach and swung his axe in a vicious arc. Blood splashed as a dog howled.

Jordan moved by in a waddling hustle. She held a bubbling pot with cloth potholders and splashed the steaming water at the hole in the door. The pink tongue blistered and an animal scream pierced the dark. "Nail that fucking window shut!" she ordered, and Percy ran for the hammer and nails.

Jordan broke the shotgun open and pulled out the spent shells. "We're not gonna make it."

Percy opened the liquor cabinet. "Then let's break out the hard stuff."

6.

"Mine's bigger," Jordan said, carving knife in one hand, shotgun in the other.

Percy grinned through a beard sticky with blood. He knelt beside the two-gallon gas can, wrapping black electrical tape around the handle of Catherine's silver knife.

"In the old religions, sacrifice was rarely a passive event," Percy said. "It involved effort and pain to demonstrate that the offering was worthy." He smiled and his eyes glittered. "The old religions were made for people like us."

He saw her shoulders straighten at the word. *Us.* Two letters placed side by side to encompass something huge.

Us.

"Pack," he said.

"Pack," she replied. "I'm ready in the other room."

He raked his eyes up and down her, bloody and torn but unbowed. Armed like a war goddess. "Leslie was a lucky sonofabitch."

"It was good while it lasted."

She limped back toward the bedroom where she would kick off phase one of the plan. "We need a name for this operation," he called after her. "Like in the army."

She paused. "Iraqi Freedom?"

He laughed, a real, honest laugh. "C'mon, you're the wordsmith."

The wind whistled around the cabin and the dogs howled.

"Let's fuck shit up." Her lip twitched but her eyes were colder than ice. Her soul filled with the cold of the deep space between stars.

"Two minutes to kick off," he said, and she touched her bare wrist.

"Watch synchronized."

She limped into the bedroom.

7.

Fire and screams blew up the night and the *crack-crack* of 9mm bullets sounded the call to war.

The pack surged in response, rushing the rear of the house as plastic sacks of high-proof alcohol flew free to detonate in splashes of fire. That was her invention, realizing that Percy's notion of Molotov cocktails needed a modern update if they were to explode against the snow. The two-gallon Ziploc bags worked brilliantly.

She had filled ten of them with Leslie's booze.

Black shapes darted among the flames as Jordan wedged herself into the bedroom window and screamed defiance, leveling the shotgun.

Percy counted to ten to give the pack time to respond to what he hoped looked like a jailbreak. He swatted aside the boards over the lakeside window in the living room, bashing through them with his axe and knocking the shutters from their hinges.

He was stripped to his jeans and t-shirt to help him fit through the window, but the rope wound diagonally across his torso caught and he had to wriggle like a fish on the line before tumbling free into the snow outside.

Stars shot across his vision, but he had no time and he kneed himself upright, pushing up with the wood axe as if it were a cane and grabbing the sloshing can of gasoline in his free hand.

His feet bled as he sprinted across the snowy crust to the humped shape of the upended boat. He dropped his gear and crouched, trying to slide his fingers underneath.

It was frozen to the ground.

He kicked at the boat and slipped. Threw his weight against it, his breath sobbing. But Jordan was the warrior in this play and he merely the priest, so he begged to whatever was listening and heaved himself against the bulk of the boat until a sudden crack announced its freedom from the ground. It shifted a foot and snow sheeted from the hull.

He flipped the metal rowboat over and dumped in the axe and gas can with a horrendous clatter.

His scream was a wordless sound, atavistic and vital as he ran alongside the boat, sliding it toward the frozen lake and onto the ice where he fell again and struggled to the front. Even as his feet broke through the crust of snow atop the ice, he used it for traction as he backed toward the dark center of the lake, pulling the boat for all he was worth.

"They're coooooming!"

Jordan's words reached him and he wasn't out far enough, damn him. Was too slow, but in the firelight of the battle on land he saw the dark shapes streaking toward the lake.

The boat tilted as he flopped inside without grace, in a place beyond pain and care. The gas can yielded its golden content without struggle and he splashed the fluid liberally around the boat in every direction before tossing it over the side where it continued to gurgle its contents onto the ice.

Numb fingers struggled to pull the metal lighter from his pocket. He ducked as the first hound sprang over the side, screaming as it snapped at his left arm while he worked the useless fingers of his right.

The lighter tumbled free but the tiny blue flame held.

Orange fire sprang forth in joyous, burning rage.

Percy caught the dog by the collar and whipped the animal out of the boat into the ring of fire.

Another dog sprang over the still-growing flames and Percy met it with his swinging axe, felling it with wild blows.

A tremendous whooshing explosion meant the flames had reached the gas can, and Percy felt the hot wind of the blast as the dogs scattered, yipping.

The boat vibrated as the ice beneath it cracked and he knew that fire and weight were working their will.

A shimmering figure from Hell appeared through the fire and smoke. It was tall and oddly elongated, its rib cage enormous as befits a running animal, its waist narrow above all-too-human hips. It sprang and swayed like nothing he had ever seen, and the single, horrible stag's antler sprouting from the socket of its missing eye seemed to weigh heavily, as if the tendons of its long neck were no match for the terrible weight of the Hunter.

Percy threw his arms wide and unleashed the primal cry of cornered prey ready to sell its life dearly.

The Hunter rushed the boat and sprang completely over the ring of fire to land on the other side, sliding and stumbling as Percy sat down hard.

He struggled up to one knee with a futile swing of his axe as the Hunter leapt over again and Percy saw the horror of its elongated legs, the knee joint reversed from man to animal.

The axe banged off the gunwale and he almost lost it in the diminishing fire outside the boat.

"C'mon! C'mon!"

Muffled by distance, shotgun blasts rocked the night and pellets spattered against the metal hull.

"I'm the Hunter. I'm the Hunter!" Percy taunted the circling monstrosity and lifted his knees in a mad jig, the boat tipping and rocking, keel sliding—

It was in the boat so quickly it seemed unfair. The speed more than animal.

But its hooves found no purchase on the metal surface and it crouched, arms flung out to catch both gunwales in long-fingered grips.

The axe flashed in a diagonal arc and struck it at the joining of shoulder and neck. A jet of black ichor shot skyward as it wrenched back, the axe blade stuck in bone.

Percy hurled himself at the wounded thing and struck the terrible antler, feeling the sharp bones puncture the meat of him to hook against his ribs. Blood flew from his lips when he shrieked, but he accepted the violent gift and grabbed the base of the antler with his left hand. His right pulled a coil of rope free and looped it over sprouting horns.

The Hunter stood and Percy wailed, mounted on the lethal antler and wriggling like a pinned insect.

It was freeing, this pain. A new language of nerve endings. In this language Percy spoke a prayer.

He gripped the tape-wrapped handle of the knife and drove its silver blade into the Hunter's good eye.

The Hunter struggled to dislodge Percy but could not free himself from the rope. As Percy dropped over the side of the boat, the Hunter's head was yanked violently on its weak neck and it tripped over the gunwale in Percy's wake.

They plunged through the ice into the freezing black of Moon Lake.

The shock was stunning. The clarity of the moment pure. Catherine told him that these places had their own spirits. Personal anima offended by the invading spirit from across the sea.

To them he offered the Hunter, bashing and grappling with the monstrosity that had taken his friend. And for the first time he had an advantage. For all its vile strength, the Hunter hoped to survive the encounter.

Long fingers found Percy's throat. His body was rent and pulled. Bones were broken. When a claw punctured his right eye he wriggled spastically, which only served to drag the tumbling combatants deeper. Percy would not be dislodged, and they sank together into the belly of the White Mountains, to the depths of Moon Lake, called *Nibi Tibik-Kizis* in the old Algonquin tongue.

8.

The fires had long since expended their anger against the ice and snow, but a greater fire rose in the east and washed Stone's Throw in a clean yellow light.

Along with the sun came the wind to blow eddies of snow over the red and black scars left by the struggle.

Inside the cabin, Jordan huddled against the bricks of the fireplace, wrapped in coats found in Leslie's closet, aware of his scent in the garments even as the stink of burnt hair clamored for attention.

Exploring fingers found stubble where she once had eyebrows and ash where she once had bangs.

She managed a pull of Cabernet from a bottle, welcoming the detonation of tannin and spices on her tongue. The quieting of pain.

It had been hours since she had seen or heard the hounds, and when she last looked, the boat was stuck in the refrozen ice of Moon Lake, upended, as if it had been carelessly allowed to drift in the days before the first freeze.

She was unaware of dozing until she blinked her sticky eyes, her attention drawn to the muffled crump of someone approaching the cabin through the snow.

Alarm klaxons blared through an empty fortress. She had no more reserves to summon, only a bare flicker of herself as she levered her body upright with the shotgun, wondering if the gun was actually loaded.

She heard a weight on the steps outside and the creak of the porch. She sucked one last time at the teat of Dionysus and tossed the bottle aside, listening to the chug of good red wine spilling free.

When the knock came, she was ready with the twelve-gauge pointed at the door.

"Who is it?" she croaked.

The door eased open, and for a moment she could make out no details, only the silhouette of a man against the yellow morning light. A shadow stretched toward her.

"Jordan?" The question a rasp.

She backed away and he stepped inside, shirt and pants frozen white, his bare skin blue with cold and his right eye a freshly gouged horror of blood and bone.

"Jordan?" Percy asked.

She pulled the trigger.

John C. Foster was born in Sleepy Hollow, New York, and has been afraid of the dark for as long as he can remember. He is the author of the crime thrillers *Rooster* and the forthcoming *The Hard Six*, as well as six horror novels, *All the Teeth in the World, Hate House, Leech, The Isle, Dead Men, Night Roads* and *Mister White*, as well as one collection of short stories, *Baby Powder and Other Terrifying Substances*. His stories have appeared in magazines and anthologies including *Dark Moon Digest, Strange Aeons, Dark Visions Volume 2* and *Lost Films*, among others. He lives in Brooklyn with the actress Linda Jones and their pitbull Coraline.